Pam EVANS

Bessie's War

HEADLINE

First published in 2020 by
HEADLINE PUBLISHING GROUP

First published in paperback in 2020 by
HEADLINE PUBLISHING GROUP

1

Cataloguing in Publication Data is available from the British Library

ISBN 978 1 4722 5684 3

Typeset in Bembo Std by Palimpsest Book Production Ltd, Falkirk, Stirlingshire

Printed and bound in Great Britain by Clays Ltd, Elcograf S.p.A.

MIX
Paper from
responsible sources
FSC® C104740

Headline's policy is to use papers that are natural, renewable and recyclable
products and made from wood grown in well-managed forests and other
controlled sources. The logging and manufacturing processes are expected to
conform to the environmental regulations of the country of origin.

HEADLINE PUBLISHING GROUP
An Hachette UK Company
Carmelite House
50 Victoria Embankment
London EC4Y 0DZ

www.headline.co.uk
www.hachette.co.uk

Dear Rea...

Hello everyone and thank you so much for buying BESSIE'S WAR. I really hope you enjoy reading this story and like the characters I have created. Because this book, like many of my others, is set in wartime I usually reflect on how different life was back then, how much harder it was and how spoilt we are in the present day. But, at the time of writing this letter, things aren't quite so cosy as the deadly Coronavirus is rampaging through the world and we are in Lockdown which means we can only go out for essentials in the hope that this will slow down the spread of the disease. We all want to help so we are st...ing indoors as much as possible in the hope of o...ding it and protecting the NHS as well as ourselves a... our families. These are troubled times for us all and e...cially health professionals. So, every era has its prob-le...'. We know this from history and are now living it.

I hope that by the time you read this, the virus h... been sent packing and you are all well enough to e... reading BESSIE'S WAR.

Thank you again for buying my book.

Happy reading and take care of yourselves.

...mest wishes

Pam

PAM EVANS was born and brought up in Ealing, London. She now lives in Surrey, near to her family and five beautiful grandchildren.

For more information about Pam and her novels visit www.pamevansbooks.com

By Pam Evans and available from Headline

Bessie's War

Chapter One

One morning in the autumn of 1940, a group of women were waiting outside Oakdene Post Office when counter clerk Bessie Green arrived for work with her colleague Joyce, whom she'd met on the way.

'Well, I didn't expect to see you lot here so bright and early this morning after the terrible night we've had,' said Bessie.

'Me neither,' added Joyce.

'I thought you'd have had a lie-in to recover from the awful bombing,' remarked eighteen-year-old Bessie to the assembly of regular customers at the post office in a parade of shops in a side street of Hammersmith in West London.

'With the old man and the family to make breakfast for? Don't make me laugh,' said Annie, a middle-aged woman with metal curlers sprouting from the front of her headscarf. As well as looking after a grown-up family, she also worked as a bus conductress and liked her hair to look smart for work, which meant the regular use of ironware.

'We're not free to lie in like you young girls are,' added Winnie, another mother of a large brood who was well wrapped up in a red knitted hat and scarf. 'We've our families to look after and we have to get up to make their breakfast.'

'My family flew the nest long ago, but I still get up to make breakfast for my old man,' said their friend Grace, a pensioner who had come out of retirement to help with the war effort and had a job in the nearby Co-op grocery store. 'But, oh dear, what a truly shocking night that was. I thought it would never end.'

'One of the worst we've had so far, I reckon, and we've had some real shockers just lately,' agreed Winnie, a tall woman with a kind heart and plenty to say for herself. 'But there were bombs raining down one after the other for most of the night, weren't there?'

'I certainly didn't think any of us would be 'ere this morning,' said Annie, who enjoyed her job on the buses and thanked the war for making it possible for her to go out to work. Her husband would never have allowed it before for fear it would have damaged his status as breadwinner. Now it was seen as the patriotic thing to do so they were both happy, especially as there was extra money coming in. 'I still feel a little bit shaky now.'

'It made mincemeat of my nerves and all,' said Ada, who was in her seventies and a widow. The loneliness of her solitary state had been very much reduced by her job as a dinner lady at the school. She was needed there because so many women preferred to work in the war factories where the wages were high.

'But here we all are again to tell the tale,' said Annie. 'During the course of every single air raid, I think my luck will run out but I'm still around the next morning.'

'And long may it continue,' said Winnie.

'Not half,' echoed Ada.

There was general agreement and more talk about the bombing that had lasted for most of the night. After such an ordeal, Bessie found it comforting to be out of the house and among such a friendly group of people and guessed that the others felt the same. Even though they had become used to the bombing, it was beyond frightening to be confined to the air raid shelter and under fire for such a long period of time, even with the family for company and everyone trying so hard to make the best of it.

'Come on then, girls, get this post office up and running,' urged Edna, a large, lively woman of advanced years who lived in a nearby block of flats and had a big family of grown-up children and grandchildren living nearby. 'I've got a lot to do this morning and I want some postal orders to send to my grandkids, who have been evacuated to the country. Poor little mites. As a family, we made the decision to send 'em away to keep them safe, but it's breaking our hearts having them so far from home. We miss 'em something awful.'

'Yeah, I can understand that,' said Annie.

'You did the right thing, though, love. They're safer where they are while these terrible raids are going on,' said Winnie. 'I know it's hard for you and your family, but at least the kids stand more chance of staying alive there than here in London. We owe that to the youngsters who have their lives ahead of them. Our grandkids went away on the school evacuation scheme. The whole family were miserable about it, but we felt we had to do it. I'll never forget seeing 'em off on the train with all the other kids. I thought my heart would break.'

'You definitely made the right decision, no doubt about it,' added counter assistant Joyce, a redhead in her forties. She was one of the many women who had recently returned to work after a good few years as a housewife. Female workers were urgently needed to fill the vacancies left by the men away at the war. Many women had headed for the services and the high wages to be earned in the war factories. Some had trained for traditionally male trades such as welding and engineering, leaving plenty of shop jobs available. As terrible as the war was, it had opened up some interesting employment opportunities for women.

'The kids are probably having a whale of a time, truth be told,' suggested Bessie. 'All that fresh air and open space will do them the world of good. I bet there'll be plenty of larking about.'

'Ours are very homesick, according to their letters,' said Edna, looking worried.

'Ah, bless 'em. Well, that's only natural at first, I should think,' said Bessie, hoping to reassure although, as she was only eighteen and single, she had no personal experience of such things. 'But I'm sure they'll be all right when they get used to it, especially as there are no bombs there.'

'The kids may very well be all right,' said Edna, who had warm brown eyes and dark hair mostly hidden under a woollen headscarf, 'but their family won't be until they're back where they belong, at home with us. We miss 'em something awful and we're going down to Dorset to bring 'em back as soon as the bombing eases up, war or no war. We ain't waiting for the victory parade. It could be years away.'

'I don't blame you, luv,' said Winnie. 'We can't wait to have ours home either. The place seems dead without them.'

'Not half,' agreed Edna.

'Can you open up, girls, please?' asked Mary, whose own

children were grown up. She worked as a cashier at the butchers in the same parade. 'It must be time by now.'

'Still a few minutes to go,' said Joyce, who had a cheerful disposition and was married with one son, Jack. He was nineteen and worked at the post office sorting depot, having failed the medical for military service, which he saw as a personal failure. After many years at home as a housewife, Joyce thoroughly enjoyed going out to work and was good at the job. 'The boss never opens for business until the dot of nine.'

'Tell him to let us wait inside then,' requested Annie. 'It's bloomin' nippy out here.'

Bessie and Joyce exchanged glances because the senior clerk, Mr Simms, wasn't the sort of man you gave orders to. He was the boss around here and he never let anyone forget it, albeit in his own quiet, rather surly way. He wasn't a local man; he lived in South London and took no interest whatsoever in the people or events of this area even though it was where he earned his living. 'All right, follow us,' said Bessie as she tapped on the door to be let in.

Mr Simms's brow furrowed slightly when the women trooped in, but he made no comment, probably because it was almost opening time anyway. Once inside, everyone had something more to say about their night in the shelter and there was speculation about where the bombs had actually landed. The current nocturnal bombing of London, generally known as The Blitz, had been relentless since September.

'Apparently, the East End is getting it a lot worse than us because of the docks,' Winnie mentioned.

'Yeah, the poor things,' came a response from Edna. 'I heard it's been terrible over there.'

'But knowing that someone else is taking more of a hammering than you don't really help when you're hunched up in the air raid shelter expecting to meet your maker at any minute, does it?' said Winnie.

There was overall agreement then the conversation became general as Bessie and Joyce went behind the counter and through to the staffroom, took off their coats and tidied themselves before taking their positions beside Mr Simms. This busy post office was a popular meeting place for the locals, who were all on friendly terms.

Bessie thoroughly enjoyed the camaraderie. She had been brought up around here so knew a lot of the customers quite well. An attractive and intelligent brunette with large dark eyes and a ready smile, she found it easy to get along with people so was well suited to the job. The occasional customer could be a bit snooty and impatient towards anyone the other side of the counter, but they were few in this working-class area and Bessie took it in her stride. Her sunny nature made her popular with the clientele.

Her first customer of the day was Mabel, a talkative regular in full flow. Bessie could almost feel the disapproving glare of the man sitting beside her as she responded to Mabel's chatter. Mr Simms, the chief clerk, rarely let them forget that he was in charge. A tall, upright man in his late fifties with thinning silver hair and watchful grey eyes behind his spectacles, he didn't have much to say, but could make his feelings known with the slightest change of expression. He rarely smiled and never at the staff. An occasional stiff grin to a customer was about the limit of his communication. Naturally he wasn't popular with the locals and Bessie got the impression that that was the way he liked it because he wanted to keep to himself. He was the most unsociable person she had ever met.

'So, what can I get for you, Mabel?' asked Bessie through the protective metal mesh near the edge of the counter.

'Sorry for holding you up with all the nattering, love,' she said, smiling and not looking particularly apologetic. 'I can't seem to stop yapping lately. Must be these bloomin' awful air raids. They play havoc with my nerves and I talk to calm myself down.'

'That's all right, my dear,' said Bessie kindly. 'We all enjoy a chat, especially in these dangerous times.' She knew she had to speed things up with Mr Simms breathing down her neck. 'So, what can I get for you this morning?' she asked again.

'Three one shilling postal orders and some stamps, please.'

'Certainly.'

Bessie completed the purchase and worked her way through the queue, dealing with a diverse array of business including postage stamps, registered letters, pension collection, a wireless licence and National Savings stamps.

'I would appreciate it, both of you,' began Mr Simms, frowning at his two underlings when the queue had cleared and they had a few quiet moments on their own, 'if you could be less chatty with the customers. All this gossiping holds things up.'

'But being friendly to the customers is part of the job, surely,' suggested Joyce.

'And it's always them who start chatting to us,' added Bessie. 'We just respond. It's the polite thing to do.'

'Then you should discourage them,' he said sternly. 'It slows everything down and people in the queue are kept waiting

7

longer than necessary. We are in charge of this post office, not the customers.'

'This is a community post office, Mr Simms, and without the customers it wouldn't exist,' Bessie reminded him, in a polite but firm manner. 'People come here in the hope of seeing their neighbours, especially after the night we've just had. They need company in these terrible times. We all do.'

'Even so . . .'

'If it's too dismal in here they can easily go to one of the other post offices in the area,' she pointed out.

'This is a place of business and should be treated as such by the staff to set an example,' he went on. 'By all means let the customers have a chat if they feel they must, but keep it brief and don't let it slow you down. You are here to serve, not socialise. As you are both very well aware, we have to maintain a certain amount of business going through this office to justify its existence.'

'We more than meet our targets,' Bessie reminded him. 'You told us that the other week.'

'And we always work while we're talking,' added Joyce, respecting the fact that he was her boss even though she didn't agree with him and couldn't bear the man, who made it abundantly clear that the feeling was mutual. 'But we can try giving the customers the silent treatment if you want to lose their custom.'

'We wouldn't lose their custom because we are very convenient for them.'

'This is a busy part of London and there are several post offices not too far away,' Bessie reminded him.

'All right, be friendly but within limits. Keep it professional and cut down on the gossip,' he persisted.

'We'll try, Mr Simms,' said Bessie, and Joyce muttered a half-hearted agreement.

But when a customer came in a few minutes later in floods of tears because she had just heard that a relative had been killed in last night's air raid, Bessie couldn't help but offer her heartfelt sympathy and allowed the woman to unburden herself. She'd have given her a cup of tea and a shoulder to cry on if she hadn't known it would probably send Mr Simms over the edge.

'Poor soul,' said Joyce when the distressed customer had left, still quite tearful.

'Yeah. It's terrible how people are suffering,' agreed Bessie with feeling. 'It really gets to me.'

'Me too,' said Joyce.

One of their regulars, Maisie, was looking gloomy as she took her turn at the counter.

'Air raids getting you down, Maisie?' asked Bessie. 'You don't look your usual cheerful self.'

'I'm not,' said Maisie, who was a pale woman in her thirties with straggly fair hair and a worried look about her. 'But it has nothing to do with the bombing.'

'Oh, what's the matter then?'

'I'm in the family way again and I'm not happy about it,' she said. 'Not happy at all. I've got four lively boys and that's quite enough for any woman.'

'Oh dear,' sympathised Bessie. 'Perhaps you'll be pleased when you get more used to the idea.'

'I expect I will and I'll love it when it comes, of course,' she said. 'But I was looking forward to a bit of freedom. I was even going to look for a job when my youngest starts school in the spring. No bloomin' chance of that now.'

'Is your husband pleased?'

'He doesn't know yet. It happened on his last leave and he's away again now. In the army. But he'll be thrilled to bits when he gets my letter. He loves kids and would like a houseful, but he doesn't have to give birth and stay at home to look after them, does he?' she said. 'Not to mention the flamin' morning sickness I'm plagued with at the moment.'

'Oh dear,' said Bessie sympathetically.

'Don't get me wrong, I love my boys to bits and I'd give my life for any one of 'em. But I didn't want any more children because I think four is quite enough for us,' she said.

Bessie nodded politely.

'It's my husband's fault,' Maisie went on. 'He doesn't like taking precautions and I think that is plain selfish. I keep telling him we're not living in the dark ages now. Well I'm gonna make sure he's more careful after this one, I can tell you that.'

'Quite right too,' approved Annie. 'You could end up with a ruddy football team.'

'There is one thing that would make me happy about this pregnancy, though,' Maisie mentioned.

'What's that?' Annie enquired.

'If I was having a girl,' she said pensively. 'I really would love a daughter. But you can bet your life it'll be another boy. That's all I seem able to produce.'

'It might be different this time,' said Bessie hopefully. 'And we'll all be keeping our fingers crossed for you.'

'Thanks, love,' said Maisie. 'I feel a bit better now I've told you lot about it. This post office has a soothing effect.'

'I'm glad,' said Bessie with a warm feeling inside. They must be doing something right. Birth, death, pregnancy, sadness, joy and everything in between; it was all discussed here. She had yet to experience many of the things the women talked about;

the trials and tribulations of marriage and motherhood mostly, but she took an interest to be polite and because she was fond of them.

'Morning all,' said Stan, one of the local postmen, a tall man in his forties with beer-brown eyes and a ready smile. 'I'm just checking that you're all still here after the night we had.'

'All present and correct,' replied Bessie, but she knew his main concern would be Joyce, whom he obviously had a soft spot for.

'Nice of you to think of us,' said Joyce, smiling at him in that special way she had when she spoke to him.

Stan had been a widower for several years and his children were grown up. He was well known and popular in the area with his easy-going charm and dry sense of humour. Not bad looking either for a mature man and his job delivering the post kept him in good shape as he walked miles every day. Past the age for the services, he did a lot of voluntary work for the war effort in his spare time. He and Joyce were very friendly and indulged in a lot of banter, but Bessie assumed it was all just in good fun because Joyce was married and she wasn't the type to play around.

'I've always got my friends at Oakdene in mind,' he was saying, giving her a friendly look as he replied to her.

'Ah, that's nice to know,' she responded.

'Glad that you're pleased, Joyce,' he said, smiling so warmly at her that if Bessie didn't know better she might have thought they were more than just friends.

*   *   *

'Anything good on the wireless tonight, Mum?' asked Bessie of her mother, Doris, over dinner that evening.

'Yeah, there's a variety show on later which might be worth a listen,' she replied. 'There's bound to be a comedian on the bill and we could do with a good laugh.'

'We'll probably be down in the shelter so we'll miss it,' said Bessie's brother Tom, who was eleven, nearly twelve. 'The siren's bound to have gone off by then.'

'Ooh, hark at you, being so cheerful,' said Bessie in a jokey sort of manner.

'I'm only saying what's true,' said Tom, at an age to be tall, long limbed and cheeky, but often in a comical way because he was a warm-hearted boy despite his tendency to lark around. He had blue eyes and a mop of fair, floppy hair that was usually untidy. 'It'll probably start wailing any minute now.'

'Let's hope we have a break from it tonight,' said Bessie's father, Percy, a man of stocky build with brown, receding hair. 'I'm on ARP duty so I'll have to leave you again. In fact, it's time I was off so I'd better get a move on and be on my way.'

'On duty again?' said Doris with an air of disapproval. 'You do much more than your share.'

'I have to at the moment, love, because there aren't enough volunteers,' said Percy, who belonged to the Air Raid Patrol and was out on the streets most nights in all conditions after a long day in his regular job as an engineer in a factory.

'It's time you had a night off,' said Doris, protective of her man.

'When the raids ease off a bit I'll stay at home more,' he said, 'and that's a promise.'

'I wish I was old enough to join up,' said Tom.

'Your turn will come soon enough,' said his mother. 'And you'll have to go in the full-time army.'

'I know and I can't wait, but the war will be over by then so I'll miss all the action,' said the boy, sounding regretful.

'I bloomin' well hope so too,' said his mother. 'I've got two sons away fighting, I don't want all three of you at it.'

'I wonder how Frank and Joe are getting on,' said Tom, referring to his older brothers.

'All right, I very much hope,' said Doris. 'We haven't heard from either of them for a while so I hope nothing has happened to them.'

'I don't suppose they often get the chance to write letters, but I expect we'll hear from them soon,' said Bessie with her usual optimism. 'They'll be thinking of us, that's for sure.'

'Yeah. 'Course they will,' said Doris.

The conversation was interrupted by the air raid siren so the family quickly finished eating and made their way to the shelter while Percy hurried off to ARP duty.

The post office seems busier than ever, recently, Bessie thought. It was a few weeks later and there was a noisy queue at the counter with the regulars in full flow with all the latest gossip. Edna was having them all in fits about how she'd been in the bath when the siren went and in the rush to get to the shelter she had forgotten to put on her knickers. They all found that very funny.

The staff had just managed to clear the queue at the counter when a noise from the telegraph machine behind them indicated that a telegram was coming in. Bessie went to attend to it, hoping it wasn't bad news from the War Office for someone.

Telegrams were sent to the nearest post office to the addressee so it would be a local person, possibly someone she knew.

It was bad news; the worst – someone's son had been killed in action. When the name of the addressee registered, Bessie's legs almost buckled and she had to grip the edge of the desk for support. With trembling hands she telephoned the sorting office to ask for a telegram boy, as was the usual procedure, then typed the message on to an official form and put it into a yellow envelope ready for delivery.

Shaking all over, she had a few words with Joyce then went to Mr Simms and explained the terrible personal situation that had just arisen. He told her to go home at once.

She ran all the way home and found her mother in the kitchen preparing lunch.

'You're home early, dear,' said Doris, whose warm, smiling eyes lit up her rather nondescript appearance. 'Your meal isn't nearly ready yet.'

'Mum,' began Bessie, her voice hoarse and trembling.

'What's the matter, love?' asked her mother worriedly, her face creasing with concern. 'Aren't you feeling well?'

'I'm fine.'

'Something's happened though, hasn't it?' said Doris, her eyes narrowing fearfully.

'Yeah. Sorry, Mum, but it has and it's really awful.'

'You'd better tell me what it is then, hadn't you?' said Doris with a worried frown.

Bessie couldn't bring herself to utter the words.

'Spit it out, girl, for goodness' sake,' urged Doris shakily.

'It's Frank,' she blurted out, barely able to utter the words as she referred to her older brother. 'The telegram boy is on his way.'

Doris's face flooded with colour then turned ashen. 'Oh, no, you mean . . .'

'Yeah, I'm really sorry, Mum,' Bessie said thickly, tears pouring down her cheeks as both women collapsed into each other's arms. 'He's been killed in action. I processed the telegram myself, but they have to send the boy. It's procedure.'

She led her mother to the sofa where they hugged each other and sobbed uncontrollably.

Bessie took the rest of the day off work to give her mother some moral support. That evening as the family sat together, an air of terrible grief hung over everything and Doris sobbed her heart out. They were all devastated and trying to help each other.

'So, Frank won't be coming home again ever then,' said Tom, the youngest of the four Green children.

'That's right, son,' said Percy. 'But you can be proud of him. He died in the service of his country.'

'I'd sooner he was coming home,' said Tom, sounding sulky because he was so upset. 'I hate this rotten war.'

'We all do, son,' said his dad, 'but don't go on about it. You'll upset your mother.'

'He's not doing any harm, love,' said Doris, who never failed to defend any one of her children.

'It isn't right that people have to die so young,' said Tom. 'Shouldn't be allowed to happen.'

'No, it isn't right, son,' agreed Doris. 'But it's what happens in wartime and there's damn all any of us can do about it.'

'What about Joe, is he gonna get killed as well?' Tom blurted out.

'We certainly hope not,' said Bessie.

'Don't even suggest such a thing,' his father put in sternly.

'It's all wrong and should be stopped,' said Tom, his voice breaking, and he left the room and rushed upstairs.

Doris got up to go after him but Bessie intervened. 'Leave him, Mum. I'll go up in a little while when he's had a chance to shed a few tears on his own and has calmed down a bit.'

Doris nodded. 'I'll see to the food, then,' she said miserably. 'We have to eat whether we feel like it or not.'

'I'll lay the table,' said Bessie sadly.

'The food is ready,' Bessie said to her brother who was sitting on the edge of his bed, his eyes red and swollen from crying.

'Don't want any.'

'Even so, you must come down and have it,' she said.

'I don't see why,' he said, 'if I'm not hungry.'

'Because Mum has got it ready for us,' she told him. 'I don't feel like eating either and I don't suppose Mum does but she has queued up for it and cooked it so we must eat it. Food is very short so we mustn't waste so much as a morsel.'

'I don't care about food,' Tom said sulkily, his voice trembling on the verge of tears. 'I only care about my brother.'

Bessie herself was devastated by the news and could barely function, but Tom was at a particularly vulnerable age; on the brink of adolescence and wanting to be more adult than he was capable of. He was trying to accept something truly awful and needed her support. The boy had always adored his older brothers, in fact he almost hero-worshipped them.

'I care deeply about Frank, too, but we have to somehow bear it and stay strong for Mum and Dad,' she said. 'It's worse for them.'

'Why?'

'Because a parent isn't meant to outlive their child,' she said, struggling to stay strong. 'Us kids are everything to them. So you and I are going to give them all the support we can and when Joe comes home he'll help as well. All right, kid?'

'I s'pose so,' he agreed miserably.

News travelled fast in this close-knit community and several neighbours called that evening to offer sympathy. Bessie found this comforting and one caller in particular raised her spirits.

'I hope I'm not intruding,' said Bessie's best friend, Shirley, who lived just around the corner. 'But I heard about Frank so I had to come and pay my respects.'

Bessie ushered her into the hall, closed the front door and threw her arms around her. 'You could never intrude, Shirley,' she said. 'You're the one person I want to see more than anyone.'

'There, there . . .' soothed Shirley, enveloping Bessie in the warmest of hugs.

'I'm so pleased to see you; I need someone of my own age from outside the family,' Bessie said emotionally. 'We are all heartbroken and don't know how to comfort each other and poor Tom can't cope at all. He's in an awful state.'

'Poor kid,' said Shirley, her blue eyes brimming with tears. She had known the Green family all her life and cared for them deeply.

'He's doing his best but I know how much he is suffering and it breaks my heart.'

17

'He adores his brothers, I know.'

'Absolutely!'

'One bit of good news, though. I had a letter from Joe today,' said her friend referring to Bessie's other brother who was also Shirley's fiancé. 'I thought you and your family would be pleased to know that he's all right.' She paused. 'Well, he was when he wrote the letter anyway.'

'Oh, that's marvellous; even more so after the terrible news we've had today; that really is something to cheer us up. Mum will be ever so pleased to know that you've heard from him. She's in pieces about Frank.'

'I bet she is,' said Shirley, full of sympathy.

'So come and see the others,' said Bessie, but at that moment the air raid siren wailed across the town so Shirley made her condolences brief then hurried home while the grieving Green family made their way to the air raid shelter.

'Do you still help at your local Brownie group?' Joyce asked Bessie a few weeks later during a quiet moment at work when Mr Simms had gone out to the bank.

'Only now and again if they are short of helpers. They don't need me all the time.'

'You're not a Brown Owl or anything, then?'

'Oh no,' Bessie said. 'I was at school with the girl who is, though, and go along if she needs an extra pair of hands. They've had to suspend it for the moment anyway as no one turns up because of the air raids. I know that adult places of entertainment are carrying on as normal and the cinemas and dancehalls are packed out every night, but when there are children involved people are more cautious.'

'Are there still enough little girls around to make up a group when the air raids stop?' Joyce enquired with interest. 'They've not all been evacuated to the country, have they? I've seen quite a few kids still around.'

'Yeah, there are still plenty in London,' said Bessie. 'Some parents just don't want to part with their nippers. They prefer to keep the family together come what may. Mum hasn't sent my brother Tom for that reason.'

'Understandable, I suppose,' said Joyce. 'My boy is grown up and a six-foot-tall postal worker so I'm well past having to make that sort of decision.'

The two women were good friends despite the age gap; united by their job, mutual dislike of Mr Simms and a similar sense of humour and attitude to life.

'At least helping with the Brownies got me out of the house of an evening,' Bessie went on to say. 'The place is like a flippin' morgue every night because of Frank's passing. We are all feeling it and it's real heavy going. We try to help each other, but it seems to make things worse somehow.'

'Why don't you go out to the pictures one night with that pal of yours?' suggested Joyce. 'There's nothing like a night at the flicks to take your mind off things.'

'Ooh, I'm not sure how Mum would feel about that, this being such a sad time for the family.'

'I thought you said there wasn't going to be an official period of mourning under the circumstances,' Joyce remarked.

'There isn't,' Bessie confirmed. 'Just a memorial service at the church. But I think Mum might disapprove of my going out for pleasure at a time like this.'

'Yeah, I can understand that. But these aren't normal times we are living in and we have to get by as best we can. I'm sure your mum wouldn't mind if you want to go out one night for a break,' suggested Joyce. 'She does have your dad's shoulder to cry on.'

'Mm, that's true,' said Bessie. 'He's been taking time off from his ARP duties to be at home with her.'

'There you are, then,' said Joyce with enthusiasm, because she really cared about her friend. 'She'll be fine with him and a night out will do you the world of good.'

'Mm, maybe I'll see how Mum feels about it and if she approves I'll pop around to see Shirley and suggest it,' said Bessie. 'Why don't you come with us?'

'Er, I don't think so,' said Joyce, flushing. 'I don't usually go out without Jim.'

'Another time perhaps,' said Bessie, but she thought it unlikely because Joyce was usually busy with her husband after work. Bessie knew Joyce's son Jack and found him to be friendly and extremely likeable; warm hearted like his mother. Bessie had only seen her husband a couple of times, but he seemed cold and she got the impression that he didn't approve of his wife going anywhere without him. Joyce never spoke ill of him, but she had mentioned that he didn't like her going out to work and she'd had to really make a stand about it. Fortunately for her and Oakdene Post Office, women without dependents were encouraged to go out to work. There was even talk about it becoming compulsory soon.

'Can I come?' asked Tom on hearing that his sister was going out to the cinema.

'No,' replied Bessie simply.

'Certainly not,' added their mother in a definite manner. 'It's far too dangerous for you to be out at night.'

'Why is Bessie allowed to go then?' he asked predictably.

'Because I can't stop her,' said Doris.

'I'm grown up, in case you haven't noticed,' added Bessie lightly.

'So am I.'

'You are eleven,' his sister reminded him.

'Almost twelve. I'm not a kid at junior school, you know,' he stated haughtily. 'I do go to senior school.'

'That doesn't make you an adult,' Bessie pointed out. 'Anyway, you wouldn't want me to come and play marbles with you and your mates, would you? Neither do I want my kid brother tagging along with me and Shirley when I go out.'

'Oh, that isn't very nice.'

He looked so dejected that she added, 'I don't mean that in a nasty way, Tom. It's just that we talk about girls' stuff and you wouldn't enjoy that, would you? But I'll go to the pictures with you another time. We'll see if we can find a film you would enjoy. Maybe one Saturday night soon.'

'Really?' he said, brightening.

'Sure,' she said.

'He isn't going anywhere of an evening while these air raids are on,' Doris declared. 'I don't think you should be going out either, Bessie, I really don't.'

'The siren hasn't gone off, Mum,' her daughter reminded her.

'Not yet, but it will do later,' she predicted. 'You can bet your sweet life on it.'

'I'll take my chances,' said Bessie. 'Sorry, Mum, I really don't want to upset you but I can't let the war stop me from ever

21

going out. I won't go if you think it would be disrespectful to Frank, but I can't let the war keep me at home every night. That way Hitler will win.'

Doris sighed. 'I don't suppose there's anything I can do about it then, is there?'

'You can hope for the best,' said Bessie. 'We're all getting plenty of practice at that lately.'

'Yeah, you go, love,' said Doris, her spirit returning. 'And make sure you enjoy yourself.'

'I will and thanks, Mum.'

The big film had just started when the cinema manager came on stage to tell the audience that the air raid siren had now sounded and would those people who wished to leave please do so quietly. There would be a notice on the screen when the All Clear went.

A few people left but Bessie and Shirley remained in their seats. In here it was warm and the film was absorbing, certainly more appealing than the damp and chilly air raid shelter. The film was *The Grapes of Wrath*, the classic story set near America's Deep South.

'What a fantastic film,' said Shirley at the end as they made their way out into the street where the air raid was still in progress. 'I was absolutely engrossed in it.'

'Yeah, and a good film certainly takes your mind off what's going on out here,' said Bessie.

Suddenly there was a loud explosion that shook the ground and sounded very close. Almost immediately afterwards some men ran in the direction of the blast, which was the opposite way to where the girls lived.

'Our families will be worried sick, thinking that we've copped it,' said Bessie shakily, breaking into a run.

Shirley agreed and they mustered all their courage and tore homewards through the streets.

There was much speculation at home as to where the bomb, which had sounded so close, had actually landed. News travelled fast among the local shop-workers and customers so within minutes of the post office opening the next morning, Bessie found out.

'It was in Bishop Street,' said Winnie, who was always a fountain of local knowledge because she made it her business to find out what was going on.

Bessie felt a reaction because some of the Brownies she knew lived over that way. 'Do you happen to know who copped it?' she asked anxiously.

'Yeah, the Masons,' Winnie replied. 'Two generations wiped out just like that. Mum and dad and grandparents, all gone. Just the little girl, Daisy, survived and that was a miracle in itself. She'd gone to a neighbour across the road on an errand for her mother before the bomb dropped.'

There was a general outpouring of sorrow amongst the assembled customers.

'Her older brother is away in the army so he's all right, but not much help to his sister now when she needs him,' Winnie went on. 'The poor little thing has been left all on her own.'

'Where is she?' asked Bessie, her heart racing because she knew of Daisy from Brownies.

'At the community centre or the church hall, I should think,' said Winnie. 'That's where they usually take people who have been bombed out until they can find somewhere permanent for them.'

'I'll go and see her in my lunch hour,' she said.

'She'll be very glad of that I'm sure,' said Maisie, who was in the queue. 'Poor little mite.'

Eleven-year-old Daisy was sitting on a thin mattress on the floor of the hall along with other victims of the bombing. There were a lot of them, Daisy noticed, some in family groups.

'Hello, Daisy,' said Bessie.

The child looked up at Bessie, her sad eyes full of tears. Although very pale at present she was a pretty girl with dark eyes and near-black hair parted on the side and fixed with Kirby grips. 'I want my mum,' she said.

A woman helper took Bessie aside. 'She has been told that her family has been killed, but I don't think she's quite ready to accept it yet, the poor little thing.'

'So, what will happen to her?'

'If we can't find anyone to look after her she'll go to an orphanage, I suppose, though I'm not absolutely sure about that,' said the woman sadly. 'Her older brother is away in the army so he can't look after her.'

Bessie knew that it wasn't possible for her to do nothing. 'Could you give me time to speak to my mother?' she asked. 'I'll be back as soon as I can. Don't let them take her away while I'm gone.'

'Right you are, my dear,' she said.

*   *   *

As it happened Bessie's mother was the least of the problems.

'I'm not going to live with a grown-up from Brownies,' said Daisy determinedly.

'Why not?' asked Bessie.

'You'd be bossing me about all the time,' she replied. 'It would be horrid.'

'I have nothing to do with the Brownies when I'm at home, you know,' said Bessie. 'And I was only helping out there anyway. I don't do it on a regular basis.'

'You're still one of them though, aren't you?'

'I'm an adult if that's what you mean,' she said. 'Having a slight connection with the Brownies doesn't mean that I'm some sort of an ogre, you know.'

One of the attendants came over to speak to Daisy. 'The caretaker has been back to where you used to live to look for your cat and there's no sign of it, love. I'm really sorry.'

'Oh, can I go and have a look?' asked the child, looking even more downcast. 'Tibs will come if I call her. She knows my voice.'

The woman exchanged a look with Bessie then turned to the little girl. 'She might have . . . I mean, it was a very powerful bomb, love.'

'Cats have nine lives,' Daisy said.

'Yes, they do say that,' said the woman. 'But I'm afraid you'll have to accept . . .'

'No, I won't,' she cut in. 'Tibs is very clever. She would have hidden somewhere when the bomb came down.'

'She might turn up, I suppose,' said the woman without much hope. 'But we'll have to leave it for now.'

'Anyway, we'd better get you home,' said Bessie.

'I've told you I'm not going with you.'

'We don't live far from your old place,' said Bessie as though she hadn't heard. 'So you won't have to change schools.'

The girl shrugged.

'And you'll have some company of a similar age,' Bessie continued determinedly, 'because I have a younger brother. He's eleven getting on for twelve.'

'Oh no, not a boy,' Daisy said with disgust. 'I hate boys. They're too noisy and rough.'

'Tom is neither of those things,' Bessie assured her.

'All boys are.'

Then the child just seemed to crumple. Her face turned red and she started to cry. Bessie tried to comfort her but she pushed both her and the attendant away and sobbed, asking repeatedly for her mother. So Bessie gave her a handkerchief and waited for her to cry some of her misery away, realising that having her at home was not going to be easy, but she couldn't just walk away from her.

'Do you want to play a game of Ludo, Daisy?' Tom asked of their new houseguest after supper, which the girl had been silent throughout despite the efforts of the family to make her feel at home. She'd been downright rude to Doris and Percy when they'd tried to be friendly.

'No thanks,' said Daisy.

'We've got Snakes and Ladders as well if you'd rather that,' he suggested hopefully.

'I don't wanna play any games.'

'What do you want to do then?'

'Nothin' except sit here,' she said, perched on the box-end attached to the fender by the fire. 'Anyway, I don't wanna be here. I wanna be in my own house with my own mum and dad. So stop trying to make friends with me.'

'He's only trying to be nice,' said Bessie.

'Well, he can shut up.'

The family were in the living room with the wireless on. Doris was knitting, Percy reading the paper and Bessie looking though a women's magazine. She was proud of young Tom who had been making a huge effort with Daisy ever since she arrived. All his attempts were rejected in a rude and definite manner, but he didn't give up.

Doris was thinking what a challenge this broken little girl was going to be. Tomorrow she would take her to the council to register formally that the child was in their care, get a ration book for her and some money to buy her some clothes as all her belongings had been lost.

But that was the least of the problems. How to help her through this tragedy emotionally and see her happy again, that was the difficult part and it would take time. But she was determined to do her best. A feeling of security was what the girl most needed and what Doris was hoping to provide. She prayed that they were spared an air raid tonight, just to give her a chance to settle in.

Bessie was expecting trouble from Daisy at bedtime because that would probably be when she would most miss her mother tucking her in. But in the end the little girl fell asleep in the corner of the sofa and had to be carried up to bed by Percy. They had moved Frank's bed from the boy's room into Bessie's and the child slept fully dressed and unwashed as they didn't have the heart to wake her.

'It won't matter this once, will it?' said Doris.

Bessie thought of the air raids they were forced to endure most nights, though mercifully they'd been spared tonight, and she remembered the many who had already lost their lives and said, 'No, Mum, it really doesn't matter.'

When Doris came into the bedroom to wake Bessie for work the next morning, she stared at the empty bed beside her and said, 'Where the devil is Daisy?'

'She must have gone to the toilet,' said Bessie sleepily.

She hadn't. She wasn't anywhere in the house.

'Oh my Lord,' said Doris anxiously. 'One night with us and she's scarpered. Now what are we going to do?'

'I don't think she's run away, Mum, and I think I know where we'll find her,' said Bessie, hurriedly getting dressed. 'I'll go and bring her home.'

'Can I come?' asked Tom, who never missed a thing that went on in the house.

'You'd better ask Mum.'

He gave his mother a pleading look.

'Go on then, but make sure you're back in time to get ready for school,' said Doris predictably.

'Yeah, I promise, Mum,' he said, rushing off to his bedroom to get dressed.

It was a cold, misty morning and they found her sitting on the front garden wall of the house opposite the bombsite that had once been her home. She looked very sad and was cuddling a black cat with smudges of white on its fur.

Her hold on the cat tightened protectively when she caught sight of Bessie and Tom.

'I had to come and find Tibs,' she said. 'I knew she'd be frightened. I'm not leaving her and you can't make me.'

'You'll have to bring her home with you then, won't you,' said Bessie, trying not to dwell too much on the fact that her mother only tolerated animals at a considerable distance. There would be much persuading to be done.

Bessie and Percy had gone to work, Tom to school and Daisy was upstairs getting washed. The little girl and Doris were going to the council to let them know officially that Daisy was living with the Greens and then to buy her some clothes. But currently Doris found herself confronted by a black cat whose yellowy-green eyes were fixed on her while it emitted a string of demanding meows. So not only had she inherited a stroppy young girl, now she had to contend with a demanding moggy, too.

'For goodness' sake stop staring at me and making that awful noise,' she said to the animal. 'Bessie gave you some food when you first arrived. You're not having any more. Food is rationed, you know. So none of us have much.' She went to the larder and took out a bottle of milk and poured some on to a saucer. The cat lapped it up and walked away, content. 'That soon shut you up, didn't it,' remarked Doris.

She had never had an affinity with animals and always tried to avoid any she saw on the streets. She would never hurt one, but she didn't feel comfortable around them. Still, cats were independent creatures so once this one settled down she probably wouldn't need much looking after beyond feeding, and she would get Daisy to take some responsibility for that. It might help to take her mind off her grief, the poor kid.

Doris sighed. First Frank's passing and now tragedy for this young girl; what next? It was a sad old world at the moment.

Chapter Two

The regulars at the post office were having a lively discussion about the first broadcast on the wireless by fourteen-year-old Princess Elizabeth, in a programme aimed at child evacuees.

'I thought she came over really well,' enthused Winnie, who was a great fan of the Royal family. 'I was most impressed.'

'So was I,' agreed Ada. 'She was really good, bless her.'

'She was all right, I suppose, but the Royals are specially trained for that sort of thing, aren't they,' said Annie, sounding much less enthusiastic. 'So she bloomin' well ought to make a good job of it, the amount of time and money that'll be spent preparing her for public life.'

'But she's young and she's only human and it ain't her fault she's been born into royalty,' Maisie reminded her. 'I think it was a really nice touch, myself, having the princess on the wireless. Makes royalty seem a bit more human if they get one of the kids to speak to the people.'

'I suppose that was the idea, to let us know that we're all in the same boat with this awful war,' said Winnie.

'Hardly in the same boat,' proclaimed Annie. 'I mean, come

on, girls, wake up. I can't imagine them climbing down into the Anderson of a night, can you?'

'They have to take shelter somewhere, though, don't they?' Winnie pointed out. 'A bomb is a killer whoever you are.'

'I'm not denying that, but they probably have a team of people helping them into some safe haven if they're not already tucked away in the country somewhere,' said Annie. 'And they'll be a damned sight more comfortable than we are. You can bet your life on it.' She laughed. 'I wouldn't be surprised if they have a shelter lined with velvet. And no shortage of hot water bottles and candles.'

'Oh yeah, that goes without saying,' agreed Edna. 'Everything possible will be done to make them comfortable.'

'While we catch our death in the cold and smelly Anderson,' muttered Annie.

'You're such a cynic, Annie,' said Winnie.

'Maybe I am, but I'm not the only one,' she retaliated. 'Some woman was of the same opinion on my bus the other day and she made her views loudly known.'

'I bet she was shouted down by the other passengers, wasn't she?' said Winnie.

'Not half,' Annie confirmed. 'You should have heard 'em go for her. A lot of people won't have a word said against the Royal family. They don't even stop to think about it.'

'It's an emotional thing, a matter of national pride, that's why,' said Winnie.

'I don't begrudge them a bit of comfort myself,' said Edna. 'Not in the least.'

'Me neither,' agreed Winnie.

'Anyway, we don't know what happens to them during a

raid so we shouldn't judge,' said Maisie. 'I hope they're comfortable, myself. I don't want our Royal family roughing it.'

'Hear, hear,' added Winnie with enthusiasm.

The queue moved on and the subject changed.

'How are you keeping, Maisie?' asked Bessie when the
expectant mother's turn came at the counter and she asked
for stamps. 'Still having sickly mornings?'

'Yeah, worst luck, and afternoons and evenings,' replied
Maisie, whose pregnancy was now common knowledge among
the locals. 'It's a flippin' nuisance.'

'When is the baby due?'

'Early summer, I reckon,' she said, taking the postage stamps
and putting them into her purse. 'But I haven't been to the
doctor's yet to get it confirmed so it isn't official. I'm not
paying out for the doc at this early stage. No bloomin' fear!'

'I don't blame you,' said Bessie, who had no experience of
such things but made sure she knew enough to have a conversation because so many of the regular customers were married
women with children. 'I don't suppose people seek medical
advice for pregnancy too early, do they?'

'First-time mums probably do because they're dead keen to
make it official, but I'm an old hand at it so I take my time
unless something doesn't feel right,' she told her.

'Sounds like a sensible idea to me,' said Bessie.

'I'm getting to be a bit thick around the middle already,'
Maisie went on. 'So this pregnancy is going to seem like forever.'

'Still, it'll be worth the wait, won't it?' said Bessie who always
tried to say what she guessed the customer wanted to hear.
'And you never know, it might be a little girl.'

Maisie smiled at the thought. 'It would be lovely wouldn't
it,' she said dreamily. 'I've been tempted to look at clothes for

little girls in the shops in town but I don't want to tempt fate.' She paid for her purchase and made to leave. 'I've got a pile of ironing to do at home so I'd better get back sharpish. Ta-ta for now, dear.'

'Bye, love.'

'Hello, Bessie,' said Joan, an occasional customer at the post office. 'I haven't been in here for a while, but last time I was in you and your family had just taken in a little girl who'd lost her parents and grandparents in the bombing. I've thought about her a lot and was wondering how she's getting on. Has she settled in?'

'Er, yeah, I think she's feeling a bit more at home now,' replied Bessie cautiously.

'That's good,' said Joan, sounding satisfied. 'It must be very traumatic for the poor little mite.'

'It's tough for her, no doubt about it,' said Bessie, moving on swiftly. 'So, what can I get for you today?'

'I'd like to send a telegram, please.'

Bessie frowned. 'Not bad news, I hope,' she said.

'Quite the opposite, my dear,' she smiled. 'It's a greetings telegram to my niece. She's getting married today.'

'Oh, how lovely for her,' said Bessie, smiling as she got a form out of the drawer.

'The wedding is up north and it's too far for us to be there,' Joan went on. 'So a telegram will do nicely and everyone enjoys it when the telegrams are read out at the reception, don't they?'

'Yeah, they do and there's nothing like a wedding to cheer people up, is there?' said Bessie, smiling.

'Ooh yeah, not half,' agreed Joan. 'And we all need plenty of that at the moment with this ruddy war dragging on.'

'Indeed we do,' said Bessie.

'Anyway, I'm glad the little girl has settled,' she said. 'My heart broke for her when I heard about it.'

'Yes it's very sad,' said Bessie. 'If you could write down what you want your telegram to say, please.'

'Of course, dear,' she said, taking the form.

'So how is young Daisy really getting on?' asked Joyce as she and Bessie made their way home together after work. 'I suspected that you weren't being completely honest with the customer who asked about her.'

'No, I wasn't,' admitted Bessie. 'I don't want to tell all and sundry what a little horror she really is.'

'Still being troublesome, is she?' asked Joyce in whom Bessie had confided.

'That's a huge understatement,' said Bessie. 'Honestly, Joyce, she's the most difficult child I've ever come across. She seemed such a nice little thing at Brownies, but there's nothing nice about her now. She's an absolute horror and is driving us all mad.'

'What does she actually do that makes her so awful?'

'She's rude and uncooperative with an absolutely vile temper,' she said. 'She hates us all, except my dad – she seems to have taken to him for some unknown reason.'

'Oh dear, it must be very hard for you and the family.'

'It certainly makes like difficult at home. She loathes my poor brother Tom most of all. The lad is battered by her hostility and he tries so hard to be nice to her. Honestly, she's upset life in our house to the extent where I wonder what is going to face me when I go in the front door of an evening. I don't know how my poor mother copes. I mean, we all have to put up with her nasty temper tantrums, but Mum gets the worst of it because she's a sort of adopted mother to her so she sees her off to school and is there when she gets home. She has to deal with most of the discipline, though we all do what we can, of course.'

'So what happens in a case like this when a child doesn't settle?' Joyce enquired with interest. 'Will your mother have to ask the council to re-house her.'

'Oh no,' said Bessie, shocked at the suggestion. 'I don't know what the official procedure is, but Mum would never even consider such a thing. None of us would dream of giving up on her, not for a second. That's the last thing we would do.'

'But if she's ruining life for the whole family surely you can't let it go on indefinitely, can you?' suggested Joyce. 'I know it might sound hard, but maybe she'd settle better somewhere else.'

'If we were to reject her now, I think that would destroy her completely,' said Bessie.

'Really?'

'Oh, absolutely! She's a damaged little girl and is fighting against what's happened to her because she can't accept it yet and we happen to be in the firing line. But we have to keep trying to bring her through it. None of us could bear to turn our backs on her no matter how hard it gets. Although I'm having a moan about her now and I get fed up with her nastiness, my heart is breaking for her.'

'Yeah, I can understand that. I feel dreadfully sorry for her myself,' said Joyce. 'But you and the family can't have your lives ruined indefinitely, can you?'

'I don't know what the future holds, but we would never

give up on her, Joyce, not after what she's been through. We just couldn't do it no matter how awful things are,' said Bessie in a definite tone. 'So we just have to keep trying and hope that eventually she'll improve. I feel sure that she will at some point when the pain of her loss begins to ease off.'

'Knowing you I'm not surprised that you are sticking with her,' said Joyce. 'But it must try your patience something awful.'

'It really does,' said Bessie. 'Sometimes we just don't know how to cope with her, but despite everything we all love her to bits. She has moments when we glimpse her soft side, the girl she really is. But they don't happen often enough.'

'And I suppose you have to be firm with her and that must be hard, with her having suffered so much already.'

'Oh yes, she gets discipline,' Bessie confirmed. 'If we give in and let her have all her own way because it's easier, she'll be even more impossible. But we could never desert her even though it sometimes feels like the only option. I honestly don't know how we are going to get through it, but we have to keep trying. We are all agreed on that.'

'You have a very kind heart and a sensible head on your shoulders for one so young,' said Joyce.

'Thank you,' said Bessie. 'It's the way I've been brought up, I suppose. We are a down-to-earth sort of a family, but Mum and Dad are very kind-hearted people and it's rubbed off on us kids. Tom is as soft as they come even though he likes people to think he's tough. He tries really hard with Daisy but she's horrid to him. Absolutely awful! He doesn't take it lying down, though. She gets a good few strong words from him but then he's back being nice to her again.'

'Aah, the poor lad.' Joyce had always found Bessie's younger brother to be a most charming boy. 'Well, good luck with

Daisy,' she said as they reached her front gate. 'If anyone can change things around, you and your family will do it.'

'Thanks for the vote of confidence. I'll let you know how tonight goes when I see you tomorrow,' said Bessie.

'Yeah. G'night, love.'

'G'night.'

As Joyce turned into her gateway Bessie wouldn't have been able to see her expression darken now that she was home to her loveless marriage. She and Jim had got married to protect her reputation because she was pregnant with Jack. Back then Jim had been a good-looking, savvy sort of a bloke and she'd been swept off her feet, but the strong attraction that had caused the pregnancy had soon faded and there hadn't been any affection to replace it. They had never been right for each other, but they were married so they made the best of it like many other people in their walk of life, in which divorce was rarely even considered.

The subject was carefully avoided but she was fairly certain that Jim saw other women from time to time and she turned a blind eye and tried to be a good wife. She reckoned she owed him that much as he'd saved her good name and had always provided well for her, having a good job as a factory manager. Because she wasn't in love with him, his infidelity didn't break her heart, but it did humiliate her and make her feel inferior. But she tried not to let it show. She still had her pride.

She had never been with another man, seeing it as her duty to be faithful to Jim and respect her marriage vows even though he didn't. Oddly enough, even though he wasn't in love with her, he was very possessive and hated her going anywhere without him. He'd be furious if he ever found out about the attention Stan showered on her. Her spirits lifted at the thought of Stan. Now there was a man she could love with all her heart if she allowed herself to. Just seeing him brightened her day.

There was one shining light in the gloom of her marriage: their son, Jack, who meant the world to her. The loveless marriage of his parents didn't seem to have affected him and he was a cheerful and popular nineteen year old. He worked at the post office sorting office in London. Having a weak chest as a child meant he'd been declared unfit for the services. Sometimes she wondered if he'd ever recover from the disappointment, especially as he was subject to abuse on the streets from ignorant people who didn't bother to wonder why he wasn't in uniform. Every so often he tried again to join up in the hope that the army might lower its standards as it got more desperate, since so many men were being lost on the battlefields. But he'd had no luck so far. Oh well, such things are sent to try us, she thought, as she turned her key in the lock. Chin up, Joyce; keep going.

There was a very loud argument in progress as Bessie stepped inside her front door.

'It isn't fair,' wailed Daisy as Bessie entered the living room. 'It's all Tom's fault but I get the blame as usual. Everything is always my fault in this house. Every bloomin' thing!'

'That just isn't true, Daisy. The cat jumped on to Tom's lap of her own accord,' said Doris, apron clad, her cheeks flaming with anxiety. 'There was no call for you to set about the boy because of it, hitting him around the head like that. You were downright spiteful, Daisy, and that isn't acceptable in this house.'

'But he's trying to take Tibs away from me,' she wailed.

'Of course he isn't,' said Doris wearily. 'That's an absolutely ridiculous idea.'

'No, it's not. You are all trying to steal her from me,' she shouted. 'She's my cat and not yours. Mine, do you understand? So, keep away from her, all of you.'

'How can we when she lives here?' Doris asked sternly. 'We can't turn our backs on the animal. If she wants to be with Tom sometimes or me or Bessie, we can't push her away. That would be really cruel. Anyway, she wouldn't give up because cats are very persistent. If she wants to be with someone else apart from you now and again, she will be and she'll come back to you again later when she's ready. Cats are free spirits and they do what they want.'

'She's my cat and I want her back,' Daisy said, reaching towards Tom as if to grab the animal.

'Oi, oi,' intervened Bessie, taking the girl by the arm and firmly restraining her. 'That's enough.'

'Leave me alone.'

'No. Not while you are behaving like this,' said Bessie. 'You can't own an animal in that way, Daisy. Especially a cat. They are independent creatures. Tibs will do what she wants.'

'You can own an animal and Tibs is mine.'

At that moment the cat sprang off Tom's lap and headed through the kitchen to the back door.

'You see,' said Bessie. 'Tibs pleases herself and right now she wants to go out.'

'You've all frightened her, that's why she wants to go out,'

Daisy said, on the verge of tears. 'I hate you. I hate the lot of you.'

And she rushed upstairs while Bessie let the cat out.

'There's no improvement in her behaviour whatsoever,' Doris confided to Bessie later when she was drying the dishes after dinner. 'I'm almost at my wits' end.'

'She is a trial, I must admit, and you bear the brunt of it,' said Bessie, drying a plate with a tea towel and putting it away in the rack above the gas cooker. 'I'm so sorry, Mum. It was my idea to have her here. I never dreamed she would be so difficult.'

'There's no need for you to apologise, love,' her mother assured her. 'Somebody had to come to her rescue and I'm glad it was us because someone else might not stick with her and she'd get moved around and never be able to settle. I just wish I was making a better job of it.'

'Oh, Mum, you mustn't think that her bad behaviour reflects on you in any way at all,' said Bessie. 'You are doing the very best you can. No one could do more.'

'If I really was doing a decent job Daisy wouldn't be so difficult; the reason she is such a trial is because she is unhappy.'

'Yes, because of her personal tragedy and nothing to do with us,' said Bessie. 'It was a hell of a thing to happen to a child. She'd be the way she is at the moment whoever she was living with.'

Doris thought about it for a moment. 'Mm, I suppose you might be right,' she said. 'It's just that it feels so personal because it's aimed at us.'

'She's taking her pain out on us but I really do think it's

just a question of time,' suggested Bessie. 'I'm hoping that eventually she'll improve, as her grief lessens.'

'Of course, we don't know how she used to carry on with her own family do we?' Doris reasoned. 'We are putting it down to her grief but she might have been difficult before that.'

'I don't think so somehow,' said Bessie. 'She was a lovely child at Brownies. Always polite and very popular with the other girls.'

'We don't know what she was like at home though, do we?' said Doris. 'She might have been a little brat then.'

'I suppose she could have been. She is the youngest and there must be a big age gap between her and her brother as he's an adult, so she might have been spoilt. But somehow I don't think so. I honestly believe that all of this is a result of the trauma of losing her family. Just think how awful that must feel for a child.'

'Yeah, I know and I do think it's why she is how she is too, in my heart. It is a huge thing for a child to have to cope with,' said Doris. 'I suppose I'm looking for alternatives because I'm desperate to make her feel better and don't seem able to do it because I can't change her circumstances. She must be feeling very unhappy to behave as she does and how can we alter that when we can't bring her family back?'

'We just have to keep trying to help her learn to live without them and give her plenty of affection if she'll allow us to,' said Bessie. 'I think we have to let some more time pass.'

'It upsets me to think how she must be hurting.'

'It breaks my heart, too.' Bessie paused thoughtfully. 'Anyway, Mum, changing the subject, there's a play on the wireless later on that sounds promising. Shall we listen to it together after the kids have gone to bed? If we're not banished to the air raid shelter.'

'That will be lovely, dear,' she said. 'Your dad is out on ARP duty so it'll just be us.'

'It's a long day for him, isn't it,' said Bessie, because her father was the foreman in an engineering factory and started very early in the morning. With the voluntary work added to his working day, she felt he must be permanently exhausted.

'Yeah, it really is but he doesn't seem to mind,' she said. 'It's all part of his contribution to the war effort. He enjoys being involved. You know your dad; he likes to be busy.'

'Just us girls, the wireless and a portion of the biscuit ration then,' said Bessie, experiencing a surge of affection for her mother. She valued their close relationship enormously.

Oakdene Post Office was packed to the doors, there was a queue at each of the three positions and people standing around talking. Bessie had trained herself to concentrate on the business in progress rather than look at the length of the queue, to help her stay calm.

'Good grief,' whispered Joyce to Bessie. 'I think the whole town is in here this morning. I know it's pension day, but even so . . .'

'It's good because it shows that there's a really strong need for a post office in this parade. The pensioners certainly enjoy coming here for a chat, but they do business as well.'

'Yeah, they're a noisy lot,' agreed Joyce. 'But a bit of a natter is the least they deserve. Most of them are out of retirement and doing a job of some sort for the war effort.'

The telegram boy arrived to collect a telegram for delivery,

Bessie having telephoned the sorting office to arrange it, and as Bessie dealt with a parcel and put it in the pile ready for the postman to collect, Stan arrived. Mr Simms gave her a warning look because he had heard her and Joyce talking. This irritated Bessie because it was petty and unnecessary; both she and Joyce were capable of exchanging a few words without interfering with their work. So she met his gaze with defiance. It really was a battle of wits between this man and his staff.

Stan went to have a few words with Joyce and the boss didn't say a word. Bessie thought perhaps he didn't have the nerve to get stroppy with anyone outside of his employ, especially another man and particularly a tall, fit one like Stan.

'Next, please,' she said, turning her attention back to the counter to find herself staring into a pair of dark-brown eyes that had a familiar look about them, belonging to a soldier with a lovely warm smile. 'Good morning, what can I do for you?'

'I'm looking for my sister, Daisy Mason,' he said. 'I've been told by my ex-neighbours that she's been taken in by the family of someone who works here.'

'Yes, that's me,' she said, smiling at him and writing down her address on a scrap of paper. 'You must be Josh.'

'That's right.'

'Very pleased to meet you, Josh. We've heard a lot about you from your sister.' She slipped the piece of paper under the mesh partition. 'Daisy will be at school now, but my mother will be in. I'll be home for my dinner break in half an hour or so. If you hang on at the house, I'll see you there.' She leaned forward and said in a low voice, 'The boss doesn't like his staff chatting to customers.'

'Ah, message understood,' he said with a wry grin as he took the piece of paper.

Josh had obviously been an instant hit with her mother, Bessie guessed, as she found them in the kitchen, him chatting to Doris while she served the food, having invited him to have lunch with them.

'They've given me ten days' compassionate leave because of the family situation,' he explained over bready wartime sausages and mashed potato supplemented by swede.

'Daisy will be thrilled to bits to see you,' said Bessie. 'I doubt if she's ever needed you more.'

His concern was obvious. 'The poor kid must be devastated by what's happened,' he said worriedly. 'I feel bad enough myself, but she's just a child.'

'Yes, she is having a tough time,' said Bessie. 'But seeing you will perk her up no end.'

'I've invited Josh to stay with us for his leave,' Doris explained. 'It'll give him a chance to see something of his sister. He's got nowhere to stay and he can have Joe's bed for the moment.'

'Good idea, Mum.'

'It makes things even worse when the family home has gone along with the family,' said Josh sadly. 'But I don't want to impose.'

'You won't be imposing, not in the least,' Bessie assured him brightly. She saw him as a gift. If anyone could get Daisy to cheer up and behave decently, it was her big brother whom she always spoke of in glowing terms. He was a very pleasant sort and had other assets too that certainly hadn't been missed by Bessie's feminine side; his handsome face and army-fit physique. How often did a girl get such a corker moving into her house? 'We'd love to have you.'

Doris struggled to keep the tears away later when she watched Daisy's emotional reunion with her brother. For a moment, the child seemed bewildered, as if she didn't know who he was, then she rushed into his waiting arms and he lifted her in the air in a joyful embrace.

'He's my brother,' she announced proudly, clinging to his hand as though she would never let it go. 'He's my real family. I knew he would come to get me one day.'

'I'm only on leave, Daisy,' he explained kindly. 'I have to go back in ten days' time.'

'Oh,' she said, her disappointment obvious.

'So you'll be staying here with Mrs Green and her family for a while longer.'

Her face fell. 'You will take me with you after the war though, won't you?' she asked anxiously.

Doris frowned. 'Aren't you happy here with us, Daisy?' she wanted to know.

The girl shrugged. 'It's all right here,' she said with a casual air, 'but I want to be with my own family,'

Josh looked from one to the other. 'I'm sure Mrs Green thinks of you as her family, Daisy,' he said.

'Dunno about that,' she replied, frowning.

'Of course we do,' said Doris in a definite tone, sad that the child should think otherwise.

* * *

'We have had a bit of trouble with her, to be honest, Josh,' Doris admitted to him later when Daisy had gone upstairs and she and Josh were chatting in the kitchen while Bessie made tea. 'And we were wondering if she was prone to temper tantrums before she came to us.'

'Not that I remember,' he said. 'She'd have the occasional sulk the same as all kids, but generally speaking she was a sunny-natured child.'

'Hmmm, the fault lies with us then.'

'Not at all,' he was quick to assure her. 'I would say that any change in her behaviour is bound to be a reaction to what's happened. But I'll keep an eye on her while I'm here and take her in hand if necessary.'

Doris smiled. 'She'll probably make a liar of me by being an absolute angel for the whole of your leave,' she suggested.

He smiled. 'Sod's law, eh?'

It didn't happen that way. After supper that evening, Daisy had a violent reaction to Tom sitting next to Josh on the sofa.

'Get off there,' she ordered. 'He's my brother not yours so move out of the way so that I can sit next to him.'

'No, I won't,' objected Tom. 'We're having a really nice chat about football.'

At which point she went into one of her rages, screaming and hitting out at Tom.

'Oi, that's quite enough of that, Daisy,' said Josh, pulling her up and holding her arms firmly with both hands. 'What do you think you are doing?'

'He shouldn't be sitting next to you.'

'Of course he can sit next to me,' he said firmly, but he was obviously upset by her behaviour. 'I thought you were eleven not two years old. I'm disappointed in you and so would Mum and Dad be if they could see how you are behaving.'

She looked downcast. 'But I really want to sit next to you,' she said sulkily.

'I know that and you can another time,' he said, 'but you do not attack someone to get your own way.'

'But . . .'

'No buts, Daisy,' he said, obviously struggling to take a necessary firm stand. 'You have embarrassed me and shown yourself up. If Mr and Mrs Green change their mind about letting us stay here I can't say that I blame them.'

She shrugged carelessly.

'You wouldn't be looking so cocky if they did ask us to leave,' he went on. 'I doubt if you'll find another family who are so kind hearted and patient with you.'

'I don't want to be with any family except my own,' she said and Bessie knew that this was at the root of the problem.

Josh seemed to be stumped by it too and didn't respond right away. He must be as devastated as his sister by the loss of their parents; Bessie knew that. 'Yeah, I realise that, kid, and I really feel for you, but, well . . . that isn't possible now, you know that, don't you?'

She nodded. 'I s'pose so,' she said.

'It's really hard, but we both have to accept what's happened. So I am asking you to try to accept this family's kindness and repay them by behaving nicely towards them,' he urged her. 'Can you do that for me, please?'

'I don't know,' she said. 'I miss Mum and Dad and you and it makes me hurt inside and I just have to be horrid. I can't help it.'

He exchanged a look with Doris.

'Yeah, I can understand that because I feel the same way but you'll have to try harder,' he said. 'I know you are young to have to cope with such a tragedy, but you must try not to hit out at other people every time you ae feeling sad.'

'It just happens,' she said.

'Mm, well, you'll just have to try harder to stay in control of your feelings. It pains me just as much as you that we lost our family, but I don't take it out on my mates who I live with in the army because that wouldn't be fair. It isn't their fault and neither are these lovely people to blame. Do you understand what I'm saying?'

'I s'pose so,' she said, head down.

'Well, let's have no more tantrums then,' he said. 'And I'll know about your behaviour when I go back off leave because I am going to ask one of the family to write to me and let me know how you are getting along. Now that Mum and Dad aren't around, I'm in charge. Because of the war, I can't be with you for much of the time so when I am not here I pass the responsibility on to Mr and Mrs Green and their family.'

'Oh,' she said looking very downcast.

'You are not all alone in the world, Daisy,' he tried to convince her with feeling. 'Far from it. You have a brother who cares about you and while I'm away you have a lovely family to look after you. But don't make it so hard for them, please.'

'I'll try,' she said, staring at the floor.

'Right! The lecture is over,' he said. 'So, come and sit down.'

'You can sit next to your brother, Daisy,' said Tom, moving up.

'Thanks, mate,' said Josh, winking at him.

'That's all right,' said Tom, feeling grown up, as though he was one of the boys.

★   ★   ★

When things had calmed down after the scene, Bessie sped around to see Shirley.

'Something amazing has happened,' she said.

'Ah, let me guess . . . Mr Simms asked Joyce to go out on a date?' she laughed.

'Don't be ridiculous,' said Bessie, giggling at the thought. 'No, we've got the most gorgeous bloke staying with us.'

'Oh yeah, who is he?'

'Daisy's brother,' she told her. 'Oh, Shirley, you should see him. Great big brown eyes, blond hair and a physique like a film star.'

'Sounds like you've seen him in the nude, but I know that you couldn't have.'

'Of course I haven't, you daft thing,' she said with giggle. 'You can tell from the way the uniform sits on him.'

'Soldier, sailor, airman?'

'Soldier.'

'Single?'

'I think so, but I intend to find out for sure.'

'I'll call round to take a look and let you know what I think.'

'No flirting.'

'Why would I when I am fixed up with Joe?'

'For a bit of fun you might, so don't,' she laughed. 'I don't want him confused.'

Their conversation was interrupted by the air raid siren.

'Oh not again,' said Bessie. 'I'll see you tomorrow and give you the latest.'

'Good luck,' said Shirley, getting her coat ready to go down to the shelter.

★   ★   ★

When Bessie got home the family were on their way to the shelter, Daisy trying to hold on to the cat who jumped out of her arms and fled as always when the siren sounded. Bessie went inside to get her scarf and gloves and was surprised to see that Josh was still in the house.

'Come on, Josh,' she said. 'Look lively. The bombers will be here any minute. They don't hang about.'

'There'll be a bit too much of a crowd in the shelter if I come too, won't there?'

'Of course not,' she said. 'We'll make room. Bigger families than ours find enough room in their Anderson.'

He looked very sad.

'Has something happened while I've been out?' she asked. 'You look concerned about something.'

'Yeah, I am, to be honest with you. I wish I could do more for Daisy and it's worrying me that I can't,' he said. 'The poor kid. I feel rotten about going away and leaving her.'

'But you don't have a choice.'

'I know, but it still upsets me,' he said. 'I mean, it's a hell of a thing for a child of her age to cope with, having her parents and grandparents wiped out. And big brother not around to give her some support.'

'She'll be all right with us.'

'I know and I thank God for it, but I still feel bad about not being with her at this hard time.'

'The war will end eventually, Josh, and you'll be back home with your sister, but right now let's go down the shelter,' she said, her nerves on edge as the rumble of the bomber planes grew louder.

*　　*　　*

51

'Seen any action, Josh?' asked Percy to pass the time when they were in the dark and damp shelter.

'A little,' he replied.

'Sooner you than me, lad,' said Percy. 'I did my share in the last war. Not something I would care to repeat.'

'I bet.'

Although Josh didn't seem to want to continue with that particular subject, the two men seemed very comfortable with each other, Bessie noticed. They carried on chatting while the bombers roared overhead and every so often an explosion shook the ground. Both the youngsters went to sleep under their blankets.

After the All Clear had sounded and the children were in their own beds, Bessie and her mother made a light supper of cocoa and cheese sandwiches.

'Thank you so much for what you're doing for my sister, all of you,' said Josh, sounding emotional. 'I feel terrible about leaving her, but at least I can go back off leave knowing that she's with people who are looking after her so well.'

'We're glad to be able to do it, dear,' said Doris. 'It was Bessie who brought her to us.'

He looked at Bessie questioningly.

'I used to help out at the Brownies,' she explained. 'So I already knew her a little. When I heard what had happened to your family I went to find her.'

'Thank goodness you did,' he said. 'And I can tell from what I've seen today that she isn't always easy.'

Bessie paused for only a moment. 'We can't deny that,' she said.

'She wasn't a difficult kid before, as far as I can remember. The odd sulk and occasional tantrum but nothing like I saw earlier.'

'It's obviously because of the trauma she's been through,' said Doris. 'A terrible shock for you as well.'

'Ooh, not half,' he said and moved on swiftly, his voice trembling with emotion. 'But you just have to get on with it, don't you, when bad things happen?' He paused. 'I can do that but my sister isn't quite old enough yet and my heart breaks for her.'

'She'll be all right eventually, I think, when she's had a bit more time,' said Doris, finishing her drink and rising. 'Well, I'm off to bed. Are you coming, Percy?'

'Yes, love,' he replied and they headed for the stairs.

It was as much as Bessie could do not to let out a cheer. Although she adored her parents, and she really did, there were times when she was glad that they weren't around.

'So, do you have a boyfriend?' asked Josh as soon as the door had closed behind Doris and Percy.

'Not at the moment,' she replied. 'How about you?'

'I'm single, too.'

'Oh really,' she said and they exchanged the warmest and most meaningful of smiles.

'Somebody is keen,' said Joyce just before closing time the next day as she glanced through the post office window. 'He's waiting for you outside. What a handsome bloke he is too.'

'Yeah, he is rather gorgeous,' Bessie agreed, feeling a pleasurable kind of nervousness.

'Don't keep him waiting then,' said Joyce. 'Get out there pronto.'

'What about Mr Simms?' she said because they had to wait until the chief clerk had cashed up before they could leave. If the books didn't balance they had to stay on until they did.

'You leave Mr Simms to me tonight,' her friend said. 'I'll be here. He can make do with just me for once.'

'Thanks, Joyce, you're a real pal,' she said excitedly, hurrying away to get her coat.

'What a lovely surprise,' she said, beaming at Josh.

'Glad you're pleased,' he said, smiling warmly at her. 'I don't want to appear too eager but the clock is ticking and I've only got nine days of my leave left.'

'You won't get any argument from me,' she said, linking arms with him. 'Life is definitely too short.'

'My thoughts exactly. I'd like to invite you to the pictures tonight, but I'm not sure if your parents would approve of my leaving Daisy. And she might have one of her tantrums because I'm taking you and not her.'

'It will be too late for her to go to the cinema anyway with school in the morning,' she said. 'She gets far too much of her own way with everyone scared she's going to kick off, so it won't do any harm for her to miss out this time. But it must be your decision. I don't want to come between brother and sister.'

'I'll do things with her another time,' he decided. 'I had a look at the cinema listings in the local paper and thought you might fancy a drama with Margaret Lockwood.'

'She's one of my top favourites,' she enthused. 'So yeah, I'm all for that, Josh.'

'Good.'

'There's a *Just William* film on at one of the other cinemas this week,' he mentioned. 'So I thought perhaps we could take the kids to see it at the weekend.'

'Lovely idea. Tom would really like that,' she said. 'Shall we do it on Saturday?'

'Sure.'

They were both smiling as they walked home through the cold and misty evening streets.

They sat in the back row of the cinema and he put his arm around her as was traditional if a chap was keen on a girl. She was well on the way to falling in love with him and when he kissed her on the way home the process felt complete.

The nine remaining days of his leave flew past in a whirl of happiness and high emotions; the thrill of getting to know someone new and the joy of falling in love. They went out dancing and walked by the river on Sunday afternoon, heedless of the cold weather in their joy at being together. He made sure to pay plenty of attention to his sister as well as Bessie and the young girl seemed quite happy with her brother's romance.

Bessie was surprised. She had expected trouble from her; jealousy about sharing his affection. But she seemed pleased by it, almost as though his attachment to Bessie made her feel more secure somehow. She was calmer altogether since her brother had been around.

'Well,' said Josh to the family when he was ready to depart on the Sunday he was due back at camp. 'I have no idea when I'll see you all again.'

'You are very welcome to stay here when you do get leave,' Doris told him.

'What if Joe is here?'

'Unlikely because he's overseas somewhere,' said Doris. 'But we'll still have a spare bed even if he is home.' She gulped back the tears for Frank. 'There will always be a place for you in this house, Josh, even if you have to sleep on the sofa. This will be your home for as long as you want it, along with your sister.' She paused, then to lighten the gloom added, 'So long as you bring your ration book, of course.'

'Thank you, Mrs Green and Mr Green,' he said, sounding emotional. 'Thanks to you all for what you are doing for Daisy and me. Tom, Bessie, all of you.'

'S'all right,' said Tom.

'Least we can do, son,' said Percy.

'I shall miss you all, even the cat.'

'Go on before we flood the place with tears,' said Doris.

'Too late,' he said with a wry grin. 'Daisy is already blubbing. Come here, squirt. Cheer up, sis. With a bit of luck I'll be back again soon. They might give me a weekend pass. It isn't as if I'm stationed abroad at the moment, is it? Anyway, I'll write to you.'

She gave him a watery smile and then he was gone. Bessie walked to the local station with him, but he didn't want her to accompany him to Waterloo. 'Mainline stations are far too emotional in wartime,' he said. 'We'll both end up blubbing.'

So she kissed him goodbye outside Hammersmith station and walked away with tears in her eyes. She couldn't face going home to the dismal quiet of a Sunday afternoon so took a stroll along by the river for a while. It was dark and muddy on this cold day, with working boats of all shapes and sizes going by carrying various cargoes. There was only one person she really wanted to be with in this mood of melancholy, so she left the riverside and headed back into town.

'Blimey, that's the speediest romance I've ever known,' said Shirley. 'Two weeks ago you hadn't even met the bloke, now you're breaking your heart because he's gone back off leave.'

'That's the war for you. Anyway, just because it was quick doesn't make it any less serious,' said Bessie. 'It probably seems a bit fast to you because you've known Joe all your life.'

'I wasn't in love with him all of my life though,' she pointed out. 'That happened later on. And it was quite sudden that I saw him in a different light.'

'And now we're both alone,' said Bessie.

'Only temporarily and at least we have each other for company.'

'Yeah, let's go to the flicks one night next week.'

'Or we could go out dancing?' suggested Shirley.

'That's what you do if you want to meet men and we're both fixed up in that department.'

'Mm, I suppose so,' she agreed. 'But I miss going out and having fun. Getting all dressed up, you know?'

'Perhaps Joe will get leave sometime soon.'

'I wish he would, but he's too far away for that. People say that once they go overseas, they won't come home until the war is over.'

'None of us knows that for sure,' said Bessie.

'They do get leave, apparently, but they have to spend it local to where they are stationed,' said Shirley.

'Mm. I suppose that's how it would work,' said Bessie. 'The military wouldn't pay their passage home just for leave very often, if ever. By the time they got here on the boat it would be time to go back. So you'll just have to be patient like millions of other people parted from their loved ones.'

'You and I can be patient together,' said Shirley. 'When I think of what some people are suffering, including you, I feel very lucky.'

'That's true.'

'How is young Daisy?'

'Her brother gave her a really good talking to when she went into one of her rages and we had no more trouble after that,' she said. 'So we are all hoping it's going to last.'

'Fingers crossed then.'

'Having him around seemed to give her confidence. Someone of her own blood, I suppose. She's got this thing about real family. I think she thought she had lost everyone, even though she knew he was still alive. Seeing is believing, I guess. She seems such a lost little thing sometimes, despite all her cheek.'

'Shame.'

'It's a terrible shame,' said Bessie, with a sad shake of her head. 'She seems to be a bit better with my mother lately. It's taken a while but they are getting on all right at the moment.'

'I thought she hated you all.'

'She did seem to, though she was all right with Dad from the start. But Mum has persisted and the kid seems to be better with her these last few days,' she said. 'She and Tom fight like cat and dog but somehow that seems normal, like a sister and brother of a similar age would do.'

'Mm,' said Shirley, but she was an only child so had no experience of siblings.

'Let's hope this better behaviour lasts now that Josh has gone,' said Bessie.

'It would be nice for you if it did.'

'I would be wonderful, but I'm not banking on it, just hoping,' she said rising. 'Anyway, I'd better go home.'

'Pictures one night next week then?'

'Definitely,' said Bessie and left.

Walking home in the silent Sunday streets, it was becoming quite foggy which would probably mean a bomb-less night. The Luftwaffe preferred clear weather to drop their lethal weapons, so maybe they would get to spend all night in their beds.

The house seemed dismal without Josh, and Bessie's mother seemed to feel it too.

'He'll certainly be missed,' said Doris. 'It was a real tonic having him here. He's such good company. Makes an effort with the rest of the family as well as you.'

'You don't disapprove of my whirlwind romance then?' said Bessie. 'I know it all happened rather fast.'

'That's what things are like in wartime,' said Doris. 'You have my blessing and I know your dad likes him.'

'I'm really pleased about that, Mum,' she said. 'Your opinion means a lot to me.'

'He's a decent lad. You'll be all right with him.'

'Yes, I really think I will,' Bessie agreed.

Chapter Three

Bessie was having a really bad day at work. Usually very punctual, this morning she'd been late because she'd slipped on the ice and had been so badly shaken up she had had to sit on a garden wall for a few minutes to recover.

Mr Simms didn't accept even the most valid excuse so he slammed into her about how bad timekeeping wasn't tolerated by the post office and threatened her with dismissal if she made a habit of it. No sooner had she recovered from that battering than a customer accused her of short-changing him.

'I gave you a pound note,' insisted the man, who was in late middle age and flashily dressed in a pin-striped suit with a brightly coloured tie and a trilby hat adorned with a feather. 'So I'd like the change from a pound, if you please.'

'You gave me a ten-shilling note,' said Bessie.

'I most certainly did not,' he insisted, his voice rising aggressively. 'I gave you a pound note and that's what I want change from . . . pronto if you wouldn't mind.'

'But sir . . .'

'I gave you a pound, no more argument.'

Bessie removed the ten-shilling note from the till and held it up. 'That is what you gave me, sir,' she said.

'That is not what I gave you,' insisted the man, his voice rising still further. 'That must be one you took earlier. It definitely isn't mine. So, will you please put your hand in the drawer again and take out the pound note that I have just given you.'

'You didn't give me a pound . . .' she began.

'So you are calling me a liar?' he came back at her quickly.

'I'm saying that you gave me ten shillings.'

There was an intervention from Mr Simms. 'What seems to be the problem here?' he wanted to know.

'The assistant here is trying to cheat me out of my money,' the scowling man explained.

'You must be mistaken, sir. A member of my staff wouldn't do a thing like that, I can assure you,' said Mr Simms.

'She did, mate, I'm telling you and don't call me a liar cos I ain't.'

'Neither is she.'

'So, she made a mistake,' suggested the customer, shrugging his shoulders. 'It happens to the best of us at times. Nothing to be ashamed of.'

'My staff are very well trained and efficient so that is most unlikely,' Mr Simms told him.

'Human error is a fact of life, mate, and it happens to us all from time to time,' said the customer. 'But I am not guilty of it today and your girl is.'

'And I'd be the first to admit it if I had made a mistake,' said Bessie. 'But on this occasion, I really didn't.'

'Right. If you are going to be difficult about this, I'll take it to the management,' said the man. 'I shall go to the head office of the General Post Office.'

'You wouldn't go to those lengths, surely,' said Mr Simms, becoming noticeably fearful.

'I most certainly would,' the man confirmed. 'I shall go to your superiors at head office and make an official complaint if we can't settle this right here and now.'

Mr Simms turned pale and his lips trembled slightly. He always seemed to be very much in awe of senior management, Bessie had noticed. When anyone of that ilk came to Oakdene on a routine visit, as they did from time to time, he was always visibly nervous in contrast to the confident way he dealt with everyone else.

'Come on, make up your mind sharpish,' demanded the customer. 'I'm a busy man. I've got things to do. I'm not waiting about here all day for you to decide which one of us is the liar. I'll take the matter to a higher level.'

The chief clerk remained silent for a few moments then did a complete volte-face. 'Give the customer the rest of his change, please, Bessie.'

'But he only gave me a ten-shilling note, Mr Simms, I swear on my mother's life.'

He hesitated for only a second. 'Give him change of a pound please.'

'But . . .'

'Don't argue,' he said. 'Just do as I say.'

With great reluctance she did as he asked and the customer left looking very pleased with himself.

'If the takings are short when I cash up tonight, you will pay the difference, Bessie,' said Mr Simms.

'They definitely will be short because he gave me a ten-shilling note,' she insisted. 'And I don't have the cash to make the money up.'

'Then you will pay so much a week out of your wages until it is all paid off.'

'That is really unfair,' she said, her temper rising. 'I didn't do anything wrong.'

'Maybe not, but the money has to be made up somehow and it was your customer so your responsibility.'

She hated him with a passion at that moment. 'Surely you must know that the customer was making fools of us,' she said.

'The customer is always right.'

'That isn't true and you damned well know it,' she said.

'No swearing in this post office, please,' he reprimanded.

Tears burned at the back of her eyes. She wasn't used to not being trusted. 'So much for staff support.'

'Bessie isn't a liar, Mr Simms,' Joyce put in. 'If she said the customer gave her a ten-shilling note then that's what happened. No doubt about it. And surely you must know that.'

'This has nothing to do with you,' he said dismissively, then turning to Bessie added, 'we are all responsible for our own actions. It's part of the job. I can't lead you by the hand.'

'I neither expect or need you to, but that customer is a thief and shouldn't have been allowed to get away with it. I needed your support on this occasion and I didn't get it,' she said, hurt and angry at the lack of backing from her boss. 'That awful man will be laughing at us all day long. He probably does that trick everywhere he goes until they get wise to him.'

'We'll see what happens when I cash up tonight.'

She knew the books wouldn't balance. How could they when the customer had blatantly stolen from them?

* * *

The incident was very upsetting for Bessie and she felt quite shaky for a while afterwards, hurt as well as angry at Mr Simms's unfair treatment of her. No sooner was she beginning to recover than she was in trouble again when the older man answered the telephone.

'It's a call for you, Bessie,' he said with a thunderous look.

Her legs turned to jelly. She never had phone calls. Staff weren't allowed them except in the case of an emergency and all her friends and relatives knew that. Something terrible must have happened at home. Someone was ill or there was bad news about her brother Joe. Oh God!

'Hello,' she said nervously.

'Hello, Bessie, it's Josh.'

'Oh,' she gasped into a very crackly line. 'What on earth has happened?'

'I got the number from directory enquiries.'

'Yeah, but why have you phoned me? What's wrong?'

'Nothing,' he replied, sounding happy. 'I just wanted to tell you that I love you.'

Tears sprung to her eyes. 'Oh,' she said, weak with relief and emotion.

'Bessie, are you there?' she heard above the hissing and crackling on the line.

'Yeah, I'm still here.' Noticing that Mr Simms was busy with a customer who was chatting to him, she said in a low voice, 'I love you too, Josh. But I'm not allowed personal calls here unless it's an emergency.'

'Oh dear, I'm so sorry, Bessie,' he said. 'Will you get into trouble?'

'Yes, very probably, but it will be worth it.'

The pips were going and she just heard 'Love you' and the line went dead.

'Sorry,' she said to Mr Simms sheepishly and went back to her position.

She thought perhaps her day was improving because he just nodded and didn't say a word.

'That is really romantic,' said Joyce when she and Bessie were talking about Josh's phone call as they left the shop together after work. 'I thought old Simms was going to explode though.'

'Was he very cross?' asked Bessie. 'I daren't look at him.'

'He seemed to be absolutely seething,' she replied.

'He didn't say a word to me about it afterwards.'

'Must have calmed down,' said Joyce. 'He does that; he flies into a rage but calms down quickly. He's a temperamental old bugger.'

'Strange sort of bloke altogether.'

'I've never met anyone more peculiar,' agreed Joyce. 'And as for making you pay back the money the conman took off you, I think that's disgusting and if he does actually go through with it he'll have me to deal with.'

'I'm still angry with him for taking the customer's side and not mine,' said Bessie. 'He must have known the man was chancing his arm.'

'Of course he did,' agreed Joyce. 'He's weird but not stupid. He didn't want to risk the customer involving the hierarchy at the Post Office's head office, that's all. He seems to be scared stiff of authority for some reason. He's always really nervous when they come to see him about anything at all.'

'Yeah, I've noticed that too. He really is the oddest sort of bloke and a nasty piece of work as well,' said Bessie. 'I'm sure he must have a heart in there somewhere because everyone does. But his is very well hidden.'

'You're telling me,' said Joyce. 'But you'd see good in the devil himself.'

'I wouldn't go that far,' said Bessie laughing. 'But I do try to see the best in people.'

'Talk of the devil,' said Joyce, noticing their boss in the shop doorway of the shoe mender's, deep in conversation with a man the girls didn't recognise.

'Goodnight, Mr Simms,' Bessie called out.

There was no reply.

'Rude bugger,' said Joyce when they were out of earshot. 'Outside of working hours we're not good enough for him to bother to speak to.'

'He was too busy talking to notice us, I think,' said Bessie.

'He must have heard you call out, though,' said Joyce.

'Yeah, I should think so.'

'He just didn't want to be bothered with us, I suppose,' said Joyce.

'He looked a bit furtive to me,' said Bessie. 'As though he didn't want to be seen.'

'Hm, I suppose he did a bit,' agreed Joyce, thinking about it. 'But don't let's waste another moment having him on our minds until we have to when we see him again tomorrow morning.'

'Suits me,' said Bessie.

★   ★   ★

Because Daisy was so possessive of her brother, Bessie had expected her to resent Bessie's romance with him, but she was absolutely delighted and seemed to see it as a chance to gain a new relative and secure a place in the Green family. Since her brother's visit she had been a lot happier altogether.

'If you marry Josh, you and me will be sort of related, Bessie,' she said happily that evening when Bessie had told the family about Josh's telephone call.

'Ooh, there's nothing like that in the offing at the moment, love,' Bessie told her.

'Why? Don't you like him enough?'

'I haven't known him long enough,' said Bessie.

'You have to know a person really well to marry them,' added Doris.

'But Josh must like you a lot if he rang you up from the army,' said Daisy.

'Yes, he does like me a lot,' said Bessie. 'And I am very fond of him too, but at the moment we are still just getting to know each other.'

'I think the whole thing is really soppy,' said Tom, who was at an age to blush if a member of the opposite sex so much as glanced in his direction. 'They're always cuddling and holding hands. It's so . . . embarrassing for the rest of us.'

'No it isn't,' said Doris. 'Not in the least.'

'It shouldn't be because it's perfectly natural,' said Bessie.

'It doesn't embarrass me,' said Daisy. 'I think you're just being childish, Tom.'

'Ooh, hark at you, being all mature,' he came back at her, grinning.

'Anyway, the phone call certainly cheered me up after Mr Simms's nastiness,' said Bessie.

'One of these days I'm going to come into the post office and sort that rotten bully Simms out,' said Tom, outraged on his sister's behalf.

'Don't you dare,' said Bessie. 'That really would set him against me and lose me my job.'

'You'd soon get another one,' he said. 'I've heard people saying there is plenty of work about.'

'Yeah, that's true because so many people are away in the services, but I like the job I've got so keep your nose out,' she said in a light-hearted manner.

Daisy had more personal matters on her mind. 'If Bessie and Josh get married will I be related to Tom as well?' she asked.

'Will you stop all this talk about marriage,' said Bessie firmly. 'And don't you dare mention anything of the sort to Josh.'

'Why not?'

'Because it's much too soon and it could put him off me altogether,' Bessie explained. 'Men don't like to think they are being lined up as potential husbands. And no, you wouldn't be related to Tom.'

'Good,' she said.

'That's a relief,' added Tom because he and Daisy still claimed to be enemies. 'I don't want to be related to her.'

'Anyway,' intervened Doris to calm things down. 'Christmas is coming up so that's something to look forward to, though it'll be even more challenging this year because of food rationing and everything else being in such short supply.'

'We'll still have a good time like we always do, Mum,' said Bessie cheerfully. 'Even if we have to have bread pudding instead of Christmas pudding.'

'You won't because I've already made the Christmas pudding,' said Doris. 'It might not taste quite the same as usual because the shortage of ingredients meant I had use my imagination, but I think it will be all right.'

'You're a wonder, Doris,' said Percy. 'Three cheers for our miracle worker.'

Daisy was a little slow to join in with the cheering, Bessie noticed. It was as though she wasn't sure if she was sufficiently attached to the family to take part in communal activities. But with a little encouragement from Bessie she was soon shouting with the rest.

'Roll on Christmas,' she said. 'Yippee!'

A couple of days after the incident with the cheating customer, Bessie saw the man waiting in the bus queue near the post office on her way to the bank to get change for the till. When he spotted Bessie he gave her a wide, victorious gin. Had she ever doubted herself she no longer did. His expression was telling her that he had beaten her. Just the sight of him set her temper blazing but she gathered her courage and went over to him.

'At some point in the future, what you did in the post office the other day will come back to haunt you because it was wrong,' she said. 'It was theft.'

'I don't know what you're talking about,' he said airily.

'Yes, you do,' she said firmly. 'You knew very well that you'd given me a ten-bob note and not a pound. You're nothing more than a common thief and you should be thoroughly ashamed of yourself.'

'Oh go away, you silly girl,' he said, obviously concerned that other people in the queue were listening.

'With pleasure now that I've said my piece,' she said and went on her way, glad that she'd found the courage to confront him but hoping she never set eyes on him again. Fortunately, people like him were very much in a minority in the post office community. Their regulars wouldn't do anyone out of a single farthing.

Bessie had been concerned about how she was going to manage her Christmas shopping with a cut in her wages to pay for the money the customer conned them out of, but in fact her pay-packet contained the full amount on Friday.

'I decided to let the matter go,' explained Mr Simms when she asked if she had to pay it back at a later date. 'Just be more careful in the future.'

He couldn't go so far as to admit that he had been wrong to suggest taking money from her, but she wasn't going to be penalised so she could let that go.

'I had a feeling he might back down,' said Joyce as they walked home together. 'He isn't always quite as nasty as he likes to make out.'

'It's a relief to me, especially with Christmas on the way and presents to buy,' said Bessie.

'I would have really gone for him if he had stopped it out of your wages,' said Joyce.

'Perhaps he suspected you might and that's why he changed his mind,' suggested Bessie jokingly.

'Oh yeah, he's scared stiff of me,' she said with irony.

'Actually, I think he might be a little bit nervous of you,' said Bessie. 'You do stand up to him rather a lot.'

'You mustn't let bullies win,' she said. 'But no, he isn't scared of me. I annoy him, that's all. He likes everyone to bow down to him and I'm a nuisance because I won't.'

'He is a bully, no doubt about that,' Bessie agreed. 'But sometimes he seems to be a little afraid of us.'

'They say that, don't they, that bullies are really cowards,' said Joyce. 'That's why they bully; to hide the fact that they are really scared stiff.'

'I don't know about that but I've got my full wages so I'm happy,' she said. 'I can start working my way through my Christmas shopping list now. Oxford Street here I come.'

'Good luck with that,' said Joyce. 'The choice isn't what it once was though.'

'I'm sure I'll find some things to buy for presents and we only get each other little gifts,' she said. 'I've got my wages, that's the important thing.'

The bombing in the run-up to Christmas was relentless and they spent nearly every night in the shelter. But by day, life continued as normal with people working and finishing their Christmas shopping, determined that Hitler wasn't going to spoil the highlight of their year. Bessie and Daisy had a wonderful surprise on Christmas Eve when Josh arrived home for the holiday.

'I struck lucky,' he told them. 'The army never tell you anything until the very last minute so I couldn't let you know that I was coming.' He looked at Bessie and gave a wry grin. 'I didn't dare telephone you at work again.'

She laughed. 'Thank goodness you didn't. I think that might have given the boss a nervous breakdown,' she said.

Although they had expected to spend Christmas Day in the shelter, the siren stayed silent so the celebrations went ahead as normal, but with less food. The Greens and their extended family enjoyed the usual games, sweet-eating and singing with Percy at the piano.

Nature made no allowances for special occasions and sent Daisy her first period at tea time. She had been told what to expect but it was a traumatic event for every young girl and she was no exception. Bessie and her mother looked after her and she shed a few tears, but the whole thing was shrouded in secrecy. Of all the days for it to happen! Bessie couldn't help but think that Daisy didn't seem to be the luckiest of people.

Although it was a wonderful day, being alone with each other wasn't easy for the couple, but they took a few walks and looked forward to the others going to bed.

'It's been the best day ever, Bessie,' said Josh with his arms around her when they were alone at last.

'For me, too,' she said, melting into his arms.

'I wish I could stay with you for longer.'

'Forever wouldn't be long enough for me.'

'After the war, we can be together all the time,' he said, adding quickly, 'if that's what you want.'

It wasn't a marriage proposal, but it was definitely a statement of intent, she thought. 'Of course it's what I want,' she assured him happily.

Life seemed very gloomy after Josh went back to camp, especially as the bombing resumed and was worse than ever. People were saying that the city around St Paul's had been bombed almost to the ground, but the cathedral remained standing.

Everyone in the post office was talking about it. News travelled fast by word of mouth so everyone in Hammersmith knew what was going on just a few miles away in the city and the West End. Weary from nights in the shelter, people still came in for their stamps, pensions and postal orders, exchanged news and most had a joke to tell. Some called in just to exchange a few words with their friends, much to the annoyance of Mr Simms. But he managed to hold his tongue because they were good paying customers at other times and he didn't want to lose them.

'Gawd knows how much longer this bombing will go on for,' said Edna. 'We're all worn out with it.'

'I'll say we are,' agreed Mary. 'Given how many thousands of people have lost their lives, it's a miracle we are all still around.'

'And for that we are very grateful,' said Edna.

The Green family, especially Bessie and Daisy, were thrilled when Josh turned up in early February.

'The army are getting generous, aren't they?' Bessie remarked. 'We didn't expect you to be back so soon.'

'You won't be so pleased when you know the reason why,' he told them.

'You mean . . .?'

'Yeah, it's embarkation leave,' he explained. 'They're sending us abroad so I won't be back for a while after this.'

Daisy burst into tears and rushed upstairs.

'She'll be all right when she gets used to the idea,' said Bessie. 'We'll look after her while you're gone.'

'You're in more danger than me with all these air raids in London,' he said.

'Yeah, I know,' she said. 'We just have to live in hope that it will end sometime soon.'

73

'Thanks again for looking after Daisy for me.'

'It's no trouble, Josh, but Mum does most of it.'

'I'll thank her and your dad again, too,' he said. 'I just don't know what my sister and I would do without this family.'

'You'd manage, but with a bit of luck you won't have to,' she said.

'I hope you'll be all right,' he said. 'London is a dangerous place at the moment.'

'It certainly is but don't let's dwell on it as there's nothing we can do about it,' she said. 'I don't suppose the army have told you where you'll be going, have they?'

'Oh no,' he said. 'I don't suppose we'll know until we get there. Secrecy is the middle name of the British Amy.'

'Probably for the best in these dangerous times,' she said. 'Apparently there are a good few spies about, living among us just like ordinary British citizens.'

'So I've heard and there are posters everywhere telling us to be careful what we say.'

'Sadly, Josh, I have to go to work so I won't be able to spend the days with you while you're on leave. I might be able to get one day off, but that's about all.'

'I'll look forward to seeing you in the evening even more then,' he smiled.

The weather was cold but the darkness of winter was beginning to lift as February progressed.

'He's out there waiting for you again, bless him,' Joyce observed as Josh appeared and stood near the letter box waiting for Bessie to finish work. 'The poor boy will freeze to death. It's bitter cold out there.'

Mr Simms made an unexpected intervention. 'Bessie, please tell your young man to wait for you inside.'

Joyce's brow went up. 'Blimey,' she said in a low tone indiscernible to the chief clerk. 'Wonders will never cease.'

'We can't have a member of the armed forces standing about in the cold, so bring him in.'

'Thank you, Mr Simms,' she said and she headed for the door. This goodwill gesture from Mr Simms showed the high esteem the military were held in by the public. She was proud to be Josh's girlfriend.

It was lovely having Josh around, but Bessie made sure that Daisy didn't feel left out by letting the siblings have time on their own together. She also sometimes included the young girl in outings to the park and the cinema when Tom usually came too. But the couple managed to have some time alone and it was agonisingly sweet because they knew it must end soon.

When he went back off leave the world seemed cold and lonely, but you couldn't mope about for long when you lived within a family.

'She's pining for Josh,' teased Tom. 'Aah, shall I go to the pictures with you, sis? Will that cheer you up?'

'No, it will not, you little squirt,' she retaliated.

'Mum, she called me a squirt.'

'Stop teasing her then and she'll stop calling you names.'

'He can't help himself,' chimed in Daisy. 'He's a proper little nuisance.'

'Don't call me names,' Tom objected.

And so the ribbing went on. Bessie realised that they were

only trying to make her feel better, but she knew that there was only one person she needed to be with at this emotional time so she got her coat and headed off down the street.

'I know exactly how you feel because I went through the same thing myself when Joe was posted abroad,' said Shirley.

'Yeah, of course you did,' said Bessie.

'But you do get used to it after a while,' she said. 'You still miss them but you do learn to accept it.'

'It seems as though there's nothing to look forward to,' sighed Bessie. 'I have no idea when I shall see him again.'

'You have to arrange things to look forward to, plan outings and so on,' said Shirley. 'Now that there's the two of us we can go out to the cinema and go to see a show every now and again. We're far too young to stay indoors every night.'

'Right now all I want to do is go to bed and cry into my pillow, I miss him that much.'

'Yeah, I was like that at first when Joe went away. But try to think of it as doing your bit for the war effort.'

'I'd rather dig Dad's allotment over every week as my contribution,' laughed Bessie, who wasn't one of life's gardeners.

'You have got it bad then,' said Shirley, giggling because Bessie had once had to look after her father's allotment when he was ill and it had been a complete disaster. She'd dug up his emerging vegetables thinking that they were weeds.

'I have,' she said. 'I really have.'

'You'll be all right once you get used to it,' said Shirley. 'And we'll go out and about together. I know I'm no substitute for your dreamboat, but in wartime we have to make do with what we have. What we want isn't an option these days. We'll keep each other company.'

'Thanks, Shirley,' she said, grateful to have such a good and loyal friend.

Walking to work the next morning Bessie was feeling guilty for making such a fuss over Josh's departure. Women all over the country were parted from their men; many of them married with children and having to bear the burden of responsibility on their own. She was lucky; she only had herself to look after and she had the backing of a loving family.

In the streets, the bombsites that had once been residential dwellings were becoming so familiar they were no longer quite so shocking. But today as she walked past the crumbled ruins of a row of terraced houses, Bessie found herself wondering about the families who had lived there and what would have happened to them if they had survived. Maybe because of Daisy she felt closer to the problem. She supposed the authorities must have found the people some sort of temporary accommodation, but to have lost your home and all your personal belongings must be crippling.

Fortunately, they had been able to provide a home for Daisy and she was young enough to put it behind her. What about all the other poor souls? The housing shortage in London was known to be dreadful so those surviving householders who had lived in these family homes could be reduced to living in one room in some hostel or lodging house, or worse.

The awful thing was the feeling of powerlessness because she couldn't help. She had no resources with which to do so. Her wages only paid for her keep, her clothes and other necessities with a small amount left for pocket money. But maybe there was something she could do for the unfortunates, something more helpful than just putting loose change into collection boxes. An idea was beginning to form and by the time she got to work she was absolutely bursting with it.

'I've thought of a way that I can help towards the war effort, in particular the people who have been bombed out,' she said to Joyce as they took their coats off.

'You already help Daisy and her brother,' Joyce reminded her. 'So you're doing your bit.'

'I was thinking more in terms of raising money for the charity that helps people who lose everything in the bombing,' she blurted out excitedly.

'It's a worthy idea but how are you planning on doing it?'

'A concert with all proceeds to the charity,' she said. 'And I want you to help me organise it.'

'I haven't the faintest idea how you'd set about it,' said Joyce. 'But I know that people do sometimes do that sort of thing to raise money, especially in wartime.'

'We'll work it out between us and rope in our friends and families and people from the other shops in the parade,' said Bessie, enthusiasm growing with every word. 'All profits will go to the wartime homeless. What do you think, Joyce?'

'Oh Bessie, you don't half come up with some mad ideas,' she said uncertainly. 'I think it's mostly show business types who put on concerts because they know how to go about it.'

'I think ordinary people occasionally do so as well, especially in wartime. I'm sure we won't be the first.'

'You could be right, I suppose.'

'The locals would support it because it's for charity and because they enjoy a night out.'

'Who would be in it though?'

'Our families and friends, people from the other shops in the town,' she suggested. 'Anyone we can find who can hold a tune, tell a joke or play an instrument. Acrobats and jugglers are also welcome.'

'Does that include you?'

'Oh no, not me,' she said. 'I don't have any sort of stage talent. I would organise it with you helping me, I hope, and I shall rope Shirley in.' Her voice rose with enthusiasm. 'We could hire the community hall in town. We probably wouldn't have to pay until later when we've sold the tickets.'

'Might have to pay a deposit.'

'I'll ask my dad to lend us that and pay him back out of the ticket money,' said Bessie. 'I'll also get him to play the piano, you know, accompany the singers. He's a brilliant pianist.'

'What singers would those be, Bessie?' queried Joyce.

'The ones we are going to find,' she replied laughing. 'There must be some people among our friends and acquaintances who can sing a song. It will be a definite contribution to the war effort, and it might be fun too.'

'Some people settle for the home and hearth when their boyfriend goes away to war,' Joyce sighed. 'You have to put on a bloody concert.'

Bessie laughed. 'So, will you help me or not?' she asked.

'Of course I will,' she smiled.

'Joyce and I are putting on a concert to raise money for the war effort, Mr Simms,' Bessie told him as she went to her place

at the counter just before they opened. 'Would you be interested in helping us?'

'I most certainly would not,' he said predictably.

'We are hoping to raise money for people who have been
bombed out and lost everything,' she explained. 'So it's a very
worthy cause.'

'I know nothing at all about the stage or how to organise
a concert,' he said.

'Neither do I, but I'm determined to find out,' she replied.

'In the meantime, perhaps you'd like to concentrate on your
work,' he said. 'And you can start by opening up.'

'Certainly,' she said, heading for the shop door. It would
take more than the negative attitude of Misery Simms to
dampen her ardour about her new project. She hadn't the
faintest idea how to organise a concert, but she intended to
find out.

'Well, you're a bit more cheerful than the last time you came
around,' said Shirley. 'Have they cancelled Josh's posting or
something?'

'Of course not, but I've thought of something to take my
mind off it,' she said. 'Something to keep us both occupied.'

'Not a couple of blokes, I hope,' she laughed. 'I'm staying
faithful to Joe.'

'Of course it isn't men,' she laughed. 'It's a concert.'

'That sounds all right,' she said. 'Is it in London? Who's in
it and have you got the tickets?'

'We're not going to a concert,' she informed her. 'We're
putting one on to raise money for charity.'

'How on earth would we do that?'

'Hire a hall, get people to take part free of charge and sell tickets,' she told her. 'Joyce is going to help us organise it.'

'I notice you are saying us which means you're roping me in.'

'Of course.'

'Oh Bessie, you and your crazy plans,' she said with a half-smile. 'We're just a couple of ordinary girls. How can we suddenly go into show business?'

'We'd be putting on an amateur show, a one-off, to raise a bit of money to help people worse off than us,' she said. 'We are not going into show business.'

'Hmm,' said Shirley, thinking about it. 'How would we find the people to perform?'

'We'd start off with friends and family and then put a notice up asking for people to audition if we don't have enough,' she said. 'My dad is a brilliant pianist so he can be the accompanist. That's one thing sorted already.'

'Mm, I suppose it might be possible,' said Shirley thoughtfully. 'You do occasionally hear of such things.'

'Of course it's possible,' said Bessie excitedly. 'So, will you help Joyce and me to organise it? I shall get the family involved as well.'

'I don't have anything more exciting to do after work so you can count on me,' she said. 'It will be something to keep us occupied and it might be a bit of fun.'

'The worst that can happen is that the show is a disaster, but at least we will have tried.'

'What do your family think about it?'

'I haven't told them yet. I'll do it when I get home. I wanted to be able to say that I have some support before I dropped the bombshell.' They were interrupted by an all-too-familiar noise. 'Whoops, there goes Moaning Minnie so I'd better get off home sharpish.'

'See you tomorrow,' said Shirley getting her coat and heading for the back garden and the shelter.

Naturally the Green clan were surprised to hear about the concert, but at least it took their minds off the air raid while they sat in the shelter.

'I'll help,' said Tom. 'But you won't get me to go on stage. Absolutely not!'

As his voice was in the process of breaking and changed from baritone to soprano about five times in one sentence she was happy to agree with him. Tom said he would make the tickets and help to sell them. Her father said she could rely on him at the piano, and her mother said she would help make the costumes, which just left Daisy.

'You've got a lovely voice,' said Doris. 'I've heard you singing around the house.'

'I could sing "You Are My Sunshine" and a couple of other popular songs if you like,' offered the girl.

'That should clear the hall,' teased Tom.

'Now, Tom,' admonished his mother. 'That isn't nice. Apologise to Daisy at once.'

'Sorry, I forgot you were the new Vera Lynn,' he joked.

Daisy slapped his arm. 'At least I'm willing to do something. You're too scared to go on stage.'

'Not scared,' he denied. 'Just realistic. There isn't anything at all I can do in that line so what would be the point of making a fool of myself?'

'You could have played a piece on the piano if you'd continued with the lessons,' said his mother.

'It was boring,' he said.

'How many lessons did he have?' asked Daisy.

'Two and then he refused to go again,' replied Doris. 'He didn't give it a chance.'

Daisy thought this was funny. 'Two lessons,' she said laughing. 'That is really bad, Tom.'

'How many have you had then?'

'None.'

'You did worse than me so you shouldn't criticise.'

'We didn't have a piano.'

'Lucky you,' said Tom. 'No one nagging you to learn.'

'I didn't nag you,' said his mother. 'The opportunity was there if you wanted it so I tried to encourage you.'

'And you refused, you silly boy,' said Daisy, teasing him.

'You're the silly one,' he retaliated. 'With all your girly talk.'

'You missed an opportunity,' she came back at him.

'I didn't want to be stuck indoors practising the scales when the street was full of kids playing.'

'That is a stupid attitude.'

'Stop it, the pair of you,' Doris intervened. 'All this childish arguing gets on my nerves.'

It occurred to Bessie that these two youngsters went into their own world when they had these slanging matches. Although they could get really insulting, she had a suspicion that they both thoroughly enjoyed it.

'When will the concert be, Bessie?' asked Tom.

'Not for a good while,' Bessie replied. 'It will take time to find the people and get everyone up to performing standard so I'm thinking in terms of late summer or autumn. Depends when we can get the hall for.'

'That's ages away,' said Daisy, sounding disappointed.

'The time will fly past as we prepare,' said Bessie.

'I can't wait to start practising.'

'Gawd help us all,' said Tom.

'Will you stop teasing her, Tom,' said his exasperated mother.

'I'm not teasing her,' he said. 'I mean what I say.'

Daisy slapped his arm and his mother reprimanded him again.

'You can't tell me to leave the room, can you, Mum?' he said cheekily. 'Not under the circumstances.'

'I can tell your father about your cheek though when he gets backs from ARP duty. Or you can apologise to Daisy.'

'I don't need to because she enjoys a bit of banter, don't you, Daisy?'

'I can hold my own against him, Mrs Green,' the girl replied. 'So don't you worry about me.'

'Well, so long as you let me know if he takes it too far, dear,' she said.

'I most certainly will,' Daisy said with spirit and it was obvious that the youngsters were very close despite all the arguing. 'So you'd better watch yourself, Tom.'

At the sound of the All Clear they all climbed out of the shelter. For Bessie there was always a feeling of huge relief when they had all survived another raid and she guessed it was the same for the others. They pretended not to be scared when the bomber planes roared overhead, but how could they not be?

But once the raid was over, it was back to normal. It occurred to her that you could live your life in wartime wondering if you would survive to live another day. Some people might think it unwise to plan to put on a concert in case they were all killed before then, but you had to look forward, to make plans as you did in peacetime or life wouldn't be worth living.

'Right, who wants cocoa?' she asked as they made their way inside.

There was an affirmative chorus. It was Sunday tomorrow so they all sat around discussing the forthcoming concert with their hot drinks. At least the proposed event had given them all something new and exciting to think about, which was exactly what they needed.

Chapter Four

Unsurprisingly, Mr Simms showed no interest whatsoever in the proposed concert, but he did allow its organisers to put one of their homemade posters on the noticeboard free of charge. They were asking for volunteers to take part in the show or help with the production. Singers, dancers, jugglers, musicians, acrobats, comics, stagehands, programme sellers, anyone who thought they might have something to offer or just wanted to be involved to call at the Green home at number six Bailey Street between seven and nine in the evening. The posters, a charming joint effort by Tom and Daisy, adorned the walls in the local shops and the library and Bessie booked the hall for a Saturday night in the autumn.

'I really don't know what made me think I could put on a concert when I haven't the faintest idea of how to go about it,' Bessie admitted to Joyce in a nervous moment at work when Mr Simms was not around. 'Why didn't you try to stop me embarking on such a crazy idea and making a fool of myself?'

'You wouldn't have taken any notice of me if I had; you were so full of it; and you're not making a fool of yourself at all,' replied Joyce. 'Anyway, why the sudden attack of cold feet?'

'The lack of talent might have something to do with it,' she replied with a wry grin. 'We haven't seen so much as a smidgeon since we've been doing the auditions. I mean, it isn't meant to be a professional show, but people will be paying to see it so they need to have some sort of entertainment. So far, we have two decent acts; Daisy singing a couple of songs with Dad at the piano and a violinist playing a few favourites. They are all really good but none of the others who auditioned had anything to offer at all. And the response to our posters hasn't exactly been overwhelming, has it?'

'No, not really,' Joyce was forced to admit. 'But it's still quite early days. The notice about the auditions hasn't been up for very long. Some people take a while to pluck up the courage to do their stuff in front of someone. I know it's only in your front room but it's still an audition, a performance. A lot of people may well have the talent but not the confidence to show it off.'

'Mm, I suppose you're right,' Bessie agreed. 'We might be able to help things along by mentioning that we need more performers to the customers and getting them to ask around. Not everyone looks at the noticeboards. Word of mouth might bring us better results. Get people talking about it.'

'We'll have to do it on the quiet, though,' said Joyce. 'Simms will have a fit if he hears us touting for performers.'

'Mm, you're right. But most of the regulars ask how plans for the concert are coming along anyway,' Bessie mentioned. 'Surely he can't object to us telling them and mentioning the need for people to take part.'

'Don't bank on it,' said Joyce. 'He's a genius at finding reasons to object to anything at all.'

'Yeah, he certainly is,' Bessie agreed with a wry grin. 'But we'll get around him somehow.'

'You two could get around anyone,' said Stan, appearing suddenly. 'But what's the problem? Maybe I can help?'

'Yes, I think you could,' said Bessie with a burst of inspiration. 'How do you fancy being the compère of our show?'

'I'd like that,' he beamed.

'The job is yours then,' said Bessie, pleased that one problem was solved at least.

'How are the plans for the concert coming along, Bessie?' asked Mary Miller later that same day when she came into the post office for stamps and postal orders. She was a chatty woman in late middle age who earned her living as a dressmaker and was reckoned to be the best in the area. Many a local bride chose Mary to make their wedding dress. 'I've ordered tickets for all the family and we're looking forward to it ever so much. You can't beat a good night out at a show.'

'It's beginning to take shape and thank you for supporting us,' said Bessie, putting her purchases on the counter. 'We'll do our very best to make sure you enjoy yourselves.'

'Got any good turns booked yet?'

'People are a bit slow in coming forward, to be honest with you,' she replied. 'Lack of confidence, I suppose. This being for amateurs, any potentials aren't used to performing in public so are nervous about it.'

'You need my nephew Ray on the job,' Mary told her with enthusiasm. 'He's got a cracking singing voice. He's a natural on stage and has bags of confidence, too.'

'He's absolutely marvellous,' added her companion Vera.

'He melts your heart when he sings. I could listen to him for hours.'

'Is he a professional singer then?' Bessie enquired.

'Oh no, nothing like that,' said Mary.

'He should be, though,' added Vera. 'He's certainly good enough.'

'Yeah, he's better than a lot of the professionals,' agreed Mary. 'He does quite often do a turn around the pubs and clubs and he packs the punters in. He gets his beer free for the night as well as a bit of pocket money.'

'Would he be willing to sing at our concert, do you think?' asked Bessie eagerly. 'Though as it's a charity show he wouldn't get paid.'

'That wouldn't worry him and I'm sure he'd love to,' she said. 'But he's away in the army – abroad somewhere.'

'Ah, what a shame; you raised my hopes for a minute then,' said Bessie with a wry grin.

'Sorry, love, but you'll find enough performers eventually, I'm sure,' she said. 'And I'll ask around. See if I can get people interested.'

'Me too,' added Vera.

'Thank you ever so much, ladies. I'd really appreciate that,' said Bessie, giving the customer her change.

'I've spread the word at work that we are looking for performers,' said Shirley, who had been sent to work in a munitions factory by the government quite early on in the war, having worked in a dress shop before that. 'So, we should be getting a few singers coming for auditions. Some of the girls sound all right when we have the music on at work and they sing along with it. We might find one or two who aren't bad. And one thing those girls don't lack is confidence. They're full of it.'

'It would be really good if you could drum up some interest, Shirley.'

'I will, don't worry. So, what else needs doing?' asked her friend, who had thrown herself into the project with enthusiasm.

'We need to concentrate on the auditions for the moment,' Bessie told her. 'And I'd like it if you and Joyce could be there when the hopefuls show us what they can do.'

'I wouldn't miss them for the world,' Shirley told her. 'Putting on a show was a really good idea of yours, Bessie. I enjoy having something else to think about apart from the air raids and how much I'm missing Joe.'

'Glad you're enjoying it,' said Bessie, excited about her new project. 'I am too. It's made a world of difference to me. Something fresh and different to think about.'

'Exactly what we both need,' said Shirley.

The air raids continued into the spring, along with arrangements for the concert. It was slow going but they eventually managed to find enough people to make up a programme of sorts; a mixture of singers, comedians, a violinist and a couple of acrobats.

But one night in May they didn't think they would live to put the show on because of what felt like the worst air raid they had ever experienced.

'Seems like we'll be in this bloomin' shelter all night,' said Bessie as the bombers roared overhead for hours on end. The whole family were cold and frightened, but managed to put up a front.

'Yeah, it is a long one,' agreed Doris. 'So we'll have to try to settle down and go to sleep.'

'With this racket going on?' complained Bessie. 'Not a flippin' chance.'

'We've slept through raids before,' said Doris.

'I don't think we've ever had one this bad before, Mum,' said Bessie. 'The noise is deafening as the planes go over and it's been going on for hours.'

'Yeah, I think this must be the worst raid ever,' said Percy, who hadn't long been home from his shift at the ARP where he'd been working on the streets helping the injured. He'd been out for hours because the length and severity of the raid meant they were short of assistance, so he'd worked for longer and was exhausted when he finally climbed into the shelter. He would never tell the family how frightened he sometimes was out on the streets on duty during the raids. He'd been among the frontline troops in the last war, but the home front was scarier somehow; probably because he was older now and the only way you could fight back was to take shelter and hope for the best. 'And we've had some shockers this past nine months. The blokes at the ARP were saying that tonight's bombardment must be the longest and most destructive of all.'

'I think they're right,' said Doris.

'Oi, Daisy, stop trying to look at my cards,' objected Tom, his everyday bickering bringing a touch of normality to the tense company.

'I'm not,' the girl came back at him. 'I'm not a cheat. If anyone is it's you.'

'No, I'm not so take that back.'

'No.'

'Yes, you will.'

'Now stop arguing, you two,' admonished Doris. 'We've

enough to put up with, we don't need you two going at it hammer and tongs as well.'

'But she's trying to look at my cards,' he protested.

'It's a wonder you can see to play cards with just the light from one little candle.'

'I can see well enough to know what she's up to,' said Tom accusingly.

'I'm not up to anything,' she retorted. 'The only cheat in this game is you.'

'Stop it, the pair of you, before I bang your heads together,' threatened Doris. 'And don't think I won't do it.'

'Sorry, Mum, but it's her fault.'

'It's him.'

'You're as bad as each other, but I don't want to hear another cross word out of either of you.'

'Play nicely,' said Bessie.

'We're not kids,' said Tom.

'In that case behave as though you're not and stop all this silly arguing.'

'Sorry,' said Daisy.

'Me too,' grunted Tom.

'Hooray,' said Bessie.

'I'll second that,' said Doris.

When the All Clear finally sounded, Bessie and the family didn't go straight in to the house. They went in to the street where their neighbours were gathered, some weeping after the terrifying experience. Everyone agreed it had been the longest and most vicious air raid of the war so far.

When the facts began to emerge the next day, Bessie and the

family were shocked to hear that every mainline railway station in London had been hit, along with St Paul's, Westminster Abbey and the House of Commons, as well as hospitals and a great many residential homes.

'What a night it was,' said Nellie when she came into the post office later, looking pale and tired. 'I really thought my end had come.'

'I think we all felt the same,' said Bessie. 'But here we all are again.'

'Plenty aren't though,' said Nellie sadly. 'I've heard that lots of poor souls lost their lives last night in various parts of the country.'

'It makes you dread the nights, doesn't it?' said Maisie, whose baby was almost due. 'My boys slept through the whole thing though.'

'That was a bit of luck,' said Nellie.

'Thank God the raids are only at night,' said Maisie as the post office began to fill up. 'At least we have the daytime to recover.'

'I hope we don't have it as bad again tonight,' said Winnie, who had just arrived, 'I don't fancy going through that for a second time.'

'We might have to,' suggested Nellie. 'There is absolutely nothing we can do about it seeing as our lives are in other people's hands.'

'We can only fight back by not letting it break us.'

'You're absolutely right,' said Maisie. 'That's about the only thing we can do.'

'Let's see what happens tonight, shall we?' said Nellie.

*   *   *

Much to the relief of everyone the skies were silent that night and the following one; in fact, the air raids stopped. No one doubted that there would be more bombs to come, but for the moment they enjoyed the peaceful nights.

'Lovely isn't it?' said Maisie a week or so later. 'I'm not really sleeping much at the moment what with heartburn and back-ache and the baby kicking, but it's nice to lie there without bombs raining down.'

'It certainly is,' agreed Bessie. 'Not long to go now, is there, Maisie?'

'Just a couple of weeks,' she said. 'Though when you get to this stage it could come at any time.'

'You'll be glad when it's over, I expect,' said Bessie.

'Not half. None of the others kept me waiting so I'm hoping this one won't.'

'I'll keep my fingers crossed for you.'

'Thanks, love.' She seemed distracted for a moment, then looked down to the floor. 'You won't have to. My waters have just broken.'

'What does that mean?' asked Bessie.

'It means the baby is coming,' she said shakily. 'I'll have to get home sharpish.'

'Will you make it?' asked Winnie, who was in the queue.

'I'll have to, won't I?' said Maisie nervously. 'I can't have the baby here.'

'You most certainly can't,' said Mr Simms looking worried.

'I'll walk home with you, love,' said Winnie kindly.

But at that moment Maisie let out a loud cry. 'The baby is coming,' she said. 'I won't make it home.'

'You'll have to,' said Mr Simms. 'You can't have the baby here.'

'She'll have to because you can't halt nature,' said Joyce, going over to the shop door and turning the sign to closed. 'Have you got a contact number for the midwife?'

Maisie got a scrap of paper out of her purse and gave it to Joyce, who handed it to Bessie. 'I'll look after Maisie if you could get the midwife.'

Joyce and Maisie disappeared into the back room and closed the door, Mr Simms turned the closed sign to open and then served Edna and Winnie, who were in no hurry to leave, while Bessie tore up the street and returned with the midwife.

Because most of the customers were regulars and knew Maisie personally, they were interested in what was happening on the other side of the door. Some stayed a while, others had things to do so left, promising to come back later for news. There were a few screams from Maisie, but nobody minded except Mr Simms who scowled at every one.

The baby was born quite quickly and there were whoops of delight from behind the door. Joyce put her head out. 'It's a girl,' she said and everyone cheered.

Bessie thought this must be one of the most uplifting moments of her life. She was very touched when Maisie said she was going to call the baby after Joyce who had been so kind to her during the ordeal. 'She'll be my little Joycie,' said Maisie, glowing with happiness as her wish for a daughter had been granted.

The midwife organised transport to take mother and baby home and very soon the post office returned to normal, all signs of the confinement gone as the back room was cleared up. But Bessie felt as though the place had been touched by magic that afternoon.

★　　★　　★

The concert really began to take shape. The tickets were produced in a joint effort by Tom and Daisy and enough performers hired to make a show. None of them really shone, but what they lacked in talent they made up for in enthusiasm. The paper shortage prevented them from producing programmes so they planned to write the acts down on a blackboard at the front of the hall on the night. It was all very amateurish but done with a great deal of heart, and excitement mounted as the day grew near.

Mary Miller came into the post office on the Saturday morning of the show to tell Bessie that her nephew had come home on leave unexpectedly and was happy to take part in the concert if she wished. Bessie didn't mind either way as they had a full list of performers, but she told her to tell him to turn up if he fancied it because the whole thing was very informal.

There was no shortage of helpers; everyone seemed willing to lend a hand, sweeping the floor and putting the chairs out. They even had donations of tea for the interval and volunteers to make and serve it.

Bessie knew that she, as the organiser, must say a few words at the beginning before she left Stan to do his job as the compère.

'Well, hello and welcome, everybody,' she began. 'What a wonderful turnout for our concert. Most of our brave volunteers have never performed in public before and I know that you will give them a warm West London welcome. Thank you all for buying a ticket and helping our charity. Now, please, sit back and enjoy the show.'

There was loud applause and the first performer came on, one of Shirley's workmates singing 'Blue Skies'. She'd never had a singing lesson in her life and didn't know middle C from the Houses of Parliament, but it was a brave attempt and she received some rousing applause. Daisy's rendition of

'Somewhere Over the Rainbow' was sweet and very well received. This concert was all about effort rather than excellence and the audience respected that, but at the same time people had paid to see some entertainment so they needed at least a little reward for it. Stan was an absolute godsend as compère with his natural humour during the introductions, but they needed more from the acts.

By the interval, Bessie was really worried. Nerves had crept in to the proceedings and none of the turns were at their best.

'The second half will probably be better,' said Joyce hopefully. 'The acts won't be so nervous then.'

Shirley appeared with a soldier in tow. 'This is Mrs Miller's nephew, Ray,' she said.

'Sorry I'm so late,' he said. 'I couldn't get away. An old mate called to see me and I haven't see him for ages so didn't want to hurry him, especially as it will probably be a while before I get home again.'

'That's all right,' Bessie assured him, noticing his deep brown eyes and warm smile. He was handsome, but in rather an ordinary way with a square jaw and snub nose.

'I'm happy to sing for you, but not to worry if you don't need me after all,' he said. 'We don't have time for an audition so you'll have to take me on trust.'

Things couldn't be much worse, she thought, but said, 'It would be lovely if you could open the second half for us then perhaps do another spot towards the end if the first number goes well.'

'Whatever you like,' he said casually, with no sign of performer's nerves as he went over to the piano and spoke to Percy about what he was going to sing.

* * *

Bessie was completely bowled over by the power and excellence of his voice, the richness and volume as he sang 'I Don't Want to Set the World on Fire'. It flowed from him naturally with a deep and melodious sound. She certainly didn't expect to be moved to tears by it, but she was. The audience were silent throughout then broke into rapturous applause at the end of the song, cheering and shouting for more.

He did another couple of numbers then came off stage to cheers and clapping, the entire audience on their feet. His outstanding performance could have daunted the other performers, but the opposite happened; he seemed to inspire them with confidence and the show really began to sparkle.

He closed the show with 'We'll Meet Again' and the audience were shouting and stamping their feet, especially when the rest of the performers joined him on stage along with Bessie and her helpers Tom, Joyce, Shirley and Stan. The show had surpassed all their expectations and they were all in high spirits. Bessie thanked all the artistes and the audience for their support. She offered special thanks to her father for his splendid work at the piano.

'All proceeds from the show are going to the charity that helps people who have been bombed-out in London. Thank you all for coming and helping us in this cause.'

There was more clapping and cheering; people were still standing. Bessie was overflowing with warmth and gratitude towards everyone involved in the show, including the audience. When they went off stage she hugged Joyce and Shirley.

'I hope you two are pleased with yourselves,' she said.

'We didn't really do anything,' said Shirley.

'You made a huge contribution,' emphasised Bessie. 'Helping me to organise it. I couldn't have done it without you.'

'And you two,' she said to Daisy and Tom. 'You've both worked very hard. You sang beautifully, Daisy.'

The others cheered in agreement and Daisy positively glowed.

'The soldier was the star of the show,' said Joyce when the youngsters had moved away.

'No doubt about that,' agreed Shirley. 'He appeared like a knight in shining armour when everything seemed to be going downhill.'

'He certainly did,' agreed Bessie. 'I want to catch him before he leaves to thank him.'

'You'll have to join the queue,' said Stan looking across to where the soldier was surrounded by admirers.

'I'm happy to wait my turn,' she said.

'Thank you so much for coming along and putting some much-needed oomph into our show,' said Bessie to Ray when the crowds had finally dispersed.

'I'm glad you were pleased,' he said, smiling warmly at her. 'I was happy to do it and really enjoyed myself.'

'How did you learn to sing like that?'

He shrugged. 'I didn't really learn,' he said. 'I've always been able to carry a tune, even as a kid. Never had lessons or anything like that. I just enjoy singing. It comes naturally to me.'

'You're very professional, though.'

'Probably because I've done quite a bit of performing,' he told her casually. 'Nothing very impressive, but being on stage builds your confidence. I sing in some of the local pubs when I'm home on leave and I always get roped in to any army concerts they put on, so that gives me experience.'

'You do more than just carry a tune.'

He shrugged.

'Don't you know how good you are?' she asked.

'I don't really think about it. People make comments,' he said. 'I'm just pleased they enjoy it.'

'You should be a professional.'

He laughed. 'Ooh, that's a bit fanciful for a bloke like me,' he told her. 'I'm a builder when I'm not being a soldier; a good solid tradesman.'

'But you were absolutely stunning tonight,' she told him with enthusiasm. 'Well, you heard the audience cheering, stamping their feet and begging for more.'

'Thanks for the praise, but it is just a local community hall,' he reminded her.

'You could fill the Albert Hall with a voice like yours.'

'Oh, now you really are getting silly,' he said, laughing softly.

'I mean it,' Bessie insisted.

He shrugged. 'In another life, maybe.'

She laughed. 'You are far too modest.'

'Just realistic.' He looked at the clock on the wall. 'It's only half past nine. Do you fancy going for a drink? I'm thirsty after all that singing.'

Seeing her hesitate, he said, 'Purely platonic, I promise. Just to wind down after the show. I'm engaged. My girl is away in the forces, the ATS.'

'A drink would be lovely then,' she said. 'I'll just have to make sure the clearing up is all done before I go.'

'I'll wait for you outside then,' he said, smiling.

'Ooh, a drink with the singing soldier,' said Shirley, grinning. 'Some people have all the luck.'

'It's just a brief after-show tipple to say thank you, nothing more,' Bessie made clear.

'I should hope so too,' said Shirley. 'Being as you are committed to Josh.'

'Ray is engaged anyway.'

Listening to the conversation, Daisy was concerned. 'What about my brother?' she asked.

Bessie spread her hands in a helpless gesture. 'What about your brother?' she said. 'I am having a drink with someone who was in the show, that's all. I'm sure Josh wouldn't mind in the least.'

'I'm not so sure about that,' said the girl, frowning.

Daisy's almost unhealthy interest in Bessie's relationship with Josh could be annoying, but she tried to stay patient because she knew it was a result of the girl's love for her brother and eagerness to be a part of the Green family. Her feelings of insecurity as a result of losing everything had left her with an overwhelming need to belong. Bessie hoped it would become less urgent as time passed and she matured because the poor kid was so vulnerable at the moment.

'Shall I come with you, sis, to make sure you behave yourself?' suggested Tom, laughing.

'Don't you dare,' she said.

'Aah, that's a shame.'

'Can I leave the rest of the clearing up to you?' asked Bessie of her helpers.

'You certainly can,' said Shirley. 'As you organised it, I'm sure we can finish up here.'

'I'll be off then,' she said. 'Thanks for everything, all of you. You've been wonderful. See you later at home, kids.'

★　　★　　★

They went to a riverside pub and sat outside as it was such a balmy autumn evening, the air moist and scented with a hint of mist, the smell of cordite from the bombs absent as they hadn't had any air raids for a while.

'Is your shandy all right?' he asked.

'Lovely,' she replied. 'Thank you.'

'You're welcome,' he said. 'I only asked because you never know what drinks are going to taste like these days with some of the publicans trying to make their limited supplies go further by watering them down. You can't blame them, I suppose.' He took a swig of his beer. 'So how come you got to put on a show?'

'I needed something to engross myself in, I suppose,' she replied. 'My boyfriend is away in the army and we were having a lot of air raids when I got the idea. I needed something to lose myself in because life was so hard.' She smiled at him. 'And, of course, I wanted to raise money for people who have been bombed-out because it's a subject that is close to my heart.'

'Good for you.' He smiled. 'So now it's over will you find some other project to fill your time?'

She shrugged. 'Maybe at some point later on but not for a while. I haven't really thought about it yet.' She changed the subject. 'Have you ever thought of going professional with your singing?'

'No. Never.'

'People must have suggested it to you.'

'Plenty have, over the years.'

'But you've never done anything about it.'

'No.'

'Because you lack the confidence?'

'Not really, though I think people exaggerate the extent of

my talent,' he said. 'I prefer to keep my feet on the ground and have more realistic ambitions.'

'And what might they be?'

'I'm a builder by trade and I want a business of my own after the war,' he said. 'I've been doing it since I left school so I know my way around a building site and I went to night school before the army. I know how the whole thing works from planning permission to building regulations. The plan is to build one house, in my spare time because I'll need to be earning, and sell it, then build another until I've made enough money to do it full-time, then I'll build one for myself and my wife. The war has got in the way of my ambitions but I'm hoping to pick it up again after demob when things get going again.'

'You'd rather do that than sing for a living?

'I know it might sound crazy, but at least it's realistic,' he said. 'I really enjoy singing. It's natural to me, but I don't see it as a career. I wouldn't have the faintest idea how to go about the management of it and you'd have to know about that sort of thing if you were relying on the income. So, I prefer to keep my feet on the ground.'

'That's surprising,' she said. 'I thought artistes always wanted to earn their living by means of their talent and would go to any lengths for their art.'

'Perhaps they do,' he said. 'And I would like that, of course. But I'm a very down-to-earth sort of a bloke. Those kinds of ambitions are just pie in the sky whereas building is a good trade and if you can eventually set up on your own you can do well for yourself. Anyway, builders are tradesmen and I've always admired them. Have you ever watched one work?'

She giggled at the oddness of the question. 'Well, no, it's never come up.'

'I admire the skill that goes into it, from the architect's plans to the finished product, and all the different tradesmen who contribute to the building.'

'I don't think I've ever heard anyone get so emotional about the building trade before,' she said.

He laughed. 'I do tend to get a bit carried away, I know.'

'The difference between singing and building is that building can be learned, but if you don't have the natural talent you can't become a singer,' she said. 'And only a few people are blessed with such talent as yours.'

He looked at her closely and she noticed in the moonlight his clear-cut features. He'd taken his cap off to reveal blond wavy hair though it was cut army style so there wasn't much of it. 'Hmm, there is that, I suppose, but builders vary. Some are better than others. There is a lot of skill involved.'

'The same as any other occupation, but singing is a special gift, you must admit.'

'Sure, I admit it but I still want to succeed as a builder.'

'So, in ten years' time can I expect to see boards around building sites with your name on them?'

'I certainly hope so,' he grinned. 'R.S. Brownlow and Co., it'll be. Look out for me.'

'I will definitely do that.'

'In the meantime, I'll walk you home then I'd better be on my way,' he said.

'So, you're going back to camp tomorrow?'

'Yeah, it was only a short pass.'

'Pity your girl wasn't around.'

'Yeah, that's the disadvantage of us both being in the services,' he said. 'We are rarely home at the same time. But we'll make up for it after the war.'

'I'm sure you will.'

'I think it will be quite a while before it's all over though,' he suggested casually.

'I've heard other people say that.'

'Yeah, it's a pretty general opinion, I think. Hitler isn't beat yet, not by a long way,' he said. 'But we'll get there in the end.'

They walked slowly to Bessie's, chatting with a kind of warm easiness all the way.

'Thanks again for your contribution tonight, Ray. Everyone enjoyed it.'

'I did too.'

'You were definitely the star of the show,' she said when they reached her gate. 'Good luck with your plans and with the war, of course.'

'Thanks.' He gave her a close look. 'You are a very pretty girl, Bessie.'

She smiled, enjoying the compliment. 'Thank you, Ray,' she said. 'What brought that on out of the blue?'

'I didn't want to leave without saying it,' he said. 'And I also admire you for putting on such a cracking concert. You really are quite a girl.'

'Oh, what a nice thing to say.'

'I mean it. You take care now,' he said. 'I hope your boy comes back safe,'

'Me too,' she said.

'Night.'

She listened to the click of his boots as he hurried down the street then she turned and went inside.

* * *

105

'Why are you two still up?' she asked as Daisy and Tom got up to greet her when she walked into the living room.

'It's Saturday night,' Tom reminded her. 'We always stay up later because there is no school tomorrow.'

'Yes, of course you do,' she said absently, because her thoughts were all of Ray.

'So, what is he like?' asked Daisy.

'He's a really nice bloke.'

'Are you going out with him again?' asked Tom.

'No, of course not,' she said. 'Josh is my boyfriend.'

'I bet you like Ray though,' said Daisy.

'Yes, I do like him,' she said. 'I like a lot of people. It doesn't mean I'm going to fall in love with them.'

'You might do, though.'

'Daisy, you have to stop this,' said Bessie.

'Stop what?'

'Worrying that I might break up with your brother.'

She flushed but didn't say anything.

'You will always be a part of this family no matter what happens between Josh and me.'

'So you are going to break up with him then?'

'No, of course not,' she said. 'But my relationship with Josh is not your concern and has nothing to do with your place in this family. You don't have to be a relative for us to love you.'

Daisy turned scarlet and said, 'I know that.'

But Bessie didn't believe her. Daisy had all the chat and wasn't short of cheek if the mood suited her, but beneath the banter and the backchat she was still as vulnerable as the first time Bessie had seen her on the mattress at the community centre, and she could weep for her.

'Come and give us a hug,' said Bessie and opened her arms

106

to her while Tom tutted and muttered something about girls being too soppy.

Daisy was thinking about her feelings for Tom a bit later as they sat in the living room with Bessie, drinking cocoa, Doris and Percy having gone to bed.

'You're quiet tonight, Daisy,' observed Bessie. 'Are you all right, love?'

'I'm fine,' she said, thinking how surprised the family would be if they knew how much she secretly adored Tom and longed for him to feel the same.

'That's good,' said Bessie. 'I thought you might still be worrying about my going for a drink with Ray.'

'No, not at all,' she said.

How Tom would laugh if he knew how she felt about him, thought Daisy. He would think it a huge joke so she must make sure she didn't show any signs of it.

'I'm bored now that the concert is over,' said Shirley when she called round to see Bessie the next day.

'Yeah, things do seem a bit flat because the whole thing was so exciting,' agreed Bessie. 'But we'll settle down in a day or two. We'll have to because we can't keep putting on concerts every time we feel a bit fed up.'

'No, but we can do other things to brighten up our lives.'

'Such as?'

'We could go out dancing at the Palais.'

'The purpose of which is to meet men and we are both fixed up in that direction.'

'No, not to meet men,' corrected Shirley. 'To dance and have fun.'

'Which involves meeting men.'

'Well, yeah, but there's no harm in it.'

'Not in itself,' agreed Bessie. 'But it could lead to trouble.'

'How old are you – twenty or forty-five?' said Shirley heatedly. 'You are such an old woman sometimes, Bessie.'

'I'm entitled to my opinion.'

'Anyway, you weren't slow in going out for a drink with that singer, were you?'

'Surely you're not suggesting there was anything untoward in that?'

'No, I'm not, which is exactly my point,' she said heatedly. 'You went out for a drink with him and there was nothing wrong in it. In the same way, dancing with blokes at the Palais is harmless.'

'It's a different thing entirely,' she said. 'I went for a drink with Ray because he'd done us a favour. Going up the Palais is making a statement. It's saying that you're available when you stand there at the edge of the dancefloor inviting partners.'

'When did you become such a prude?' asked Shirley.

The remark hit home to Bessie suddenly. 'Yeah, I suppose you're right,' she said thoughtfully. 'I'm sorry, Shirley. I'm sure a night out at the Palais can't do any harm. As long as you don't want me to go with you.'

'I'd like to go with you but if you don't want to come I can go with the girls from work. They go regularly,' she said. 'But you can come with us if you want.'

'I'll pass on that one,' she said. 'But I hope you have a good time.'

'I shall do my best,' grinned Shirley. 'And I'll tell you all about it afterwards.'

'I'll look forward to it,' said Bessie, feeling about sixty.

Bessie spoke to Joyce about it in a quiet moment the next day at work.

'Am I being a dreadful prude?' she asked, having explained the situation.

'A little, maybe,' said Joyce. 'I think some girls do go out dancing while their men are away and I'm sure there's no harm in it, but the usual reason for going is to meet someone. They say the Hammersmith Palais in the most successful marriage bureau in London, though not all the men have marriage in mind when they go there looking for girls.'

'I've always thought the idea of going was to meet someone special and Shirley already has one of those.'

'Mm. But there is a certain atmosphere at a dancehall, isn't there? The lights, the music and so on. It is exciting and your friend probably enjoys that. Anyway, what she does is nothing to do with you.'

'Not even if her boyfriend is my brother?'

'I can see why you are concerned, of course,' said Joyce. 'But people are free to make their own decisions so I think you should stand back and let her do what she wants. It's bad enough having all the wartime restrictions to cope with. It's only natural your friend wants to go out and have fun if she's that type of girl. But it's only my opinion and you must make up your own mind.'

The conversation was cut short by one of their regulars in tears. She wanted to send a telegram.

'My sister's husband has died suddenly,' explained Rita. 'She's in too much of a state to come down here to organise a telegram to her daughter herself so I'm doing it for her.'

'Sorry to hear that,' said Bessie. 'Is her daughter away somewhere then?'

'Yeah, she married some bloke and went up north to live,' she explained tearfully. 'She'll have to come home now, though, for the funeral anyway. It will be a shock to hear her dad has died. He seemed to be as fit as a fiddle.'

'I'm sure she will be shocked and upset,' said Bessie, feeling sad for the customer who was obviously in an emotional state. 'Could you write down what you want to say on this form and I'll send it right away.'

'Thank you, dear.'

'Why not have a sit down for five minutes before you leave,' she suggested because poor Rita looked pale and shaky. 'Give yourself a chance to recover.'

'Thank you, I might do that,' she said.

Bessie took the details then went to the telegraph machine to do the job. When she came back to the counter she noticed that the weeping customer was sitting down and talking to Winnie and Edna. That was the marvellous thing about this place; customers usually saw someone they knew and had someone to confide in. Maybe not always welcome for everyone, but in a case like this it was a godsend.

The distressed customer had stopped crying and was clearly enjoying the company. The conversation was morbid; all the details of the sudden death, but talking about it was obviously helping Rita. There was so much more to Oakdene Post Office than just business, thought Bessie, and long may it continue!

* * *

'Hello, Joyce,' said Stan the postman one Saturday afternoon when he happened to see her in Hammersmith Broadway. 'Doing some shopping?'

She gave him a beaming smile; always pleased to see him. 'I've got some clothing coupons to use up so I'm going to treat myself,' she told him.

'Good for you.'

'Not much choice in the shops, though,' she said. 'Still it'll be nice to have something new to wear to work.'

'You won't be keeping it for best, then?' he said. 'That's good because I'll get to see you in it.'

'I don't really go out anywhere much besides work,' she told him.

'Doesn't that husband of yours take you out then?' he asked. 'No.'

He frowned. 'Oh, but he likes a night out. I've seen him in the pub.'

'Yeah, he likes to go out, but he doesn't want me to go with him,' she found herself telling him. 'He likes to be with his mates.'

Stan made a face. 'He must be mad. If you were my wife I'd want to have you on my arm at every opportunity.'

She laughed nervously. 'Oh Stan, you don't half come out with some stuff.'

'I mean it, but then you know how I feel about you, don't you?' he said.

'Yes I do, Stan.' The two of them had hit it off ever since she'd started work at the post office and she'd got to know him better when she'd run into him in town one day and had gone to Lyons with him for a cup of tea and he'd poured his heart out to her. His wife had died of pneumonia before the war and he'd been broken by it for a while, but had somehow got over it. He made no secret of the fact that he very much liked and admired Joyce, but appreciated her married status. She more than just liked him but kept her feelings under control because she respected her marriage vows even if her husband didn't respect his.

'Can I be cheeky and suggest that we go for a cup of tea before you start dress hunting?' he suggested.

'You certainly can. I'd really like that, Stan,' she agreed, smiling. This unexpected meeting had brought a touch of magic to her day.

Chapter Five

Much to everyone's relief the bomb-less nights continued through the winter into the new year of 1942. There was always a threat of their return while the war continued, but people got used to sleeping in their own beds again and hoped for the best. It was a huge boost to public confidence to know that America had now joined the war as an ally.

'God bless every single one of them,' said Doris when the family were discussing it over dinner.

'Hear, hear,' responded Percy.

'America is a big and powerful country,' said Doris. 'We couldn't have anyone better on our side. All the extra troops will make a world of difference, I should think, as well as the weapons.'

'Definitely,' Percy agreed. 'It'll give our forces a boost too, I reckon, having some help.'

'Perhaps we'll get some good news from the front soon, then,' said Bessie.

'Given a little time I'm sure we will,' said Percy.

'Hooray,' cheered Daisy who knew nothing of the technicalities of the war, but welcomed any news that might suggest an end to it. There was a very happy atmosphere over dinner that evening.

The post office closed on Wednesday afternoons so one day in early January, before Daisy went back to school after the Christmas holidays, Bessie took the opportunity to go to Oxford Street with her mother and Daisy to get the latter a new winter coat. It was rather sad to see the West End looking so shabby, Bessie thought when they arrived. Some of London's most elegant stores like Selfridges and John Lewis had been damaged by the bombs, but shopping continued as normal, despite the rationing.

The West End still had its special atmosphere, Bessie noticed, even though the buildings could do with a lick of paint and a good deal of repair work. People created the atmosphere of a place and there were plenty of those about as always in Oxford Street; they had probably saved their clothing coupons to spend where there were so many stores to choose from, the same as us, Bessie guessed.

They got Daisy a red coat in one of the lower-priced shops and the colour looked lovely with her dark hair.

'Do you think Tom will like my new coat?' she asked as they headed for Lyons teashop for refreshments.

Bessie and her mother exchanged a glance. Despite her argumentative attitude towards Tom, Daisy clearly adored the boy, which made her acutely vulnerable.

'Boys of that age don't usually take much notice of clothes, love,' said Doris tactfully. 'But I'm sure he'll think you look lovely in it even if he doesn't say so.'

'I shall ask him if he likes it,' she said.

'Is his opinion that important to you then?' Bessie asked.

'No, not especially,' she said with unconvincing breeziness. 'But it's a nice feeling if people think you look smart, isn't it?'

'It certainly is,' agreed Bessie.

There were so many crowds in the West End there was a queue to get into Lyons and even when inside, Bessie and the others had to wait a while to find a table, but they eventually managed to get seated.

'I really love it here,' said Daisy, spreading the meagre portion of margarine on to her bun.

'You mean Lyons?' asked Bessie.

'No, not the café in particular though I do like it a lot,' she said. 'But I mean the West End in general, the shops and lots of people. It feels good here. I'd like to work here when I leave school. In one of the big stores.'

'Well, that's a definite ambition anyway,' said Bessie approvingly. 'We'll have to look into it when it gets nearer the time. They might send you on to war work, though. I don't know the rules about that. You might be too young.'

'If they do send me in to a factory I'll get a job in one of the big stores when the war is over,' said the girl. 'It's what I'd like to do as a job and that's definite.'

'You certainly know your own mind and that's a good thing,' said Bessie, smiling at her.

'Both you and Tom will be wage-earners soon,' mentioned Doris. 'Though Tom will be doing an apprenticeship so he won't get much money while he's training. It's just that you'll be so grown up, going out to work every day. You're growing up too fast for my liking.'

'We can't stay children forever,' said Daisy. 'And I can't wait to go to work.'

Doris looked thoughtful. 'I shall have to look for a job myself when the kids leave school,' she said to her daughter.

'Yeah, I suppose you will,' agreed Bessie. 'Work outside the home is compulsory now for women without children of school age and no other dependents, isn't it?'

'Yeah, it is. I want to do my bit anyway,' said Doris. 'In one of the local shops, probably. Most are short-staffed because of people going on to war work for the big money you can earn in a factory. But I suppose I'll have to go where the labour exchange sends me.'

'I'm not sure about that, Mum, but you might have a few jobs to choose from,' she said. 'They won't send you into a factory at your age, I shouldn't think.'

'Anyway, we've a few months to go before the changes happen,' said Doris. 'A little bit more time for me to pluck up courage.'

Bessie raised her eyes questioningly because her mother had always seemed supremely confident. 'You're not worried about it, are you, Mum?' she asked.

'I'm scared stiff,' confirmed Doris. 'I haven't been out to work since before I got married. The world has changed a bit since then so I'll be terrified.'

'You'll be fine,' said Bessie reassuringly, realising that she had only ever seen her mother in her own domain where she reigned supreme. Working outside of the home must seem a bit daunting for her.

'I shall certainly do my best.'

They stayed for a while drinking their tea and chatting, but noticing the queue of people waiting for a table they didn't leave it too long. Back outside in the crowds Bessie was surprised to find herself looking at Mr Simms standing talking to another man. She tried to attract his attention, just to be friendly, but he was engrossed in conversation with his companion then they parted company and her boss disappeared into the crowds.

She made a mental note to mention that she had seen him when she saw him at work tomorrow. Just to be friendly.

'It looks very nice on you, dear,' said Percy that evening when Daisy sashayed around the living room in her new coat. 'You look really smart in that.'

She did look lovely, Bessie thought. She was a natural for red with her dark hair and eyes and she was becoming a very pretty young woman. 'What do you think, Tom?' she asked her brother who was deeply immersed in this week's edition of *The Beano*, the cat asleep on his lap.

'What?'

'Daisy's new coat. Doesn't she look smart?'

He ran his eyes over the young girl who was looking at him expectantly. 'Yeah, it's quite nice,' he said and disappeared behind his comic.

'That's boys for you,' said Bessie disapprovingly. 'No interest in clothes whatsoever.'

'I don't care what he thinks anyway,' said Daisy and left the room hurriedly.

'Honestly, Tom,' said Bessie in a tone of admonishment. 'That wasn't very nice.'

'What have I done now?'

'You could have shown a bit more interest,' she said, reminded again of the depth of Daisy's feelings for him. 'Your opinion means a lot to Daisy. She cares about you more than you realise.'

'It's just a bloomin' coat,' he said irritably. 'Am I supposed to get all poetic about the latest bargain from C and A? Daisy looks nice whatever she wears.'

'You might like to tell her that sometime,' suggested Bessie.

'And have her get conceited? Not likely!'

'I doubt if anyone could make Daisy conceited. She lost her confidence when she lost her parents, poor kid, and it would take more than a compliment from you to restore it. Just imagine how you'd feel if that had happened to you at such a young age.'

'All right, I'll tell her I like the flippin' coat,' he said with an impatient sigh. 'Now can I get back to my comic, please?'

'Yes, you may,' said his mother, sharing a look with her daughter.

Actually, Tom absolutely adored Daisy, but she must never know how he really felt about her.

'Very crowded in Oxford Street yesterday, wasn't it, Mr Simms?' said Bessie casually in a quiet moment at work the next day.

He gave her a puzzled look. 'Was it?' he asked. 'I really wouldn't know.'

'But you were there. I saw you in the crowds outside Lyons near Marble Arch,' she said.

'I wasn't anywhere near Oxford Street yesterday,' he said with an edge to his voice.

She frowned. 'But I saw you,' she said. 'You were deep in conversation with another man.'

'You are mistaken,' he insisted, his voice rising with irritation. 'I wasn't in that area at all. Haven't been for a while.'

'Oh, it must have been someone who looked like you then,' she said as he seemed so touchy about it.

'Yes, it must have been because it certainly wasn't me,' he said adamantly.

'The boss was a bit huffy, wasn't he,' mentioned Joyce when she and Bessie were leaving the shop after work. 'When you said that you saw him in Oxford Street.'

'Yeah, he was very prickly,' she agreed. 'It definitely was him too. I've no idea why he would deny it.'

'It makes no odds to us what he does in his spare time, does it?' said Joyce.

'Of course not,' agreed Bessie. 'I couldn't care less where he goes or what he does and only mentioned it to be friendly. But I was wasting my time as usual because the last thing he wants is to be friends with us.'

'I've seen him talking in the street several times,' said Joyce. 'I'm amazed he's got any friends to talk to as he's such an unsociable man.'

'They are always strangers to us,' remarked Joyce. 'Never any of the customers. He'd cross the road rather than speak to them outside of the post office.'

'Yeah, I think he would too. He certainly is a weird bloke,' said Bessie. 'Sometimes he seems almost human and you think you are making headway then he goes all cold and peculiar again.'

'Oh well, it takes all sorts . . .' said Joyce.

'It certainly does.'

*   *   *

'How are things here?' asked Annie one bitterly cold morning when she came in to the post office for stamps. 'I haven't been in for a week or two. Are you all well and enjoying the cold weather?'

'We're well but could do with the temperature going up a bit,' said Bessie. 'We're looking forward to the spring.'

'Ooh we've a while to wait for that,' said Edna. 'A good few chilly days to go yet.'

'There was ice on the inside of our windows first thing this morning,' said Annie, who was looking smart in her conductress's uniform.

'And ours,' said Edna chattily, ignoring Mr Simms's look of disapproval at the lingering dialogue. 'Always is when it's really cold. We've told the landlord umpteen times but he won't do anything about it. He just says what do we expect for the rent we pay; a palace?'

'Much the same for us,' said Annie and the conversation moved on to the shortage of everything.

'I reckon we'll all eat ourselves sick after the war when food is plentiful again,' said Edna.

'At first I expect we will,' said Annie. 'But we'll soon get used to it and eat normally after a while.'

'Got time for a cuppa at mine, Annie?' asked Edna as they prepared to leave.

Annie paused for a moment then said, 'I'm on duty in an hour, but yes I'd love one and I fancy a chat, Edna,' she said smiling. 'Half an hour won't hurt.'

The two pals went off together leaving Bessie and Joyce feeling touched by the warmth of their friendship.

★　　★　　★

Bessie called at Shirley's house to ask her if she fancied going to the pictures on Saturday night and she didn't seem keen.

'I suppose you're going dancing with the girls from work again?' said Bessie.

'Err, well, yeah . . . that's right.'

Bessie had known Shirley all her life and she knew when she was telling fibs. 'You're not, are you?'

She made a face. 'Not exactly, no.'

'Why can't you come out with me then?'

'Well I . . .'

'Oh, for goodness' sake, Shirley, either tell me what's going on or tell me to mind my own business.'

'I met this bloke at the Palais . . .'

'And you're going out with him?'

She nodded, looking guilty. 'He's absolutely gorgeous,' she enthused. 'A pilot in the RAF.'

'Oh, you are going up in the world.'

'You know that sort of thing doesn't matter to me,' she said. 'But he does have bags of charisma.'

'What about Joe?'

'It's only one date,' she said, having the grace to look guilty. 'Joe doesn't need to know anything about it.'

'I'm not going to write and tell him if that's what you're suggesting,' said Bessie. 'I wouldn't dream of it. I just wondered if you'd forgotten that you are committed to him. He is my brother so naturally I'm concerned.'

'Honestly, Bessie, you are such a prude lately,' she said, her voice rising irritably. 'It's one flippin' date. Just a bit of fun. You remember fun, it's that stuff that makes you laugh.'

'There's no need to be nasty.'

'Just standing up for myself,' she came back at her. 'Anyway, you are a fine one to lecture me when you went out with that singer.'

'That wasn't a date,' she said. 'Nothing like it. You know that very well.'

'What was it then?'

'Just a brief after-show chat over a drink,' she said. 'A spontaneous one-off. And besides, it was months ago.'

'Well, I can see no harm in a one-off night out with a man for me,' said Shirley.

'In that case, you're more naïve than you should be,' said Bessie. 'I presume your engagement ring is stashed away in your drawer at home while you go out dancing, so that this bloke thinks you're free.'

'Free,' she said mockingly. 'Which century are you living in? Anyone would think these were the days when an engaged woman was expected to give up her friends and stay indoors all the time.'

'Of course I wasn't suggesting that, but I don't think you are expected to go out with other men,' said Bessie. 'Isn't that the idea of getting engaged; it's meant to be a serious commitment!'

'One night out, for God's sake,' she blasted angrily. 'What a lot of fuss about nothing.'

'You can't blame me for being concerned about my brother,' said Bessie, making as though to leave.

'You're sounding like Daisy! What about me, I'm your best friend,' she reminded her. 'Do I mean nothing to you?'

'Don't be ridiculous.'

'Look . . . none of us knows how long we've got while this terrible war is on, Bessie. We might be blown to bits tonight or tomorrow. I know you feel loyalty towards your brother and I understand that. All I want is a little fun to brighten my life up a bit. Working in a factory is very hard going and monotonous.'

'You do what you want, which you will anyway,' said Bessie. 'You always do.'

'Yeah, I will.'

'Ta ta then,' said Bessie briskly. 'Let me know if you're free for the flicks any time.'

'Bessie . . .'

'I'll wait for you to contact me. I won't be getting in touch with you again and that's definite. You know where I am,' said Bessie and hurried out into the night.

Her eyes were stinging with tears as she headed for home along the blacked-out streets. Her friendship with Shirley was hugely important to her and she didn't want to lose it, but she really didn't think she could cope if Shirley started to see this man on a regular basis. Her feelings for her brother were too strong. Perhaps it would just be something and nothing. But she had a very bad feeling about it.

The next day at work all thoughts of Shirley's love life were banished by the sheer volume of work caused by Mr Simms being off sick and no one available in the system to stand in for him.

'Phew,' Bessie said to Joyce when they closed for lunch. 'It seems as though the entire neighbourhood has been preparing mail that needs to be sent by registered post or having news important enough to warrant a telegram.'

'Wireless licences and saving stamps too,' said Joyce. 'I know Mr Simms is one hell of a pain, but we miss his contribution when he isn't here. It's the responsibility too.'

'I don't mind that,' said Bessie, realising as she spoke that she really rather enjoyed it.

'Maybe so, but he gets paid extra for that.'

'Yeah, that's true,' Bessie agreed, wondering if there was any chance of promotion for her at some point in the future at a post office somewhere in London. Managing a post office was a good job. She was surprised by these thoughts because she had never before considered any sort of a career. Girls like her usually saw employment as a bridge between school and marriage and her thoughts had always run along those lines.

But the war had changed things; it had created all sorts of interesting job opportunities for women and made new skills available, so maybe she should change the way she viewed things. Still, there was nothing to be done for the moment except get on with the job she had and do her best. At least the extra work had taken her mind of Shirley and her new man.

The weather softened into spring and felt sweet indeed after the bitter winter days. Splashes of colour brightened the gardens as crocuses and daffodils began to break through.

'Ain't it lovely to feel a bit warmer,' said Edna one sunny morning when she came into the post office to send most of her sweet ration to her evacuated grandchildren.

'Not half,' agreed Mary, who was there for her pension. 'I don't know how long the sunshine will last, but let's enjoy it while we can. I really enjoy sleeping in my own bed too after all those cold and miserable nights in the shelter.'

'Me too,' said Bessie and Edna agreed.

A tall young man with fair hair and smiling eyes came in. 'Morning, ladies,' said Joyce's son.

'Morning, Jack,' came a communal greeting; they all knew and liked him.

'Lovely day.'

'Not half,' said Edna.

'What are you doing here, love?' asked Joyce, smiling. 'It's lovely to see you, but aren't you supposed to be at work?'

'I've been sent out on an errand,' he explained. 'So I thought I would call in to see if you are behaving yourselves.'

Bessie glanced surreptitiously in Mr Simms's direction and said in a low voice, 'No chance of anything else when you work here.'

'Nice to see you, Jack,' said Mary.

'It would be even nicer if I was in army uniform though, wouldn't it,' he said with a wry grin.

'No, not at all,' said Mary firmly; they all knew how sensitive he was about his civilian status. 'You do a good job at the sorting office. You're doing your bit.'

'I don't have any say in where I am anyway,' he said, a bitter edge creeping into his voice.

'So stop punishing yourself,' said his mother.

'Your mother is absolutely right,' came a supportive chorus from Mary and Edna.

'It isn't easy when you get nasty remarks thrown at you on the streets because you're not in the forces,' he said.

'Not again,' said Joyce frowning,

'Yeah. I think I'll have to have a notice strapped to my chest saying that I keep trying to get into the forces but they won't have me.'

'People should have the sense to know that,' said Joyce.

'And anyone who matters does, so don't take any notice of the others.'

'Easier said than done, Mum,' he said. 'Anyway, I'd better get back to work. See you tonight.'

'Yes, love,' said Joyce warmly. Her son kept her sane in her mockery of a marriage and she adored him.

Bessie didn't hear from Shirley and she missed her terribly. She was obviously too caught up with her new love to bother about her old friend. Bessie was tempted to go and see her, but she'd said she would leave it to her and she wanted to keep to her word because it hurt to think of her friend cheating on Joe.

Then one evening in spring Shirley knocked at the door.

'I miss you, kid,' she said.

'Have you finished with your new boyfriend then?'

'No, quite the opposite.'

'Aren't you too busy with him to think about me?'

'No. I'm in love with him, Bessie, and I'm so happy I want to share it with you,' she said.

Bessie was shocked. 'You've come around here just to tell me that?'

Shirley nodded. 'I want you to meet him,' she said.

'No thanks.'

'It would mean a lot to me, Bessie.'

'What about Joe?'

At least she had the decency to look sheepish. 'I will write to him sometime soon, I promise,' she said. 'I just haven't got around to it yet.'

'Too busy with your new man, I suppose.'

'It isn't that,' she said. 'It's because I don't want to hurt him.

Maybe I'll wait until he comes home to tell him. That might be better. It's a bit cruel to have him receive a letter like that when he's stuck in some hellhole with nothing nice to take his mind off it.'

'I'm surprised you're concerned about his feelings,' said Bessie, but she did actually agree with Shirley. It must be hard to be jilted when you are so far from home.

'Of course I care about his feelings,' she said vehemently. 'I'm very fond of him still.'

'But you like your new man better,' said Bessie.

'It's a different sort of feeling.'

'You mean you fancy him more.'

'No, I mean I am totally spellbound by him.' She was adamant about it. 'I never felt quite this way about Joe.'

'Could that be because Joe doesn't wear a pilot's uniform?' she asked sharply.

'Don't be so ridiculous, Bessie. I would feel the same about Bernie if he was a sweeper at Victoria Station.'

Bessie very much doubted that but she said, 'Well, knowing how I feel about it, given that you are engaged to my brother, why have you come to tell me about it?'

'Because I miss you and I want you to be part of my life again. That's why I want you to meet Bernie.'

'No, absolutely not.'

'Oh please, Bessie' she implored. 'My parents have met him. It's just you now.'

'Why do you want me to meet him when you know that I thoroughly disapprove?'

'Because you have always been an important part of my life and I want you to be so again,' she said.

'I can't be disloyal to my brother, Shirley.'

'And you wouldn't be,' she assured her. 'Just meet him so you're not a stranger. Please.'

'What would be the point exactly?' she asked.

'You're my best friend and I want you to get to know the man I'm going out with,' she said. 'It's all very normal.'

'Not when you're engaged to my brother it isn't.'

'Mm, I can see why you would be against him,' she said. 'I thought if you were to actually get to know him a little and were to see how nice he is, you and I could still be friends.'

'Surely you can see the position I'm in,' said Bessie. 'You're cheating on my brother and you're asking me to condone it.'

'No, I'm not,' she said in a definite tone. 'Bessie, there's a war on. Bernie could be killed the next time he goes on a shout. Joe could be killed in action. You and I could cop it in an air raid. All we have is the moment. So, we have to live life to the full.'

Bessie sighed, weary of her friend's relentless attempts to persuade her. But she also knew in her heart that it wasn't her place to judge. 'All right,' she said. 'I'll meet him, just to please you. When and where do you want me to be?'

Shirley was all smiles. 'Thanks, Bessie. I'll fix it up and let you know,' she beamed.

'I'll await instructions then.'

The meeting took place in a pub in a side street near Marble Arch. It was obvious at once to Bessie why Shirley had fallen for him; he was outstandingly handsome with dark seductive eyes, a dazzling smile and charisma in gargantuan proportions. Well spoken and charming, he was definitely a cut above the men they usually mixed with. Smart, too, in his RAF uniform with his wings proudly on display.

'I'm so pleased to meet you at last, Bessie,' said Bernie. 'I've heard so much about you.'

'Likewise,' said Bessie.

'I feel as though I am on trial, though, I must admit,' he told her in a matey sort of manner. 'I know how important you are to Shirley. So, if I don't get your approval, I think she might give me my marching orders.'

'Don't overrate my importance,' she said lightly, entering in to the spirit. 'Shirley doesn't take any notice of me.'

'She certainly does,' he contradicted. 'I don't feel good about stealing her away from your brother, but some things are beyond our control, aren't they?'

'If you say so,' said Bessie coolly.

'Anyway, let me get some drinks. What would you girls like?'

'Gin and whatever you can get to go with it please, darling,' said Shirley in the manner of a girl about town.

'Bessie?' he said, looking at her questioningly.

'Just a soft drink, please.'

Up went his brows.

'Enter into the spirit, Bessie, and have a proper drink, for goodness' sake,' said Shirley in a tone of admonishment.

Bessie shrugged. 'All right,' she said, looking at Bernie. 'I'll have the same as Shirley. Thank you.'

'You're welcome.'

Despite Bessie's reservations, the evening went really well and she thoroughly enjoyed herself. They talked and joked and laughed a lot. He was polite, articulate and friendly and Bessie was absolutely certain that he was going to hurt Shirley in the same way that she was going to break Joe's heart.

✶   ✶   ✶

Despite Bessie's doubts, Shirley's love affair with Bernie continued through the summer, during which the air raids stayed away. Daisy and Tom both left school. He started an engineering apprenticeship and she went to work in one of the West End stores, having not been considered fit enough for factory work because of a tendency towards bronchitis that she had had since childhood.

Doris also got a job outside of the home: in the local Co-op grocery store as a part-time counter assistant.

'I've never been so scared of anything in my life,' she confessed the night before she was due to start.

'Now that isn't true, Mum,' said Bessie. 'What about that terrible air raid we had last May?'

'Yeah, that was very frightening,' Doris admitted. 'Funny, you'd think we'd never be scared of anything again after the air raids. But this is a different sort of thing altogether. I'm not scared of dying like in the raids, just afraid of making a fool of myself.'

They all encouraged her and said she'd be fine, which she was, and within a few days she was enjoying the job and thrilled with her first pay packet. 'I'll treat you all to the pictures,' she said joyfully. 'I can't buy you anything fancy because there's nothing much in the shops to buy.'

Shirley's romance with Bernie carried on, but Bessie had to make do with a rare letter from Josh that said very little. It wasn't easy to feel attached to someone when all you had was an occasional contact heavily censored by the army. She was beginning to understand a little of why Shirley had become involved with Bernie. It was lonely without your man around and it must be easy to fall in love with someone else if the opportunity presented itself. She'd had a letter from Josh a month or so ago, but it had been very brief. Their time together had been so short she was finding it hard to remember what it had felt like to be with him. He was beginning to seem like a stranger.

One evening in the autumn of 1942, Shirley came to Bessie's door sobbing her heart out.

'Bernie has finished with me,' she wept when Bessie had taken her up to her bedroom for privacy. 'Just like that, it's over. He doesn't want to see me again.'

'Did he say why?'

'Yeah. He said it was never meant to be serious and it's time we parted because I'm getting too attached to him,' she said. 'He doesn't want to be tied down.'

'Charming,' said Bessie sarcastically.

'A long-term relationship just isn't what he wants,' she continued tearfully. 'He said he never promised me anything and it's true, he didn't. I can see that when I look back on it.'

'He was seeing you regularly and seeming keen,' said Bessie. 'Most girls would take that as some sort of commitment.'

'Mm, I suppose so.'

'Heartless bugger,' said Bessie.

'I was expecting a marriage proposal when he said he had something important to say to me, so it was a terrible blow,' she sobbed. 'Made me feel quite ill.'

'I'm sure.'

'I suppose he's met someone else.'

'Did you ask him?'

'Yeah, he denied it. Just said he isn't ready to settle down yet so it's best if we part.'

'It could be true, I suppose, but that doesn't make it any less painful,' said Bessie. 'I don't expect you feel as if you can contact him to try and change his mind, do you?'

'I couldn't even if I wanted to,' she said thickly. 'I don't know how to get in touch with him. I don't have an address or a telephone number. He made sure of that. All I know is that he lives on the other side of the river somewhere when he's on leave. Anyway, there's no point in chasing after him if he doesn't want to know, is there?'

'No, I suppose not,' agreed Bessie, not at all pleased that her prediction had come true, and filled with sympathy for her friend. 'So, you'll just have to get on with your life as best you can. I'm no expert, but I suppose the healing process takes time.'

'It really hurts, Bessie,' she said. 'There doesn't seem any point in anything without him.'

'That sort of talk isn't like you, Shirley,' her friend replied. 'I know very little about these things, but you're bound to feel better with time although it might take a little while. I know it isn't much of a substitute, but you've got me to keep you company.'

'You're a good friend, Bessie,' she said. 'I know I've deserted you lately. It happens when you've got a boyfriend.'

'Yeah, I understand that. And don't forget you still have Joe,' said Bessie. 'Or did you write and tell him it was over?'

She bit her lip. 'No, I didn't have the heart,' she said. 'But I will have to because Bernie changed my feelings towards Joe. You can't be in love with two men at the same time, at least I can't. My feelings towards Bernie haven't changed because he's dumped me. Unfortunately, you can't just turn them off.'

'I suppose not,' agreed Bessie.

'I am not going to use Joe by staying with him just because Bernie doesn't want me.'

'It's awkward with him being away, though,' said Bessie. 'We've agreed it must be awful to get a letter saying you've been dumped when you are miles away from home.'

'Mm, that's what I've been thinking,' she said. 'I'll give it some more thought before I do anything at all. Maybe I should leave it until after the war when he comes home.'

'That's worth considering. Anyway, you don't have to make any hasty decisions. You just need to work your way through this personal setback before you do anything as important as that,' said Bessie. 'And you've got plenty of friends to keep your spirits up; there are the girls at work and me.'

'I don't want the girls at work to know he's chucked me,' she said. 'That would make me feel even worse. I'll tell them he's been sent away somewhere.'

'Is it a good idea to lie to your friends, though?' wondered Bessie.

'Probably not, but I'll do it anyway,' she said. 'My pride has been battered enough already. I can do without that lot talking about me behind my back.'

'Oh well, you know best.'

'In this case I really do,' said the tearful Shirley.

The sale of National Savings Certificates was boosted by the government's recent advertising campaign, with the idea of enhancing the wartime economy.

'I've sold quite a lot of them today,' Bessie said to Joyce as they finished work one day in October and were getting their coats on to go home.

'Sales seem to be well up these last few weeks.'

'That's one good thing about the war,' said Bessie. 'More people are working so they can afford to save a bit. They help themselves and the war effort too.'

'I'd sooner be poor than have this rotten war though.'

'I think we all would,' said Bessie. 'I suppose I saw something positive and leapt on it.'

They both laughed as they put their gloves and scarves on.

'We're off, Mr Simms,' said Bessie as they passed him doing something at the counter on their way out. 'Goodnight.'

'Goodnight,' he said and as Bessie caught his glance, a touch of malevolence in his eyes sent shivers through her.

'See you tomorrow,' said Joyce.

'Don't be late.'

'We wouldn't dare,' replied Joyce lightly and the women left the premises.

'Sometimes I don't know what to make of Mr Simms at all,' said Bessie as she and Joyce headed home.

'There's never any doubt in my mind,' said Joyce with a smile in her voice. 'He's a miserable old sod, there's no two ways about it.'

'He can be scary sometimes too.'

'I don't think he's going to jump on you, love,' said Joyce laughing. 'He's well past that, I reckon.'

'No, I don't mean that.'

'What then?'

'I don't know exactly,' she said. 'He just gives me the creeps at times. There's something in his eyes that's really mean, evil almost. He's shady. We've both seen him in conversation in the street and he always seems furtive somehow.'

'Yeah, he does but I think he's harmless,' said Joyce to reassure her. 'Just a bit lacking in the social graces and completely devoid of a sense of humour.'

'I don't think he's smiled in years,' said Bessie.

'Probably laughs his head off at home with his sister,' suggested Joyce. 'He doesn't do it at work in case he spoils the stern image he likes to project to keep us in our place.'

'I almost feel a bit sorry for him at times,' said Bessie. 'It must be hard work being so miserable all the time and never having a friendly conversation or a laugh with your work colleagues.'

'Oh well, it's another day tomorrow,' said Joyce. 'Maybe we'll get a smile out of him then.'

'I wouldn't bank on it,' said Bessie lightly.

Surrounded by the warmth of the family, Bessie soon forgot all about Mr Simms. Sitting around the table eating and sharing the events of their day there was plenty of banter and laughter. It might only be spam fritters and mashed potato mixed with swede, but all the plates were cleared.

'We get some really posh people coming in to the store,' said Daisy, who was on the haberdashery counter and longing to get into the women's fashion department.

'So you put on your hoity toity voice, I suppose,' said Tom, affectionately teasing.

'No, I most certainly do not,' she said in a firm tone. 'I just speak in my normal way.'

'Blimey, that's enough to send them straight to the shop next door,' he said laughing.

'He's teasing,' said Bessie quickly, because Daisy was ultra-sensitive when it came to Tom.

'The customers like me anyway,' said Daisy. 'My supervisor said I have a way with people.'

'And I agree with her,' said Doris kindly. 'You're a very nice young girl so of course the customers like you.'

'Don't tell her that, Mum, for goodness' sake,' said Tom. 'She's vain enough as it is.'

'You're the vain one,' Daisy came back at him.

'No, I'm not.'

'Yes you are,' she insisted. 'You're always looking at yourself in the mirror.'

'I only check to make sure my hair is tidy before I go out,' he said. 'There's nothing wrong with that.'

'He's hoping that some girl might notice him, I reckon,' said Daisy, laughing.

'No, I am not,' he denied hotly. 'I've been brought up to take pride in my appearance and not go out looking scruffy, that's all. That's true, isn't it, Mum?'

'You've been encouraged to be clean and tidy, yes,' she confirmed. 'Not to spend every minute looking at yourself in the mirror.'

'And I don't.'

'Ooh, not much,' said Daisy. 'It's a wonder you haven't worn a hole in the rug by the fireplace.'

'I thought it was looking a bit thin the other day,' said Doris, entering into the fun.

They all laughed. No so long ago Tom had had to be persuaded to comb his hair before he went to school. Nowadays he was much more attentive towards his appearance. It was probably connected to an invasion of hormones at around this age, Bessie guessed. He was becoming a young man.

'Was that a knock at the door,' said Percy. 'You're all making such a racket I'm not sure.'

'There's only one way to find out,' said Bessie, getting up and leaving the table.

There had indeed been a knock at the door and Bessie opened it to find Shirley standing there, sobbing her heart out.

'What on earth . . .?' said Bessie, putting her arms around her friend and gently easing her into the hallway. 'Whatever is the matter?'

'I'm pregnant, Bessie,' Shirley wept. 'And I don't know what the hell I'm going to do.'

'Oh blimey,' exclaimed Bessie worriedly. 'That's a bit of a shocker, I must admit.'

'It's a flaming disaster.'

'Well, you've got me,' said Bessie kindly, wanting to support her friend in any way she could. 'And I'll do what I can to help you.'

'Thank you, Bessie,' she sobbed.

Chapter Six

'I'm here for you come what may, but you need to tell your parents as soon as you can pluck up the courage,' Bessie said to her friend later that evening. She and Shirley had gone out for a walk, a half moon and familiarity with the area showing them the way.

'I'm absolutely dreading it, Bessie,' she said.

'I bet you are, but you might not feel quite so powerless about the problem once they are in the picture,' suggested her friend. 'Whatever their reaction it can't be worse than the worry of hiding it from them.'

'Oh Bessie, they'll be so upset and disappointed in me,' she said, her voice trembling.

'Yeah, I expect they will be, but they'll get over it and I can't see any other way forward. Once they get over the shock they might be all right about it.'

'I just want the problem to go away.'

'If you really mean that there's only one other alternative then,' said Bessie. 'Your workmates might be able to help you with that. You're not the first girl this has happened to. I've heard it costs quite a bit though.'

'I don't mean that,' she said, shocked at the suggestion. 'No, I really couldn't have an abortion.'

'I didn't think so,' said Bessie. 'So, you'll have to tell your mum and dad.'

'It's easy for you to talk,' snapped Shirley. 'You're not the one in trouble.'

'Sorry, love, but I'm only trying to help,' said Bessie. 'You don't have the support of Bernie so your parents are your only other option. I mean, I'll do what I can but neither of us have any power. We're young and we're skint. Anyway, your mum and dad always seem really nice.'

'They are normally, but something like this will floor them,' she said. 'The worst shame that can fall on a family. They'll be devastated. Especially as I'm their only child.'

'Mm. At first I expect they will be upset and might give you a hard time, but once they get used to the idea they'll probably be all right,' suggested Bessie hopefully. 'I know I might seem hard but I honestly don't know what else to suggest. It's happened so it needs sorting. If it would help I would tell them for you, but that might only make things worse.'

'Phew, not half; the fact that the terrible secret is known outside of the family, even only by you, would infuriate them,' said Shirley. 'They'll guess soon because I'm being sick in the mornings. I've been pulling the chain to hide the noise, but they're going to wonder about that before long, not to mention the fact that I'll start to get fat.'

'Still, no matter what happens now and how awful things seem, there is a baby on the way and that has to be good news.'

'Not to me it isn't. I can't even think of it as a baby,' said Shirley. 'It's just one big problem.'

'Yeah, I suppose it might seem like that at this stage, but once the secret is out in the open with your mum and dad, you might relax a bit and feel better.'

'My life seems to be going downhill fast; first Bernie leaves me and now this,' she said. 'It would be different if Bernie were around to give me his support, but I'll just be a creature of scorn: an unmarried mother. Oh God!'

'But apart from all that, it will be lovely having a kid, won't it? As you are an only child your parents might welcome a grandchild once they get used to the idea.'

'There will be fireworks when I tell them though,' she said. 'Anyway, Bessie, I don't want a child. I hate the idea of being a mother. I'm not ready for it. The whole thing gives me the creeps and makes me feel trapped.'

'You'll feel differently when the time comes, I expect,' suggested Bessie, trying her best to stay positive against a tide of negativity. 'And I'll be around to give you some moral support.'

'That means a lot, Bessie,' said Shirley, fresh tears falling. 'I feel so alone.'

'You're not alone because you've got me and your parents. So, come on, let's go home,' said Bessie kindly, linking arms with her in a friendly gesture as they found their way through the dark streets.

It was almost closing time at the post office, but a few people were still waiting to be served.

'I reckon we've more than earned our wages today,' Joyce said to Bessie. 'I'll be giving out stamps and postal orders in my sleep tonight.'

'We have been very busy but not long to go now,' said Bessie. 'We can close up in a minute.'

'As much as I like the job, I've had enough for one day.' Joyce looked at the clock. 'I'll go and put the closed sign up. It's time now.'

Bessie carried on serving but looked up at the sound of a sudden disturbance and found herself staring at a man who was holding a gun in one hand and Joyce in the other, the gun pointing at Joyce. People in the queue were screaming, some were trying to open the door.

'The door is locked so you can calm down and wait until I'm ready to open it,' said the man in a gruff voice. 'And keep quiet; stop that bloody yelling. It's upsetting my concentration. I'll use the gun on you if I have to.'

Silence fell upon the room.

'Give me the takings,' the man said to Mr Simms. 'You look like the guvnor so hand over the dough. I know there must be plenty of it because it's nearly time to close up and this little goldmine has been busy all day. I've done my homework.'

'I took a lot of the money to the bank earlier,' said Mr Simms. 'There'll still be enough for me.'

'The money isn't mine,' said Mr Simms. 'It belongs to the Post Office so I can't hand it over.'

'Don't mess me about,' said the man, who looked to be about thirty and was wearing civilian clothes that looked dirty and unkempt. 'Just give me the dosh and you can have the lady back. Otherwise.' He jabbed the gun at Joyce. 'She gets it.'

'All right. You're not in some gangster film so cut the dramatics,' said Mr Simms, seeming calm. 'I'll give you the money but only after you have assured me that you won't harm her.'

'You can have her back all in one piece as soon as I get the dough,' he said, his voice shaking. 'But get a move on. I don't have time to hang about.'

Mr Simms looked at Joyce. 'It's all right,' he said in a tone of voice Bessie had never heard before; he sounded almost gentle. 'You'll be fine. I'll give him the money.'

Joyce looked pale and scared, but she said, 'It isn't your money to give.'

'Don't worry about that now.'

'Stop yapping' said the man. 'And get the money out of the bloody till.'

Mr Simms went to the till, removed the money, put it into a bank bag and walked towards the robber.

'Not in the services then?' he said conversationally.

'Does it look like it?'

'No, but you could be in civilian clothes for some particular reason.'

'I'm in civvies because I am a civilian and not ashamed of it,' the man said aggressively.

A customer decided to have her say. 'You should be with the rest of the boys, doing your bit in the war, not threatening innocent people. You wicked bugger.'

Even from her position behind the counter Bessie could see that the man was trembling. At the slightest provocation, the gun would go off. Joyce looked terrified and Bessie's heart was racing.

'Keep your mouth shut,' said the man.

Mr Simms made an announcement. 'If you could all keep quiet, please, and leave this to me we might get somewhere.'

'Yeah,' said the man. 'Keep your noses out.'

Mr Simms was face to face with the man, and holding the

money in the bag. The robber didn't have a free hand so he said, 'Put the money on the counter.'

'Certainly, after you release my colleague.'

'I'll let her go when I have the money.'

Mr Simms was quiet for a moment then he walked to the counter and put the money bag down.

'Put it in my coat pocket,' ordered the man.

'Very well,' said Mr Simms removing the money bag from the counter and making as though to put it into the man's pocket.

But with extraordinary deftness he knocked the gun from the man's grip, pulled Joyce away, picked up the gun and pointed it at the man. 'Call the police please, Bessie,' he said.

'Certainly, sir,' she said.

Mr Simms was the hero of the hour; everyone wanted to shake his hand after the police had taken the man away. All the customers praised his bravery and the cool way he had handled the dangerous situation. Bessie and Joyce were full of admiration for him.

'You were really brave, Mr Simms,' said Bessie.

'I owe my life to you,' added Joyce.

'Let's not get carried away,' he said modestly. 'I am in charge here so it was my job to deal with the situation.'

'Well, we think you were marvellous, don't we, Joyce,' said Bessie.

'Absolutely,' her colleague agreed.

He did manage an attempt at a smile, but Bessie sensed that when the fuss had died down he would revert to being his usual bad-tempered self and she and Joyce would complain about him in private as always. But when he was being horrid she would try not to forget how he had behaved today. He deserved that.

Feeling as he did about Joyce, Stan was absolutely horrified to hear that she had been in danger. By the time he called into the post office on his way home, the drama was over and Mr Simms had rushed off to a meeting at head office.

'I'll shake your boss's hand when I see him,' said Stan. 'I can't bear the thought of anything happening to you, Joyce.'

She flushed, smiling. 'All's well that ends well so we can put the whole thing behind us,' she said.

'I'm not so sure how Mr Simms will feel about you shaking his hand, Stan,' said Bessie with a wry grin. 'Might be a bit too personal for him.'

'There is that,' said Joyce and the three of them burst out laughing.

Of an age to enjoy any sort of drama, Tom thought the whole episode was marvellous when Bessie told the family about it over their meal that night.

'Cor, I wish I'd been there,' he said enviously.

'I'm very glad you weren't,' said his mother. 'With someone waving a gun about? No thanks! It's bad enough that Bessie was there.'

'Did the police know who the man was?' wondered Percy.

'Yeah. A deserter on the run, apparently,' said Bessie. 'They'd been looking for him for a while. He's from west London somewhere, but I didn't recognise him.'

'Sad, really, isn't it,' said Doris. 'I mean some men just aren't cut out for the army. So the poor devil has ended up in trouble with the police.'

'I don't suppose many men enjoy the front line,' said Percy, who had been in action in the last war. 'But you have to get on with it and do your duty for your country. You don't threaten innocent people with a gun.'

'Well that one fell by the wayside, the poor thing,' said Doris. 'It happens. We are all only human and some are not as strong as others.'

'I can't wait to join the army,' said Tom.

'You've a few years to go 'til you are eighteen and I'm hoping the war will be over by then, though I suppose you might still get called up,' said his mother.

'I wouldn't mind seeing some action,' said Tom.

'You wouldn't like it, son, I can absolutely promise you that,' said his father.

'Change the subject, please,' said Doris. 'I've lost one son to this war. I don't even want to think about the possibility of losing another.'

'So stop talking about it, Tom,' said Daisy. 'You are upsetting your mother.'

'I was just saying . . .'

'Well don't,' said Daisy.

'Here she goes again, telling me what to do.'

'Now now, you two,' Doris intervened. 'I want no arguments at this table tonight.'

'Sorry, Mrs Green, but he is so annoying.'

'Annoying? Me?' countered Tom. 'You're the annoying one. Always trying to boss people about.'

'I've never seen her doing that,' said Bessie.

'Nor have I,' added Doris. 'And you can get that cat off your lap, Tom. I know you are hiding her under the tablecloth.'

'She doesn't like to be left out and she isn't doing any harm,' he said.

'It isn't hygienic, having a cat at the meal table, so put her on the floor.'

'She isn't hurting, love,' said Percy.

'Honestly, you are all barmy about that damned moggy,' she said, tutting.

'I didn't notice you shooing her off our bed when she slept there the other night,' remarked Percy, with a smile.

'That was just a one-off because she hadn't been well,' said Doris. 'Cats are supposed to go out at night.'

'That one doesn't if she can possibly help it,' he said. 'She usually manages to be missing when we go to bed so that we can't put her out.'

'I'll start putting you out at night if you don't shut up,' she said. 'See how you like it.'

The whole family erupted at this and Tom and Daisy resumed their bickering.

'I would never bring Tibs to the table,' fibbed Daisy. 'I know it isn't right.'

'Ooh, you little liar,' he challenged. 'You had her on your lap under the tablecloth the other night.'

'No, I didn't.'

'Yes, you did.'

'That's enough, you two,' said Doris. 'You're making the mealtime into a battleground.'

'It's her.'

'It's him.'

'Stop it the pair of you,' said Bessie. 'You're upsetting the rest of us. Mum has cooked us a nice meal, the least you can do is to let us enjoy it in peace.'

'Sorry,' said Daisy.

'Me too,' added Tom.

'I should think so too,' said Bessie firmly, very much aware of the growing strength of feeling between the two young people. Most of the time it seemed as though they loathed each other, but Bessie wasn't so sure about that. They had become very close. When they laughed together magic filled the house.

Shirley came to see Bessie with good news.

'Mum and Dad are being really good about you know what,' she said. 'Mum went off the deep end at first when I told her, but she calmed down eventually. They are not pleased, naturally, but they will be behind me. I'm glad they know about it. You were right to twist my arm.'

'So, what's going to happen?'

'I'm keeping the baby and living at home.'

'Have you got to pretend it's your mother's child?'

'No, nothing like that,' she said. 'Mum said it's happened so we must do our best for the baby and ignore the gossip. She even broke the news to Dad for me. He seemed more embarrassed than angry. He still thinks I'm about five, I think.'

Bessie smiled. 'Dads are a bit like that about daughters,' she said.

'I think Mum always wanted more kids but it didn't happen so perhaps she'll enjoy having a grandchild,' said Shirley. 'I still don't want it though. I'm not ready for motherhood, so I feel really miserable at the prospect.'

'Even though your parents are being so good?'

'That doesn't alter the fact that I'm going to be a mother

147

before I'm ready,' she said. 'I'm relieved that I'm not going to be out on the street, of course, but I really don't want this baby.'

'Oh Shirley . . . that's an awful thing to say.'

'I'm just being honest,' she said. 'I can't make myself want it, can I?'

'I expect it will be different when it's actually born.'

'I bloomin' well hope so. If not, I'm going to have a miserable life and so is the kid.'

'Are you hoping for a boy or a girl?'

'Couldn't care less,' she said. 'I have no interest whatsoever; it's just a cross I have to bear.'

'I'm shocked to hear you say this.'

'Maybe you are, but if I can't be honest with my best friend it's a poor show.'

'Yeah, that's very true,' said Bessie sadly. 'I'm just sorry you feel that way.'

'My life is ruined,' she said miserably. 'I have accepted that. It was broken into a million pieces the day Bernie said he didn't want to see me any more.'

'Come here,' said Bessie and put her arms around her. Shirley was selfish at times. Being an only child she had been indulged all her life, but she was a good and loyal friend. 'I'll be around to keep you company through it all.'

'Thanks, kid,' she said. 'I'll need you because I think Mum might try to suffocate me. She keeps telling me to put my feet up when all I want to do is go out dancing.'

Bessie laughed. 'You keep away from the dance halls,' she said. 'That's where your troubles started because that's where you met Bernie.'

'I know that,' she said. 'But I just want to have fun, Bessie, not a baby.'

'Please don't say that,' said Bessie. 'It really upsets me.'

'Why?'

'It just seems so cruel.'

'The baby can't hear,' she said. 'It's not much more than a seed at the moment.'

'It still doesn't seem nice.'

'Easy for you to be sentimental,' she said. 'You're not the one who's had her life ruined.'

'I know,' said Bessie kindly. 'But you'll get through it.'

'That's what I have to look forward to now, isn't it? Getting through things rather than enjoying them.'

'People do enjoy having a little one around,' said Bessie. 'You might do too.'

'Not a chance.'

'We'll see,' said Bessie.

Joyce's son Jack was in high spirits one morning when he opened a letter that had come for him in the post.

'I'm in. At last I'm in,' he told his parents, who were eating their morning porridge.

'In what?' asked his mother.

'The army,' he said, delighted. 'My persistence has paid off. These are my call-up papers.'

'But you're not fit enough for the services,' said Joyce, worried at the thought of her boy going away to war. 'They turned you down.'

'I've been going to the recruiting office regularly to try to persuade them to change their mind and at last it's worked,' he said.

'They've lost a lot of men so they'd be lowering the bar, I

suppose,' suggested Jim. 'Well done, son. I know it's what you want.'

'It really is, Dad.'

'I'm none too happy about it,' said Joyce. 'I mean, how can you not be fit enough one minute and fit enough the next?'

'Change of circumstances,' suggested Jim. 'They won't send him to the front, though. He'll probably have an office job somewhere.'

'I don't mind what they do with me so long as I'm in the army,' Jack said. 'At last I'll be like my mates – in uniform.'

Although Joyce had reservations about his going, she was very proud of him. 'Well done, son,' she said. 'I know it's what you want.'

'It really is, Mum,' he said, hugging her and bringing tears to her eyes.

Stan was very sensitive towards Joyce's feelings and he knew when she was upset, no matter how hard she tried to hide it.

'So would it help to talk about it?' he asked when he called at the post office the next day. 'I know something is wrong so don't bother to deny it.'

She didn't intend to burden him with her problems, but the kindness in his eyes loosened her tongue and out it all came.

'It's only natural that you would be upset that your boy is going away,' he said kindly when she had finished speaking. 'You're his mum and that's what mums do. But at least he wants to go, so that's a good start.'

'Yeah, I realise that.'

'The time will soon pass.' He smiled at her reassuringly.

'He'll be back before you know it. And I'll be around to cheer you up.'

'Thank you, Stan.'

'Why are you thanking me?'

'Because you're so kind,' she said, thinking how different his attitude had been to that of her husband, who had become irritable with her for being upset. Stan seemed to understand her in a way her husband never did.

'All part of the postal service,' he laughed, making a joke of it, though she could tell that he was upset for her. He was such a dear friend and that was so important.

'We need something to take your mind off things,' said Bessie when Joyce told her about Jack, 'so why don't we put on another charity concert?'

'Good idea,' said Joyce.

'We could start getting it organised right away,' suggested Bessie.

'I see no reason to hang about,' agreed Joyce.

So they wasted no time, and the experience they had gained from their last efforts stood them in good stead now. The star of their last show, Ray, wasn't there but most of the other acts were pleased to take part, especially Daisy who started rehearsing right away.

Much to the amazement of Bessie and Joyce, Mr Simms offered to take part with a magic act, explaining that magic was a hobby of his.

'That man never ceases to surprise me,' Joyce said to Bessie. 'He's as horrid as can be for most of the time, then he offers to take part in our show without even being asked.'

'I can't imagine him as a magician, can you?' said Bessie.

'I really can't,' said Joyce. 'God knows what he'll be like. I'm embarrassed for him already.'

As it happened she had no need to be embarrassed because Mr Simms entertained the audience brilliantly with some very clever card tricks. At one point a playing card was transported into the pocket of a member of the audience in the back row and another into a man's sock. The crowd loved it and shouted for more, which he provided.

Throughout the entire performance, he kept a straight face which suited the act perfectly.

'Well done, Mr Simms,' said Bessie when they were backstage afterwards. 'You were incredible.'

'As I've said, it's a hobby of mine.'

'The audience loved it.'

'Good,' he said. 'I'll be on my way now.'

'Are you not staying for the finale?'

'No. I have important things to do at home so I have to go.'

'As you wish,' said Bessie. 'Thank you for taking part. You were the star turn.'

He nodded and hurried away and the show continued. Bessie couldn't help but think of Ray and the huge contribution he had made to the last show. Maybe this concert didn't have quite the same sparkle, but the performers had all done their best and it had been a sell-out so they had achieved their aim and raised money for their charity. It had been fun to organise, too, and had served its purpose of keeping her busy.

* * *

Bessie and her family and friends were in high spirits as they walked home through the town.

'You did really well, girls. It was a lovely show,' said Doris. 'When is the next one?'

'Give us a chance, Mum,' said Bessie, laughing. 'These concerts take a lot of work.'

'I was only kidding,' said Doris.

'We will do another one,' said Shirley. 'But not just yet.'

'We'll come whenever it is,' said Doris.

Bessie felt a hand on her arm suddenly and turned to see that Joyce had grabbed her. 'Look, Bessie,' she said, pointing towards the open window of a pub.

Looking inside the pub Bessie saw Mr Simms at the bar deep in conversation with a man, a stranger to her. 'So much for important things to do at home,' she said.

'Why lie about it?' wondered Joyce. 'Why not just tell us he was meeting someone for a drink?'

'I have no idea,' said Bessie. 'But I wouldn't trust that man further than I can throw him.'

'Well, he's certainly a dark horse, that's for sure,' said Joyce.

'I think we might be wise not to mention seeing him in the pub at work on Monday,' Bessie suggested. 'He'll probably deny being there anyway.'

'I think you're right,' agreed Joyce, and the two women went on their way thinking about the deviousness of the man they worked for.

'There are a lot of American servicemen around in the West End,' said Daisy over dinner one evening in December. 'Very smart they are too. We see them when we go out for our dinner break and they sometimes come in to the store to buy things to send home to their wives and girlfriends. They are very polite and friendly.'

'You keep away from them,' said Tom.

'Why should I?'

'Because they are only after one thing from a girl,' he said, sounding grumpy.

'I don't think they are going to have their way with me in the crowds in Oxford Street, do you? Or behind the haber-dashery counter,' she said giggling.

'You can laugh,' he said in a serious tone. 'But I know what I'm talking about.'

'How exactly?' she wanted to know. 'How do you know any more about them than I do? I doubt if you've ever even spoken to one.'

'I've heard what they get up to,' he replied, becoming heated. 'Everyone knows except you. If you hang around with them, you'll get yourself a bad name.'

'I don't hang around with them. I just happened to mention that I've seen some Americans and you're carrying on as though I'm planning to sleep with one.'

'Daisy,' admonished Doris. 'Let's not have that sort of talk at the table.'

'Well, Tom's always going on at me,' she said.

'Stop going on at her, Tom,' said his father.

'It's only because he cares about you, Daisy,' said Doris.

That was the problem, thought Bessie. He did care about her and she was growing up and eager to explore the world. As was he. But he was protective towards her and she didn't like it. Or did she? Maybe the protests weren't as genuine as they seemed. Could it be that their feelings for each other were changing now that they were growing up?

She herself must stand back from it. It wasn't easy to watch two people you loved struggling to readjust their feelings for each other as they approached adulthood.

'I'll be all right, Tom,' Daisy was saying in a gentler tone. 'Thank you for caring about me, but I can look after myself.'

Tom just nodded and the conversation became general.

'Are you going out again tonight, Tom?' asked Daisy as he patted his hair in front of the mirror above the fireplace.

'Yeah, not that it's any of your business.'

'Just taking an interest,' she said airily. 'You go out a lot at night lately.'

'So what if I do? I'm a young man and it's what young men do,' he told her. 'I'd be a bit of drip if I stayed at home every night, wouldn't I?'

'Have you got a girl?'

'None of your business.'

'So you have then?'

'I didn't say that, but it would be none of your business if I had,' he said.

'I'm like a sister,' she said. 'So I'm almost a relative and relatives tell each other things.'

'Not always,' he said, turning away from the mirror to look at her and catching his breath at her loveliness, sitting on the sofa with her legs tucked underneath her, those huge eyes resting on him.

He absolutely adored her, but she must never know that. It was like falling in love with your sister so he must stifle his feelings and continue to treat her like an irritating relative. He did have flights of fancy when he reminded himself that there was no blood tie between them, so there was nothing actually wrong with him loving her, but it didn't feel right to fancy her in the way that he did and it tormented him.

'What about you?' he asked. 'Are you seeing your giggly girlfriends tonight?'

'A couple of them are coming round later.'

'Just as well I'm going out then,' he said. 'All their jabbering and tittering gives me a headache.'

'You sound about forty.'

He shrugged. 'I'll be off then. See you later if you haven't gone to bed when I get back.'

She nodded. 'Have a good time.'

'I will,' he said and left the room. How she would tease him if she knew that he was only going to his mate's house for a game of cards with a few of their pals. She would laugh even louder if she ever found out how he really felt about her.

The war and the winter dragged on. Bessie felt as though she would never be warm again. The coal shortage meant they were sometimes without a fire at home when they were waiting for a delivery and it was very draughty in the post office because the door was being constantly opened.

'Roll on the spring, eh, Joyce,' said Bessie one cold February day in 1943.

'Not half,' she said. 'It seems a long time coming. It's freezing in here.'

'The draught when people come in and out is like ice.'

Bessie turned to Mr Simms. 'Joyce and I are very cold, Mr Simms,' she said. 'We need some sort of heating in here as we can't get paraffin for the heater.'

'There is a war on,' he said in his old grumpy manner.

'But it's freezing,' she said. 'My feet are aching with the cold and I've got terrible chilblains.'

'So have I,' added Joyce.

'You'll just have to put up with it, I'm afraid,' he said. 'I can't be held responsible for the fuel shortage.'

The next morning, he brought in a small electric fire.

'Keep it quiet, though,' he said. 'We're all supposed to be saving energy.'

'Thanks, Mr Simms,' said Joyce.

'I'll benefit as well from a bit of warmth.'

'Of course,' said Bessie politely. What a strange man he was!

'He's a funny old bugger, isn't he,' said Joyce when they were walking home. 'Just when you think he can't get any worse he does something nice like that.'

'Yeah, it was the same with the attempted robbery,' said Bessie. 'He saved the day and seemed pleasant for about five minutes afterwards, then he went back to his miserable old self. I'll never work him out.'

'But having the fire makes all the difference to the working day, doesn't it,' said Joyce.

'I'll say,' agreed Bessie. 'It was quite cosy in there today. And as for Mr Simms, I don't think we'll ever get to know him if we work here until we're ninety. He's one of life's mysteries.'

'He certainly is,' said Joyce. 'But one thing we can rely on is that spring will come. The sun might not shine every day because this is England, but it will be a damned sight warmer than this.'

'Roll on, spring,' said Bessie.

Spring came and was sweet indeed. There had been no air raids for a while and people got used to the peaceful nights.

Shirley gave birth to a daughter in June but it wasn't a happy occasion for her because she didn't bond with her baby. 'Take it away,' she said weeping. 'I don't want anything to do with it.'

So the baby was handed over to her mother and put on the bottle while Shirley stayed in bed crying for a lot of the time. About the only contribution she made was to choose a name; she called her Gloria.

'She'll probably feel differently when the baby is a bit bigger,' suggested Bessie to Shirley's mother, June, when she called to see Shirley on her half-day off.

'That's what I'm hoping,' said June.

'You don't think she should see a doctor then?'

'No, it'll be a passing thing,' she said. 'I don't want to involve the doctor in case they put her away as she clearly isn't in her right mind at the moment. I'm hoping we can manage this ourselves. We've been putting on a show for the midwife. I had to be very firm with her about the bottle feeding. She strongly disapproves so I had a job to get pills to dry up the milk. Shirley was having such trouble with it, she gave in in the end.'

'I'll do anything I can to help,' said Bessie.

'Thank you, dear,' she said. 'That means a lot. She needs her friends.'

It's such a shame,' said Bessie looking at the scrap of humanity in her crib, 'She's such a lovely little thing.'

'Yes, I am completely under her spell,' June said.

'Just as well, the way things are.'

'Indeed.'

'I'll go and see Shirley,' said Bessie. 'Is she in the living room?'

'No, she's in bed.'

'Still!' Bessie, who had visited regularly since the birth, was shocked. 'The baby is a month old.'

'Maybe you can persuade her to get up.'

'I'll do my best,' she said and headed upstairs.

'Well, you're dragging it out, aren't you?' said Bessie. 'Three o'clock in the afternoon and you're still in bed. There's a baby downstairs who needs looking after.'

'She's all right with Mum,' Shirley said, looking sheepish.

'But she's your daughter. You need to be with her.'

Shirley started to cry. 'I feel so awful, Bessie,' she said.

'Awful? In what way?'

'Frightened.'

'What of?'

'Being a mother.'

'I suppose it could be a bit daunting at first,' said Bessie. 'I expect most new mums feel like that with a first baby at the beginning. But you'll soon get used to it.'

'The feeling is overwhelming,' she said. 'I feel as though I can't do anything. That's why I'm staying in bed.'

Bessie took her hand. 'How about you get up now while

I'm here and we'll go downstairs and have a chat. You might feel better when you're washed and dressed.'

'Will you stay for a while?' she asked.

'Yeah, I'll stay.'

When Shirley came downstairs, Bessie suggested that her friend's mother go out for a break if she fancied it. Shirley looked stricken.

'I'll be here with you and Gloria,' said Bessie, 'so you won't be on your own with the baby.'

'I wouldn't mind popping round to see my friend Betty next door. She's not been well but I haven't been able to pop in to see how she is,' said June. 'I haven't seen anyone since Gloria arrived. I won't be gone long.'

'Take as long as you like,' said Bessie. 'I won't go until you get back.'

'Thanks ever so much, love.'

Obviously glad of the break the older woman left and Shirley looked terrified.

'It's all right,' said Bessie, putting a comforting hand on her arm. 'I'm here.'

'Mum is really good with Gloria though.'

'And so will we be if she needs anything,' said Bessie, looking towards the cradle in which the infant was sleeping.

'Mum and Dad have been so good in every way,' said Shirley. 'They paid for all the baby stuff, the cot and pram and clothes and so on. I don't have a penny piece now that I'm not working.'

'It's unusual for parents to be so understanding about a baby born out of wedlock.'

'Mm, I know,' she said. 'I think it might be because they always wanted another child after me but it didn't happen, so a grandchild is the next best thing, even under the circumstances. They're not the type to be upset by gossip and scandal. Dad earns good money as a factory manager so he's happy to keep us.' Her eyes filled with tears. 'All that and I can't look after my child properly.'

'Of course you can,' said Bessie. 'There's no harm in letting your mum help until you are ready to take more part. She obviously enjoys it, but you'll have to make more of an effort.'

'I know.'

'We can start right now,' said Bessie. 'Let's take Gloria for a walk in her lovely new pram.'

'Oooh, I couldn't, Bessie,' she said 'My legs are too weak.'

'That's probably nerves,' suggested Bessie. 'It'll wear off once we're out.'

It took some more persuasion but eventually they set off with Gloria in her shiny new pram.

'Park or shops?' asked Bessie.

'Park,' said Shirley. 'There'll be people I know at the shops.'

'Surely you're not worried about being an unmarried mother?' said Bessie. 'You are the most self-confident person I know.'

'I was. Not now,' she said. 'But it isn't the unmarried thing. That's the least of my worries, though it doesn't help. It's feeling so nervous. I don't want people to see me like this. It's as though childbirth has shattered my confidence.'

'It doesn't show,' said Bessie. 'But we'll go to the park if you'd rather.'

As they walked, with Bessie pushing the pram, and the

sunshine gently warming them, Bessie felt her friend relaxing. They sat on a bench.

'Thanks for making me come out,' said Shirley. 'That awful feeling has eased off a bit. I feel more like myself when I'm with you.'

Bessie could see that the haunted look had gone from her eyes and only then did she realise how awful she must have been feeling. She also guessed that whatever they were and however silly her fears may seem to others, she really had been suffering and probably would again. One trip to the park wasn't going to offer a permanent cure.

But company of her own age might help while she learned to accept the responsibility of being a mother, which in turn would probably settle her nerves. Bessie was going to give her as much of her time as she could possibly manage. Shirley's mother was a wonderful support, but sometimes the company of a close friend was very welcome.

'We'll do this again, Shirley,' she said. 'I'll come and see you as often as I can. Between us we'll get your confidence up and running again.'

'Thank you, Bessie,' she said taking her hand.

Chapter Seven

Bessie kept to her word and spent a lot of her spare time with Shirley and the baby, hoping the company would boost her friend's confidence. It did seem to help, but Shirley's was not an instant cure. There were still dark times for her, especially when Gloria showed the slightest sign of ill health. Even a sniffle would worry her and the tiniest rise in temperature sent her into a complete panic. But things were better and Bessie felt closer to Shirley than ever before. She also adored the baby, who had wispy blond hair and a chubby smile as she grew out of the newborn stage.

Shirley had been too preoccupied with the baby and her ailing nerves to bother about spending her clothing coupons, most unusual for her as she loved to stay up to date. So one Saturday afternoon in summer Bessie offered to look after Gloria while her friend went shopping. As well as helping Shirley, she also wanted to give her friend's parents a break because they were both very supportive of their daughter and stepped in to help out without the slightest hesitation. Her father had Saturday afternoon off so she thought they could relax together without worrying about the baby.

So, while Shirley headed to the Broadway and her parents enjoyed some free time, Bessie wheeled the baby in the pram towards the park with the sunshade up as it was a sunny afternoon.

'Well, you've been busy since I last saw you,' a voice said and she looked up to see Ray, the singing soldier.

She explained that the baby wasn't hers and they chatted generally for a while.

'I expect you're married by now, aren't you?' said Bessie. 'I remember that things were heading that way when we last met.'

'No, sadly not,' he said. 'We broke up soon after that.'

'Oh, what a shame,' she said. 'I remember that you seemed keen.'

'She met someone else,' he explained, not sounding too bothered. 'But it's all right, I'm over it now.'

'I suppose that sort of thing is bound to happen in wartime with people being parted.'

'Oh yeah, I'm sure there are plenty of other couples breaking up as we speak. Are you still with the same boyfriend?'

'Yeah,' she said.

'You don't sound too sure.'

'I am,' she assured him. 'But it isn't easy to feel as though you are with someone when you never see them.'

'I suppose so.'

'Have you been overseas yet?'

'No, not yet,' he said. 'I must be more use to the army in this country at the moment for some reason, but I very much hope to go abroad at some point.'

'You make it sound as though the war is going on indefinitely.'

'I didn't mean to,' he said smiling. 'But it isn't going to end tomorrow or next week.'

'I don't think anyone has any illusions about that.'

'We'll get there eventually,' he said.

'I bloomin' well hope so,' she said. 'It seems to be going on forever.'

'Yeah, it's much longer than anyone expected at the beginning,' he said. 'But on a more cheerful note, have you put on any concerts lately?'

'Yes, we did a second one.'

'Did it go well?'

'Yes. Everyone really enjoyed it,' she said. 'Are you still singing?'

'Yeah, mostly in the bath,' he laughed. 'But I always give them a few songs in the pub when I'm on leave. I've been doing that since I was old enough to have a pint.'

'As I've said before, you should be singing at the London Palladium, not your local pub.'

'Don't start that again.'

'I mean it,' she said. 'When the war is over you should look into it.'

'I expect I'll be too busy trying to earn a living,' he said, 'but thanks for your interest.'

'No need to thank me,' she said. 'Just take note of what I say.'

'Aren't you the bossy one?'

'Not bossy, just definite if I feel strongly about something.'

'I might give it some thought after the war if my building plans don't come off,' he said. 'Meanwhile, would you think it very cheeky of me to ask you out tonight if you've nothing planned? Just as friends. No funny business.'

'What sort of thing did you have in mind?'

'Whatever you fancy,' he said. 'The Palais or the pictures or just for a drink if you prefer.'

She hadn't been dancing for years and the idea of a night at the Palais was almost irresistible.

'If I was in a position to come I'd choose the Palais,' she said. 'But obviously I can't because of Josh.'

'How will he be hurt by it?'

'I suppose he won't,' she said thoughtfully. 'But I'll feel guilty because it wouldn't be right.'

'I'm asking you out as a friend,' he said. 'I have no intention of persuading you to be unfaithful.'

'Promise?'

'I promise.'

She thought about it for a moment. 'All right then,' she said, grinning broadly.

'I'll call for you about seven,' he suggested.

'No, don't do that,' she said quickly. 'I'll meet you somewhere.'

'Your parents won't approve, eh?'

'My boyfriend's sister lives with us and she definitely won't approve. She's overly protective of her brother. I shall tell her I'm going out with you, but I'd rather spare you from her rampant disapproval.'

'As you wish.' He seemed about to say more but changed his mind.

'I'll meet you somewhere.'

'Outside the station at eight o'clock,' he suggested. 'And we'll walk over to the Palais together.'

'I'll see you later then,' she said and hurried towards the park with Gloria, her face wreathed in smiles.

*   *   *

'You're going out on a date then?' asked Daisy disapprovingly when Bessie told the family of her plans at teatime.

'No, I am going out dancing with a friend who happens to be a man.'

'Which is a date,' insisted Daisy.

'Not in this case, it isn't,' said Bessie. 'Ray is a friend who helped out with our concert and I haven't been dancing for ages so we are going together. That is all.'

'So, you won't mind if I tell Josh when I next write to him,' she said.

'Yes, I will mind,' said Bessie firmly. 'I don't want you upsetting him for no reason.'

'If it's so innocent why would you care?'

'Because he will almost certainly do what you're doing and jump to the wrong conclusion. Josh is thousands of miles away fighting in a war and the last thing he needs is an unnecessary piece of information.'

'Bessie is right, love,' said Doris.

'Leave well alone,' added Percy.

'Well, you would take her side, wouldn't you,' snapped Daisy, her face turning scarlet with rage. 'Because she's family.'

'That isn't fair,' said Doris. 'You know we think of you as family. We are taking her side because she happens to be right.'

'You are all ganging up against me,' she said, on the verge of tears, and rushed from the room.

Tom went after her.

'You need to calm down,' he said kindly, sitting next to her on the edge of her bed.

'How can I when Bessie is about to betray my brother?' she sobbed.

'She said he's just a friend, but even if it does turn out to be more than that it's none of our business.'

'So you do think it's a proper date then?'

'I have absolutely no idea' he said. 'But whatever the truth is, it's nothing to do with us.'

'But my brother is her boyfriend and he isn't here to do anything about it.'

'You shouldn't interfere, Daisy.'

'I can't just sit back and do nothing.'

'That's exactly what you must do.'

'How would you like it if someone was cheating on Bessie,' she said.

'I expect I'd feel just like you.'

'You'd probably throw a few punches.'

'Maybe I would, but it wouldn't be right,' he said. 'We have to mind our own business.'

'When did you get to be so wise?'

'I'm growing up, Daisy,' he said. 'We both are. So you need to stand back from Bessie's business.'

'I don't know how to,' she said. 'It hurts when I think of her cheating on Josh.'

'You must learn to let it go over your head,' he suggested. 'You don't want to lose Bessie's friendship, do you?'

'Of course not.'

'So get over it and concentrate on your own life,' he said. 'Have a look to see what's on at the pictures tonight. Maybe the two of us can go. It'll take your mind off what Bessie is doing.'

'You won't get around me that easily,' she said sharply.

'I'm not trying to,' he said. 'I just thought it might cheer you up.'

'Thank you, Tom,' she said thickly. 'I'll see what's on.'

The print was blurred by tears as Daisy looked at the local paper. She didn't seem able to get anything right as far as this family was concerned. They had done so much for her and she adored them all but she never seemed to share their views. She was so afraid of losing them yet she made that more likely by the way she behaved. When Tom had offered to go to the cinema with her she had sounded ungrateful.

Why couldn't she say the right thing? She managed it at work even if she did have to tell a few fibs to please the customers, and everyone seemed to like her. But this family she adored seemed to get the worst of her.

'Come on, Daisy,' called Tom. 'Where's the paper? We'll miss the beginning of the big film if you don't get a move on.'

'Just coming,' she replied, wiping her eyes and forcing a smile.

Doris was thinking about Daisy as she and Percy settled down to listen to the wireless after the youngsters had gone out. Daisy was so acutely vulnerable she sometimes brought tears to Doris's eyes. The whole family had taken her to their hearts, but she still seemed uncertain of her place among them. It was unspoken but you could sometimes see it in her eyes.

She was obviously fretting about Bessie's night out with Ray because she saw it as a threat to her brother. Doris herself had been surprised by the outing because her daughter was the most loyal of souls, but she was young and she hadn't heard from Josh in almost a year. It was only natural she wanted to have fun sometimes, especially as she had spent so much time with Shirley lately, who had apparently had some sort of emotional breakdown after her baby was born. So that must have been depressing for Bessie.

Hopefully this date with Ray would be a one-off. She really did hope so because of Bessie's commitment to Josh. Oh dear, the youngsters' love lives had been made so complicated by the war. They did say that absence makes the heart grow fonder, but that wasn't always the case. Well, there was nothing she could do about it. Bessie was old enough to live her life as she saw fit. And any parental interference would definitely not be welcome. So, keep your opinions to yourself, Doris!

Bessie was having a wonderful time. She hadn't been to the Palais since the Americans had arrived in England and what a difference they had made to this dancehall. A new kind of energy seemed to emanate from it because of the jiving and jitterbugging they had brought with them.

The jitterbuggers were twisting and jumping near the band. As of one mind Bessie and Ray moved closer to watch, but were soon trying out the steps for themselves. Breathless but smiling they stepped and twirled to the catchy tune of 'Chattanooga Choo Choo'.

'Oh, isn't it wonderful,' she said to Ray in the interval when they went upstairs to the cafeteria. 'I just love this new sort of dancing.'

'Yeah, it is good fun,' he agreed.

'It wasn't like this the last time I was here,' she said. 'It's absolutely buzzing.'

'The Yanks have started a craze.'

'And I'm all in favour.'

The choice of beverage was limited to tea because soft drinks were rarely available and the establishment wasn't licensed for alcohol.

'Sorry I couldn't get anything more interesting,' Ray said lightly, putting the drinks on the table.

'No need to apologise,' she said. 'You can't help the shortages. I'm having such a lovely time I'd be happy with water.'

'I'm enjoying it too,' he smiled. 'I love the jiving. I've never been much of a foxtrot man.'

It would have been tactless to mention how smart and good looking the Americans were so she just said, 'It seems we have more to thank the Yanks for than just their support in the war.'

He nodded. 'They've certainly put new life into this place.'

'It's been ages since I've had any fun,' she said thoughtfully. 'I was almost beginning to forget that I'm young.'

'Why the shortage of fun?'

'Well, my boyfriend is away so I don't normally go dancing and I have a friend who has had a problem so I've been worried about her,' she explained. 'But tonight is pure enjoyment and I'm loving it.'

'I'm glad,' he said warmly and she felt the impact of his charisma, which he had in abundance.

'I can't wait for it to start again.'

'Me neither,' he smiled.

*   *   *

171

The second half was even better because they were both more familiar with the steps. Bessie was quite sad when it came to an end, but they were both singing the songs softly as they waked home.

'Thank you for tonight, Ray,' she said. 'You've reminded me how to be light hearted.'

'I've enjoyed it too,' he said. 'I have one more night left of my leave. I suppose you'd think I was taking liberties if I asked you to do all this again tomorrow night.'

'Why don't you try it?' she suggested.

'Do you fancy doing it all over again tomorrow night?'

'I'd love to,' she replied, smiling.

'So you're going out with him again tonight then?' said Daisy with disapproval the next evening as Bessie got ready to go out dancing.

'Yes, I am, as it happens,' she replied, giving Daisy a challenging look, partly because she didn't much care for disapproval from a slip of a girl and also because she was feeling guilty about this second date with Ray.

'Are you going to the Palais again?' asked Tom.

She nodded.

I shall go there when I'm old enough,' he said. 'Everyone else seems to.'

'Yeah, it's one of London's most popular dance halls,' said Bessie. 'We are lucky to have it so near.'

The room was filled with tacit disapproval. All of them except Tom disagreed with her plans to see Ray again. She had arranged to meet him at the station again so she left early to escape.

172

'I couldn't shake off my own disapproval though,' she said to Ray when she told him about it as they walked to the dancehall.

'But we're only going dancing,' he said.

'It still doesn't feel right.'

He stopped in his tracks and took her arm. 'Look . . . would you rather forget it and go home? I don't want you to feel bad on my account.'

She looked at him. 'Not on your life,' she said. 'For once in my life I am going to be the bad girl.'

'Ooh, that sounds promising.'

'Not that bad,' she said and they both roared with laughter. He really was a tonic.

Ray was such good company. They danced and talked; laughed and joked. Bessie found herself feeling gloomy when the dance ended and they walked home, the night air infused with the scent of late roses. The fact that this was their last meeting added an air of melancholy to the mood after the fun of the evening.

'So you are going back to camp tomorrow then,' she said.

'That's right. I'm getting an early train so I'll be gone before you wake up.'

'Should you really have gone back tonight then?' she wondered.

'Probably, but as long as I go early enough, I'll be all right.'

'Why didn't you tell me?' she said.

'Because I wanted to see you.'

'But if you get into trouble it will be my fault.'

'Don't be daft,' he said. 'It was my decision. You knew nothing about it.'

'I certainly didn't,' she said. 'I wouldn't have let you risk trouble with the army on my account.'

'It will be fine,' he assured her. 'I might even try for the late train tonight just to be sure.'

'Go then, Ray, go now,' she urged him. 'You don't need to come right to my house. I'll be fine.'

'Another few minutes won't make any difference,' he assured her.

At her gate she said, 'We both know this will have to stop, Ray. I am committed to Josh.'

'It's just been a couple of nights out.'

'I think we both know it could very easily be more.'

'Yeah, I can't deny it.'

'I just couldn't do that to Josh,' she said. 'Your girl did it to you so you know how it feels.'

'I survived,' he said. 'Life has disappointments for us all. But we pick ourselves up and get on with life. I don't know where I'll be from one day to the next while I'm in the army. They could send me anywhere and life could be cut short for any of us while this war is on. But if you would really rather I didn't stay in touch . . .'

'It would probably be best.'

'Fair enough,' he agreed. 'If that really is what you want I won't get in touch again.'

'Thank you for two wonderful nights,' she said sadly. 'I'll never forget them.'

'Goodbye, Bessie,' he said and turned and headed off down the street.

She knew she had done the right thing but it felt so wrong. Her spirits were low as the turned the key in the door.

Everyone was in bed so she crept up the stairs as quietly as she could and was careful as she opened the bedroom door so as not to wake Daisy.

'Did you have a nice time?' asked the young girl in a whisper.

'Why are you still awake?'

'I've been waiting for you.'

'Checking up on me, are you?'

'No, of course not.'

'Well you can stop fretting because I won't be seeing Ray again,' she told her.

'I wasn't worrying.'

'Yes you were,' said Bessie in a harsh whisper. 'And it has to stop, Daisy. How I live my life is my business and has nothing to do with you, even though you are Josh's sister.'

'Yeah, I have finally accepted that,' she said. 'Tom has had a chat with me about it. I wasn't checking up on you, honest. I was just interested.'

'I'm relieved to hear it,' said Bessie. 'But I don't feel like talking now and you need to go to sleep.'

'G'night then,' said Daisy.

'G'night.'

Bessie went to the bathroom knowing that Daisy would be upset by her firm attitude, because the girl was so vulnerable. But she had felt compelled to adopt a strong stance or have her trying to tell her how to live her life. But back in the bedroom she planted a kiss on her head and whispered 'Goodnight, love' before she got into bed.

''Night, Bessie.'

She felt better for having done that, but she was still feeling sad and deflated. It felt like the day after a very special party. There would be other parties, but no more Ray and that was surprisingly depressing.

'I'm going back to work,' Shirley told Bessie when she called at the house with the baby in the pram the following Sunday morning.

'Really?'

'Yeah,' she confirmed. 'Mum is going to look after Gloria. She'd rather be at home anyway, but it's illegal now for a woman without dependents not to work; even older women, as you know. I need to be earning to pay my way and support Gloria so it suits us both. Well, it doesn't really suit me because I enjoy being at home with my daughter now. After those initial wobbles, I've loved being a mum, but I need the money. I can't keep sponging off Mum and Dad.'

'No, I suppose not,' Bessie agreed. 'So, will you go back to the factory?'

She nodded. 'It isn't the most pleasant job, but I can earn good money there if I put in the hours. My daughter won't want for anything if I can possibly avoid it.'

'Good for you,' said Bessie.

Gloria's admirers realised she was here and came to pay homage.

'Oh, isn't she coming on,' said Doris.

'What a little sweetheart,' added Daisy.

'You're doing a good job, Shirley,' said Percy.

It occurred to Bessie that not once had any member of her family mentioned Shirley's status as an unmarried mother in a detrimental way. But there had been plenty of gossip in the neighbourhood; Shirley had had more than enough spiteful comments. Bessie sometimes wondered if a common criminal got less abuse.

'Are you staying for a cuppa, love?' Doris asked Shirley.

'If you're making one, yes please, Mrs Green,' she replied.

Gloria was lifted out of the pram and they all piled in to the living room. Bessie felt blessed by the warmth of the company. She was so glad her parents still welcomed Shirley into their home. They were fond of her and that hadn't changed because she had 'got herself into trouble'.

'Morning all,' said Winnie as she approached the post office counter. 'Is everybody all right?'

'Yeah, we're all fine,' replied Bessie happily. 'I think we can put up with this war as long as we don't have air raids and it's been a while since we've had one of those.'

'Don't tempt fate, for Gawd's sake,' said Winnie. 'I doubt if Hitler has finished with us yet.'

'The boys need to get on and get the bloomin' job done,' said Mary, who had just been served and was on her way out.

'I'm sure they're doing their best,' said Bessie.

'Yeah, I know they are,' Mary agreed. 'I shouldn't have said that. Poor devils. God knows what they are going through.'

'Can we get on with the business, please,' said Mr Simms as more customers came in and the queue began to lengthen.

'Sorry if it upsets you, mate,' said Winnie. 'But I enjoy a

chat and if you can't have one in your local post office when there's a war on, it's a very sad day.'

'Hear, hear,' said Mary.

Silence fell and the atmosphere felt awkward. Bessie got busy heating the sealing wax for a registered parcel and the post office chatter flowed as usual. It would take more than Mr Simms's bad temper to upset her today.

'What are you so pleased with yourself about?' Joyce asked of Bessie later on during a quiet period when Mr Simms had gone for his break. 'Have you had a letter from your soldier boy or something?'

'Something like that,' said Bessie.

She had indeed had a letter from a soldier, but not Josh. It was from Ray. He said he knew that she was spoken for and he should stay away from her, but he hadn't been able to stop thinking about her and wanted to see her again when he could get away from camp. 'Much against my better judgement I have fallen in love with you,' he wrote.

'Well, anyone who makes you look that happy is all right with me,' said Joyce.

Bessie smiled but she knew her happiness couldn't last. She would write to Ray tonight and tell him not to contact her again. In wartime, it was apparently very common for an attached woman to meet someone else while her man was away. The agony aunts' pages in the women's magazines were filled with letters from readers who had done exactly that. The advice was always the same. Do not be unfaithful to your man, whatever the temptation. Get rid of the new love.

She knew they were absolutely right. It was an appalling thing to do and she must abandon any such flights of fancy about being with Ray. But just until tonight, when she put pen to paper, she would allow herself to enjoy knowing that her feelings for him were reciprocated.

That evening, after a great deal of serious thought, Bessie got Daisy on her own in the bedroom where she was sitting on her bed cuddling the cat.

'I want to have a chat with you,' said Bessie.

'Oh! What about?' the girl asked nervously. 'Am I in trouble?'

'No. Not at all,' Bessie assured her. 'But I need to tell you something.'

'What is it?' asked Daisy looking worried.

'I have just written a letter to Ray telling him that I feel for him as he does for me,' she said. 'I know you will be upset because of your brother and I was going to turn Ray down. Right until I put pen to paper, but then I realised I just couldn't do it.'

'Oh,' said Daisy sadly.

'I know you are hurt on Josh's behalf, but this has happened to me and there is nothing I can do about it.'

'You could put Ray out of your mind,' she suggested. 'People do. I've read about it in the magazines.'

'I'm not going to do that, Daisy, I'm sorry.'

'Poor Josh,' she said, her voice breaking. 'Are you going to write and tell him?'

'No. Absolutely not!'

'So you are going to carry on behind his back?'

'For his own good, yes, if you want to put it like that,' she said. 'Can you imagine how hard it would be for him to get a letter from me to say that I have fallen in love with someone else. I mean, he can't go off and have a good time to try and forget about it. It would be too cruel. So I shall wait until he comes home and tell him then.'

'I think what you are doing is terrible.'

'Of course you do and it is,' said Bessie. 'If I was in your position I would probably feel exactly the same. I am telling you now so that you can get used to the idea before Ray comes here again. He'll probably get posted abroad sometime soon, but until then I'd like to enjoy seeing him on the odd occasion he can get here.'

'Do the others know?'

'No, not yet. I wanted to tell you first because of Josh,' she said. 'The others won't be happy about it and I don't blame them. But just this once I must follow my heart and do what is right for me.'

Daisy shrugged.

'One thing I would ask is that you are civil to Ray when he comes to the house and if you don't feel able to then please make yourself scarce while he's around.'

'All right,' she said with a shrug.

'And one more thing, Daisy . . .'

'Yeah?'

'Don't spend all your time worrying about your brother's feelings. You have your own life to live. One day soon you'll met someone special and you'll be more able to understand how I am feeling now.'

'Maybe,' she said, sounding doubtful.

'So, are we still friends?' asked Bessie, taking her hand.

'More like sisters, I hope.'

'And sisters disagree sometimes, so I've heard.'

'I s'pose so.'

'I have to tell the others now,' said Bessie. 'And I won't be very popular with them either.'

'Good luck,' said Daisy, managing a smile.

Chapter Eight

The family didn't exactly welcome the news about Ray, because they were fond of Josh. But they knew that Bessie was no fly-by-night and that she was serious about Ray, so he was treated well whenever he came to the house. He was very likeable, too, which helped, plus the fact that he had been the star of their concert hadn't been forgotten.

The population in general wanted to see some sign of an end to the war, which continued to drag on. There had been vague rumours about an Allied invasion, but nothing else had been heard so as far as people knew it hadn't materialised.

'I suppose they have to be careful what they put in the papers,' said an elderly man who had come to the post office for his pension. 'They don't want the Germans to know too much.'

'Mm, there is that,' said someone else. 'We do get some war news, but I reckon it's chosen carefully.'

The days got shorter and colder with November fogs and frosty mornings. People were still eager for some positive news about the war, but none of any consequence came. There was more talk about an Allied invasion, which would, apparently, lead to the end of the war. No one seemed to know when or if it was actually going to happen, but it was something for people to cling on to as rationing bit even harder.

'At least we're not having the air raids,' said Doris. 'And we can cope with all this other stuff so long as they stay away.'

There was a murmur of approval.

'Ray doesn't get home so much lately, does he?' Doris remarked.

'No, he doesn't,' said Bessie. 'It might have something to do with the invasion, but he never talks much about what's going on in the army. I suppose he isn't allowed to.'

'Perhaps he's got another girlfriend,' said Tom, teasing her. 'And he goes to see her instead of you.'

'Tom, that's an awful thing to say,' said Daisy, giving him a playful slap.

'Yes, it is,' added Doris in a tone of admonishment.

'Only joking,' he said. 'If I really thought he would do something like that, I'd keep quiet, wouldn't I?'

'It doesn't worry me, Mum,' Bessie assured her. 'I trust Ray.'

And she did. She hadn't queried why he hadn't been around much because she had faith in him. She missed him but she would never question him.

'And so you should, dear,' said her mother. 'He's a thoroughly decent chap.'

'You lot are far too serious,' said Tom, who was always larking around and absolutely longing to be old enough to join the army. 'You need to relax more and have a laugh.'

'And you need to quieten down,' said his mother.

'I will when I'm too old to have a laugh,' he said.

'You'll never be too old to do that.'

'No, with you as my mother, I don't suppose I will.'

They all laughed. They always did plenty of that despite everything.

Ray managed to get home for Christmas, but he told Bessie the army was cutting back on weekend passes as well as ordinary leave so he didn't know when he would be home again after this.

He spent some of Christmas Day with his own family, but came to the Greens in the evening. They had a few drinks, played some games and sang a few songs with Percy at the piano. On Boxing Day night, he and Bessie went dancing at the Palais, where they jived and smooched and had a wonderful time. Bessie couldn't remember ever being this happy before. Sadly, though, he had to return to camp the next day.

Soon after they had welcomed in the New Year of 1944 the air raids returned.

'I thought we'd seen the last of the shelter after nearly three years without bombs, but let's find everything and get down there sharpish,' said Doris. 'No long faces. We won't give Hitler the satisfaction.'

'He won't know if we are smiling or crying our eyes out, Mum,' Tom pointed out.

'But we'll know,' said Doris, wrapping herself in a coat and scarves. 'That's the important thing. So hurry up and get your warm clothes on.'

They all trooped down the garden.

'Ugh, it's colder and smellier than ever,' said Bessie, lighting a candle.

'It seems like that because we haven't been down here for three years,' said Doris. 'But it is horrid, I must admit.'

'We'll soon get used to it again,' said Percy who had a rare night off from the ARP after several continuous nights of duty out on the streets.

'Let's hope we don't have to,' said Doris. 'It might just be a one-off.'

'Fat chance,' said Tom.

'Stop moaning and deal the cards,' said Daisy, who had slipped a pack into her pocket.

'Well done,' said Bessie, 'for remembering to bring them.'

'Yes, dear,' echoed Doris as the sound of the bomber planes rumbled in the distance. 'We need something to occupy our minds as those buggers come overhead.'

In the freezing-cold candlelight, they all joined in a game of rummy as the sound of the planes grew louder. Doris thought how nice it was to have her husband around for a change. He deserved a night off duty.

The air raids became regular, everybody got used to the sheltering habit again and life went on as usual. People still went to work, to the pubs and cinemas as though nothing had changed.

Bessie was in the queue at the chemist one day at the end of January when someone tapped her on the shoulder.

'Hello, Eve,' she said, turning to see Ray's sister. 'How lovely to see you.'

'And you,' she replied.

They chatted for a while then Eve said, 'How was the Palais on Saturday night?'

'I haven't been there for a while.'

'Oh, I thought you went last Saturday,' she said. 'Ray said he was going so I assumed you were going with him.'

'Ray was home at the weekend?' said Bessie in surprise.

'Yeah,' said Eve, beginning to look uneasy. 'Didn't you see him?'

'I didn't even know that he was home.'

'Oh.' She bit her lip. 'I'm sure he had his reasons for not catching up with you.'

'I'm sure he did,' said Bessie, trying not to show how upset she was.

Fortunately the queue began to move so she made her purchase, said goodbye to Eve and left the shop. She was absolutely devastated. She and Ray had missed each other, had longed to see each other again, or so she had thought. But apparently, it was only her. He'd been home and hadn't even bothered to tell her, let alone come around to see her. Instead he had gone out dancing on his own. Not the actions of a man in love.

She couldn't face going home just yet, so headed for Shirley's.

'Perhaps he just wanted a weekend on his own,' suggested Shirley.

'But he's supposed to be in love with me,' said Bessie. 'In his letters, he says he's longing to see me.'

'Mm,' said Shirley. 'Words are easy, especially in a letter. I can understand why you are upset.'

'I feel so rejected and sick inside,' Bessie confessed. 'I don't know what to do, whether to write and ask what's going on or leave it until I see him again.'

'It's difficult to know what to do for the best,' her friend replied. 'I think if it was me I'd leave it until you see him.'

'And answer his letters as normal,' she said. 'If I get any. Perhaps this means he's finished with me.'

'I shouldn't think so, but I'm no judge of men,' she said. 'Look what happened to me.'

'Mm.'

'But Ray is a different type altogether to Bernie. Ray is a decent bloke,' said Shirley. 'I'm as surprised about this as you are, but I should wait it out. Answer his letters and bring it up with him when you see him.'

'If I do,' she said. 'Perhaps he doesn't want to see me again.'

'Wait and see what happens,' Shirley suggested. 'Meanwhile you can give the baby a cuddle. It might cheer you up.'

She did adore little Gloria, but even her loveliness failed to raise Bessie's spirits today.

It was a month before she saw Ray, but she had answered his letters in the normal way. He was waiting for her outside the post office when she finished work on the Friday night and she raised the subject uppermost in her mind early on in the conversation.

'Yeah, I did get home one weekend,' he said casually. 'Just a twenty-four-hour pass.'

'But I didn't see you.'

'No, I needed a weekend on my own.'

'Oh.' She caught her breath at his brutal honesty. 'But you went to the Palais. You don't go there to be alone.'

'That's true.'

'So you wanted a weekend off from seeing me?'

He stopped walking and turned to her. 'Yes, that's right, Bessie.' He paused. 'You and I need to talk.'

'I'm listening,' she said, with dread in her heart.

'We can't talk here in this crowded street,' he said. 'Let's walk up to Lyons.'

'This, us, Bessie,' he said in Lyons teashop over a pot of tea. 'I enjoy it and I absolutely love being with you.'

'But . . .?'

'I am not planning on settling down at the moment. Not with all the uncertainty of the war and not knowing if I'll come back alive. So there will be no marriage proposal.'

'Who said I was expecting that?'

'No one said it, but you were probably expecting it at some point,' he said. 'We are good together so it's the natural course of events. But not for me.'

'Is that why you didn't see me the last time you were home?'

'Yeah,' he said. 'I needed to feel free again. So I went out on my own and I liked the feeling.'

'Oh.' It was like a blow to the chest.

'Bessie,' he said, reaching across the table for her hand. 'I do love you, very much.'

'But not enough to give up your freedom.'

'I would never love anyone enough to do that.'

'So why did you let it go on for so long?'

'Because I was enjoying myself,' he said. 'I love being with you, but then I realised I was getting in too deep. I didn't see you that weekend I was home because I wanted to see how it felt without you.'

'And you liked the feeling?'

'I wouldn't go so far as to say that,' he said. 'But I felt like my old self again.'

'So this is the end for us then?'

'Don't say that.'

'It's what you mean, isn't it?'

'I just want to be straight with you, Bessie,' he said, still dodging the question. 'We can still have the odd night out together if you fancy it. I think I'm being sent abroad soon anyway.'

'So you don't want to see me again, then?'

'This isn't easy for me, Bessie.'

'Just say it, Ray, at least have the courage to do that.'

'It's probably best.'

'Fine,' she said through dry lips. 'I'm very hurt, Ray, of course I am, but I am not going to fall apart.'

'Are you sure?'

'Of course I'm bloody sure,' she said angrily. 'The world doesn't begin and end with you.'

'Bessie . . .'

'I'm going,' she said. 'Thank you for being honest with me. I hope you enjoy your freedom.'

She got up and walked out with her head held high. But she was hurting, *so very much.*

'Well, I'm shocked, Bessie, I really am,' said Shirley to whom Bessie had flown, not able to face home yet. 'I really thought you two were going to make it.'

'So did I.'

'Still, at least he wasn't cheating on you with some other

girl,' said Shirley, who had just bathed Gloria and was putting her nappy on. She finished work early on Fridays so was able to do the baby bedtime routine.

'As far as we know.'

'You don't suspect that, do you?'

'Not really. But he was like a stranger to me today,' she said. 'I felt as though I had never really known him.'

'That would be the shock of what happened making you feel like that,' she said. 'Men and their precious freedom, eh. They always want to hang on to it.'

'I suppose if he had felt enough for me he'd have wanted to give that up.'

Shirley nodded. 'Anyway, kid, you can rely on me as a shoulder to cry on. When I'm not at work I'm here and I'll enjoy your company any time.'

Her warmth and eagerness to help brought tears to Bessie's eyes. 'Thanks, Shirl,' she said. 'I'd better be going now. I'll have to tell the family. Oh dear, what a dead loss I am. I can't even hang on to a fella.'

'It's only Ray you couldn't hang on to,' said Shirley. 'There are plenty more fish, not to mention Josh.'

'Losing Ray doesn't mean I am suddenly going to start loving Josh again,' she said. 'I haven't seen him for so long he seems like a stranger.'

'Give yourself time,' said Shirley, giving Gloria a cuddle. 'Things usually work out. Look at me. I thought it was the end of the world when Bernie ditched me and it hurt for a long time. But now I've got my little princess and I'm happy.'

'You've done wonders,' said Bessie.

'With plenty of help from my parents,' she said. 'I couldn't have done it without their support. They've been marvellous, Bessie. Once they got over the initial shock when I told them I was pregnant, they have been behind me all the way.'

'You've been lucky then,' said Bessie. 'Most girls in that position have a terrible time.'

'I know, but Mum and Dad have been really good.'

'I suppose you've had your share of disapproval from the public at large, though.'

'Oh yeah, and plenty of it,' she said. 'But it's water off a duck's back now. And God help anyone who says anything to Gloria when she's older.'

'Everyone will have forgotten it by then.'

'I hope so,' she said. 'But I shall be keeping a protective eye open.'

'Well, I'd better go home,' said Bessie. 'I have the job of telling the family and I'm not looking forward to it. They'll be disappointed. They really like Ray.'

'They won't be so keen on him when you tell them what happened,' she said.

'And the silly part is I shall probably want to defend him,' she said.

'Yeah, I didn't want to hear a word against Bernie. I could say it but flew to his defence if anyone else dared to,' sighed Shirley. 'Men, eh? They make fools of us all.'

'They certainly do,' agreed Bessie, and went on her way.

Bessie waited until everyone had finished eating before she broke the news.

'What do you mean finished with him?' asked Doris. 'You and Ray are lovely together.'

191

'That's what I thought, but apparently not,' said Bessie. 'He doesn't want to settle down.'

'Oh, doesn't he,' said Doris. 'He should have thought of that before he strung you along.'

'I was a willing party, Mum,' said Bessie, still wanting to defend him.

'Maybe you were, but he had no right to let it go on for so long if he wasn't serious.'

'He probably had his reasons,' said Tom. 'Ray is a good bloke and no one will convince me otherwise.'

'He can't be that good or he wouldn't have dumped Bessie,' retorted Doris.

'It isn't a crime to break up with a girl, Mum. We weren't engaged,' Bessie reminded her. 'And I don't want to hear any of you saying bad things about him. We were courting and now we're not. Those are the plain facts. So can we now please change the subject?'

Silence fell over the room.

'There's a lot of talk on the wireless about this invasion they are supposed to be having,' said Doris.

'There has been for a while,' said Percy. 'But that's all it is – talk. Nothing happens.'

'At least the air raids seem to have stopped,' said Doris. 'And that cheers everybody up.'

'I'll say,' said Percy, trying to assist his wife in steering the conversation away from the end of their daughter's romance.

The only person at the table who looked happy at the news of the end of Bessie's romance was Daisy, and as soon the meal had finished and they left the table, she said to Bessie, 'Will you go back to Josh now that Ray isn't going to be around?'

'No, I will not,' said Bessie furiously. 'What an awful thing to say.'

'I thought . . .'

'Well you thought wrong and you had no business making assumptions,' said Bessie, her voice rising to a shout.

'Oi,' said Tom. 'There's no need to take it out on Daisy just because things have gone wrong for you.'

'It was such a stupid thing to say.'

'No it wasn't,' said Tom. 'It was perfectly natural she might think that.'

'It doesn't work that way,' said Bessie.

'We don't know that, do we,' said Tom. 'You're the experienced one.'

'I do think you're being a bit hard on them, dear,' said Doris.

'Oh, I've had enough of you lot,' she cried, grabbing her coat and leaving the house.

The light was fading outside but she could see well enough, having become accustomed to the blacked-out streets. She had no destination in mind and wasn't sure why she had come out except that she had needed to get away from the family and be on her own with her broken heart. It really was a horrible feeling. She wanted to cry but she was too tense for tears.

It occurred to her that this was what she was going to do to Josh if he was spared and came home after the war. Not having Ray didn't mean she wanted Josh. She didn't want anyone except Ray. Seeing him had been the light in her mundane life. His weekend passes had shone in the dull ordinariness; the air raids, the blackout, the shortage of everything had been bearable with him in her life.

Now there was nothing to look forward to and she missed him already; the sound of his voice, the smell and feel of him close to her. How could she ever be happy again without him to look forward to? She pulled herself up before she drowned in self-pity and turned back towards home. She had been mean to Daisy and she needed to put it right before any more time passed.

'Are you two doing anything tonight?' she asked of Tom and Daisy.

'I'm going to the youth club with my mates,' said Tom. 'Someone from the Civil Defence is giving us a talk and then we might play some records on the gramophone that someone is bringing in.'

'What about you, Daisy?' asked Bessie. 'Are you going with him?'

'No, I'm staying in.'

'Do you fancy coming to the pictures with me?' she said. 'My treat to make up for being mean to you.'

When Daisy smiled she looked very pretty, and she beamed at Bessie now. 'Ooh, yes, please,' she said.

'Go and get ready then,' said Bessie, 'while I have a look at the paper to see what's on.'

She ran up the stairs and Tom turned to his sister. 'Well done, sis,' he said. 'That's just what she needs. She gets very upset when you're cross with her.'

'I know,' she said. 'I wasn't cross with her, not really. I just feel shattered. I shouldn't have taken it out on Daisy.'

'A night at the flicks might cheer you up, too.'

It would take more than that, thought Bessie, but she said, 'You never know.'

Ray was standing at the bar of his local pub, deep in thought. He had done the right thing for Bessie, but his own heart was broken. The prospect of life without her was hardly bearable. But it had got too serious; the next step was marriage and kids and he couldn't do that. The worry of it all would make him miserable and he would take it out on Bessie.

He'd seen what it had done to his own father. Four kids and a wife to keep. It must be a terrible strain, especially before the war when there wasn't so much work about. Dad had looked haggard then and was often bad tempered. It was the responsibility that must have worn him down.

Never a word of complaint though. He just did what he had to and seemed to love his wife and kids. You got a hiding if you deserved it but Dad didn't hold grudges. Once you'd had your punishment, that was the end to it. Of course, things were easier for him now. Ray and his brother were both grown up and self-supporting so there were only two still at school and they'd be leaving soon. But Ray would never forget the haggard look of his dad when Ray had been little.

It wasn't that Ray didn't want to do it, but that he thought he couldn't. Bessie was the first girl he'd felt this strongly for, that he'd wanted to marry and spend the rest of his life with, and it scared him to death.

He wasn't proud of himself. Other men fell in love and got married and took the responsibility in their stride. But not Ray. He'd backed off as soon as he realised how deeply he felt for Bessie. He'd hurt her and that hurt him. But better now than a few years down the road when they had kids and he wasn't able to provide. He thought back to that weekend he'd been home and hadn't seen Bessie. He'd gone to the Palais and felt as miserable as sin. He'd told her he'd enjoyed himself as part of the process, but he hadn't stayed long. He'd left and gone to the nearest pub. He'd missed Bessie so much that weekend he'd been glad to go back to camp.

Now the landlord of the pub came over and spoke to him.

'Home for the weekend, Ray?'

'Yeah.'

'Will you give us a song later on, Ray?' he said. 'The punters would love that.'

'Sorry, mate,' he said. 'I'm leaving in a minute.'

'Oh, never mind,' he said. 'Got a date, have you?'

'Something like that,' said Ray who had absolutely no idea how he was going to spend the rest of the evening. But singing was the last thing he felt able to do. His spirits were far too low.

Bessie and Daisy saw a Fred Astaire film called *The Sky is the Limit*. It was a light-hearted romantic comedy and it barely registered with Bessie, she was far too upset. But at least nothing was expected of her for almost two hours so she could sit in darkness and wallow in her misery.

'Did you enjoy the film, Daisy?' she asked when the lights went up.

'I loved it,' the girl replied. 'Must be really good to be able to dance like that.'

'It would take plenty of hard work,' said Bessie. 'Dancers have to practise for hours, I think.'

They made their way out of the cinema and set off for home arm in arm. 'I'm sorry I upset you earlier,' said Daisy.

'It's all right,' said Bessie. 'I shouldn't have taken my misery out on you. But I feel so awful, Daisy.'

'So how will you get better?'

'I have no idea,' she replied. 'I suppose the pain will fade in time. There's no medicine for a broken heart. You just have to let it do its worst.'

'Did you feel like this when Josh went away?'

'No, I was sad that he was leaving but he hadn't rejected me, so no, it was nothing like this.'

'If he'd not gone away, it wouldn't have happened because you wouldn't have got together with Ray.'

'Who knows?' said Bessie. 'I'm a great believer in fate. I don't think it was ever meant to be with Josh so fate intervened.'

'Oh,' said Daisy and Bessie knew she was disappointed because she was still hoping that somehow Bessie and Josh would get back together. But it wasn't going to happen. Absolutely not!

Much to Bessie's relief Daisy finally seemed to accept that there wasn't going to be any more romance between her brother and Bessie. She was her usual cheerful self by the next day, entertaining them in the evenings with chatter about her work in the West End. She was an entertaining storyteller and really brought events to life. They heard all about the awkward customers as well as the nice ones and there were plenty of laughs to be had in the way she recounted her days.

Then one evening she came home from work in tears, went

straight to her bedroom, buried her face in her pillow and stayed there sobbing her heart out and refusing to tell anyone what was wrong. After much persuasion, she emerged to eat her meal, her tears having subsided, but returned to her bedroom immediately after. The family decided that she was entitled to some privacy and stopped trying to find out what could have happened to upset her so much. But they were worried because she was clearly distraught.

She was subdued for a few days then seemed to return to her normal self, so the incident, while not exactly forgotten, slipped into the past. Bessie suspected they might never know the cause of her unhappiness, but guessed that everyone had certain things they wanted to keep private. Daisy seemed to have recovered so had obviously manged to deal with it. That was the important thing.

Chapter Nine

One morning in June 1944 there was an air of excitement in the Oakdene Post Office as news came that the long-expected Allied invasion had actually happened. It had first been announced on the eight o'clock news that morning and was officially confirmed later when the post office staff relied on the customers to keep them up to date as there was no wireless set on the premises.

People had waited so long for what they believed would be the last act in this terrible war that there was almost a feeling of celebration. But the thought of all the lives that would be lost before this operation was over struck fear into Bessie's heart. All those young men, who should have so much ahead of them, could have no future at all by the time this latest operation was over. But it would be insensitive to verbalise her thoughts because many of these women had husbands or sons at the front.

An elderly man came in beaming and said, 'Invasion at last, God Save the King,' and all the customers cheered.

'At last something is happening,' said Joyce. 'This war can't go on forever.'

'Exactly right,' said a customer. 'Do you have anyone involved in it?'

'My son, I think,' said Joyce, 'but I don't know for sure because the whole thing has been shrouded in secrecy and any letter I get just says that he's well. I have no idea where he is.'

Bessie thought of Ray who very probably would be involved, but she didn't know about Josh because she'd gathered from the very few letters she'd had that he was further afield somewhere.

She was still hurting from Ray's rejection of her, but tried to make the best of things. Something like today helped to get the situation into perspective. Compared to the enormity of the invasion, her broken heart was nothing. It didn't feel like that though.

All day the sense of festivity remained at the post office; every customer was full of it. As always Mr Simms tried to retain a serious atmosphere in his domain but today he really was fighting a losing battle.

Things were no different at home. Both Bessie's parents respectfully stood up for the King's speech on the wireless and Doris was sniffing into her handkerchief by the end. There was patriotic fervour everywhere. Doris even agreed to go to the pub with her husband for a celebratory drink that night, a rare thing indeed as she was old fashioned and of the opinion that pubs were a male domain.

'The war isn't over yet,' Bessie reminded her parents.

'No, but we've had a significant move forward,' said her mother. 'Why don't you come with us to celebrate?'

'No thanks, Mum, but you go and enjoy yourselves.'

'It's a time to be with people,' said Doris.

'I'll make do with the company of Tibs and the two young-sters, if they're not going out.'

'Just as you like, dear,' said her mother and went to get her coat.

Bessie was sitting listening to the wireless with the cat on her lap and feeling lonely when Tom came into the room looking worried.

'Can you come, Bessie, please,' he said in a quick urgent tone. 'Daisy isn't well.'

'She was all right at teatime,' recalled Bessie. 'What's the matter with her?'

'I think it's something to do with that thing girls have, but she's in terrible pain,' he said. 'Please will you come.'

Bessie tore upstairs and found Daisy sitting on the bed, hunched up and shivering.

'It's my period,' she said.

Bessie turned to Tom. 'Can you make some tea, please, and bring some aspirin up with it.'

'Sure.'

As soon as he was out of earshot Daisy said, 'My period was late. I've been really worried. And now it's much more painful than usual.'

'Periods aren't always on time,' said Bessie. 'A late one is nothing to worry about and some are more painful than others.'

'It is a worry if you think you might be pregnant.'

'What!' gasped Bessie shocked. 'You haven't been . . . oh, Daisy. How late are you?'

'About a month.'

'You might well be having a miscarriage then.'

'Yeah, that's what I thought,' she said, crying now. 'Oh, Bessie, I don't know what to do.'

'I don't know much about these things either, but I suppose it will just come away,' she said. 'I'll stay with you.'

'Please don't tell anyone.'

'Of course I won't,' she said. 'As far as anyone else is concerned you're feeling a bit off colour.'

Bessie was managing to seem calm for Daisy's sake, but she was actually terrified. What else could she do but stay with her and hope for the best? As far as she knew there was no help available for an unmarried girl in this situation. She really didn't want to worry her parents with it unless there were complications because they would be upset and angry with Daisy and that was the last thing the girl needed now.

'I'm curious to know how this came about, Daisy,' she said to help keep their minds occupied. 'You haven't mentioned a boyfriend.'

'I don't have one,' she said. 'The boy who did this to me works at the store in the menswear department as a junior. He's been bothering me every time I see him in the canteen or in the corridors if I've been sent on an errand. We are both juniors so we have to do a lot of running about.'

'How old is he?'

'About sixteen, I think,' she said. 'Anyway, this particular day, I'd been sent to the stores to collect something that had been ordered by a customer and I met this boy in the corridor. There was no one about so he started following me and before I realised what was happening he dragged me into a storeroom.' She paused. 'That's when it happened.'

'Oh Daisy, how terrible,' said Bessie, unable to conceal the look of shock on her face. She put her arms around Daisy and held her close.

'I didn't know what was happening. He was laughing at first, but then he went all serious and it was all over so quickly. I tried to fight him off, begged him to let me go, but he wouldn't stop.'

Bessie sat still, almost unable to bear what she was hearing.

'I haven't had any trouble with him since, though,' Daisy said. 'I suppose he achieved his aim so lost interest. I hardly know him,' she said. 'Anyway, there's only one boy for me.'

'Oh yeah. Who is that?'

'Tom.'

'Oh Daisy,' Bessie cried. 'But the two of you are always arguing.'

'I still love him though.'

'But you are both so young.'

'Old enough to know how we feel,' she said. 'At least I am. I don't know about Tom.'

'You'll probably feel differently when you're a bit older,' said Bessie.

'No, I won't,' she said in a definite tone. 'He might go out with other girls for a while, but he'll still mean the world to me and somehow we'll be together eventually because we are meant for each other. I know I'm young, Bessie, but I am absolutely certain about this.'

'Does he know how you feel about him?'

'Of course not,' she said. 'He'd run a mile at this stage in our lives if he did. When the time is right he'll know, so please don't tell him.

'I promise,' said Bessie, but she was worried by Daisy's innocent belief that Tom would return her feelings eventually. There was nothing she could do. People had to live through their own disappointments. The girl would probably fall in love a few times before she was done.

'Thanks, Bessie.'

'That's all right, but for God's sake, in future please watch out for boys like the one at work,' said Bessie.

'I thought he was just being friendly because we both work at the same firm.'

'I know you did, love, but not all boys are as decent as Tom,' Bessie warned.

'I know that now,' she said, drawing in her breath as the pain returned.

Tom knocked at the door with the tea and aspirin. 'Thanks, Tom,' said Bessie. 'I'll stay with her if you want to go out.'

'Is she all right?'

'She will be.'

'I'll go around to my mates for an hour or so then, if you're sure,' he said and left.

'Right, madam,' Bessie said to Daisy lightly. 'Perhaps this aspirin will help.'

'Thanks for looking after me, Bessie,' she said. 'I don't know what I'd do without you.'

'You'd manage, but you won't have to because I am here for you and will be for as long as you need me.'

'Blimey, you look a bit rough, Bessie,' said Joyce the next morning when they met on the way to work. 'Were you out celebrating last night?'

'No, nothing like that. Daisy has a touch of flu and she was restless so she kept me awake for most of the night,' she fibbed.

'Oh, you poor things, both of you.'

Last night when Bessie's parents got back from the pub, her mum had been more than a little inebriated and had gone to bed singing 'There'll Always Be an England' so wouldn't have noticed if Daisy was giving birth to triplets in the other bedroom.

So, as far as anyone besides her and Daisy were concerned, including the family, Daisy was a little off colour with a touch of flu. Bessie was going to telephone the store and tell them Daisy wouldn't be in for a couple of days. She should be on the mend now that it was over. Of course, she should really see a doctor, but it wasn't possible so they had to hope for the best. Bessie knew girls who had been in trouble and got it sorted by some mysterious woman in a back street and they were often back at work very soon as though nothing had happened.

'Come on, you two,' said Mabel, who was waiting outside the post office. 'Get this place up and running.'

'Still a few minutes to go till opening time,' said Joyce.

'But come on in,' said Bessie as she and Joyce went inside. 'We won't keep you a minute.'

The day's business got started and everyone was talking about their invasion celebrations the night before, though the mood was more serious than yesterday as people thought more about what the boys would be going through.

Bessie greeted an elderly man who had come for his pension. 'Hello, Mr Roberts. How are you today?'

'I'm all right, dear,' he replied.

'Still busy with the Home Guard?'

'Oh yes,' he said with enthusiasm. 'Whatever happens we'll be ready.'

'Good for you,' she said, putting his money along with his pension book on the counter. 'You're doing a good job.'

In the early days of the war when a German invasion was expected, a group of civilian men, either too old or unfit for the services, prepared to defend their country by joining a military-style organisation called the Home Guard, which they attended in their spare time.

'We do our best,' he said.

'Take care of yourself,' she said as he turned to go.

'And you,' he said. 'See you again next week.'

'I'll be here,' she said and he went on his way.

The next customer wanted to talk about her son who she thought had been involved in the invasion. 'I don't know for sure though because of all the secrecy,' she said. 'It's good news and all that, but there's bound to have been lives lost.'

'All you can do is try to stay positive,' responded Bessie, while getting the stamps the customer had asked for. 'At last we can start thinking in terms of an end to the war. I'm sure your boy will be fine and he'll write to you as soon as he can.'

'Yeah, of course he will, dear,' the lady said, smiling. 'You've cheered me up no end.'

A large part of this job was listening to the customers, saying what they wanted to hear and never mentioning yourself unless they specifically asked. She thought she'd probably got the balance about right, but Mr Simms thought otherwise and told her so when they closed for lunch.

'As I have told you before, Bessie, you spend far too much time in conversation with the customers instead of concentrating on the job in hand,' he said, and turning to Joyce added, 'in fact you could both do with cutting the chatter.'

'I'm guided by the customer and the situation,' said Bessie.

'If I have a chatty customer and a long queue I try to wrap it up quickly without making them feel hurried.'

'This is a business, not a lonely-hearts club.'

'We've had this discussion before, Mr Simms,' she said. 'And as I have told you many times, I do my very best to keep a balance between friendliness and efficiency.'

'We both do,' added Joyce. 'But this isn't the sort of place where you can keep it totally professional. You might be able to do that in a big town centre post office, but not here in a neighbourhood one.'

'Well, try harder,' he said. 'I want to see a much faster turnaround in this establishment.'

'But why?' asked Bessie. 'You won't necessarily get any more customers. In fact, you could get fewer if they think they are being rushed. In these terrible times we are living in it's especially important for people to be able to socialise.'

'Make it shorter then,' he suggested firmly. 'You don't see me wasting time chatting to customers.'

'That's why customers head for Joyce and me,' she responded.

'Oh well, I shall be keeping a close eye on things.'

I bet you will, thought Bessie but said, 'Yes, Mr Simms.'

A week later it was impossible to rush the customers or keep them quiet because of an unexpected and frightening development in the war. Strange pilotless aircraft appeared in the skies over London and fell to the ground, causing huge loss of life and terrible damage.

'Our boys must be shooting them down,' said Annie. 'I saw one on my way to work this morning and it just seemed to fall out of the sky.'

'It's worrying that they come in the daytime as well as at night,' said Winnie. 'At least the other bombers only came at night.'

Everyone had their own opinion about what the new aircraft could be and the mystery was solved when a government minister announced that pilotless aircraft were now being used against the British Isles. He explained that when the engine stops and the light at the end of the machine goes out the aircraft will fall to the ground and an explosion will follow in five to fifteen seconds.

'At least we know what they are now,' said Winnie. 'But everyone seems to be carrying on as normal and not taking much notice of the siren.'

'We can't bring the country to a halt by staying in the shelters all day long, can we,' said Bessie. 'So we'll just have to dodge them as best as we can.'

'Creepy, isn't it,' said Mabel, 'That they can come by themselves without a pilot.'

There was general agreement about this and post office business carried on as usual. Bessie did try to abide by Mr Simms's wishes and not allow the gossip to go on for too long, whilst still remaining friendly. He did run the place after all, so deserved some respect.

'I saw one go overhead in my dinner hour,' said Daisy, now fully restored to health. 'My friend and I were in the park eating our sandwiches when this thing clattered overhead.'

'I hope you took shelter,' said Doris, frowning.

'No, we didn't because the engine didn't stop,' she explained. 'We watched it until it went out of sight. But we did hear the explosion. We don't take much notice, to be honest.'

'Well, you should,' said Doris, looking worried. 'You should always take shelter if you can when the siren goes.'

'I thought it was only if the engine cut out,' said Daisy.

'It's best to be on the safe side,' put in Tom wisely, sounding about forty.

'Oh yeah,' said Daisy grinning. 'So, I rush off to find a shelter and everyone else is carrying on as normal when it passes over. I'd look a right fool.'

'Sooner that than be dead,' said Tom.

'Yeah, I know,' she said, becoming serious because she knew only too well the lives that had been lost because of these new German bombs, and was very frightened of them. But she tried to make light of them in an effort to lessen her fear.

'People just seem to dive into shop doorways when these things come over during the day,' Percy mentioned. 'Nobody bothers to make much of a fuss about it. I noticed it in my dinner hour when I went for a walk.'

'We're all so used to fear and disruption now we're getting a bit careless, I suppose,' suggested Doris.

'You still need to be careful though,' said Percy. 'And you shouldn't be sitting in the park when they come over, Daisy. You really must be more careful.'

'I will, Uncle Percy,' she said.

'Well said, Dad,' said Tom. 'You're about the only one in this family Daisy takes any notice of.'

'Not true,' said Bessie, laughing. 'She might not take any notice of you, but she does of me, don't you, Daisy?'

'Not half,' said the girl. 'You're my big sister.'

The siren went just after they had finished their meal. 'That's decent of Hitler, to let us finish eating,' remarked Doris.

'Creepy,' said Bessie. 'Having robots coming over to bomb us.'

There was a murmur of agreement and they all headed for the shelter except for Percy who put on his coat and tin hat and headed for duty on the streets.

A woman was screaming hysterically by a pile of bricks and rubble that a few minutes ago had been a house.

'My daughters are under there,' she sobbed. 'I'd gone to see if my elderly neighbour across the road was all right when the bomb fell and the girls were on their own. I'd only been gone a minute. Get them out, please get them out.'

'We'll do our very best,' said Percy and he and his mates began moving bricks and debris as quickly as they could.

Although Percy seemed calm he was actually sick with dread at what they might find, but he never let his fear show when he was on duty. He had to stay strong at all times in this job. After moving much of the wreckage, they found a girl of about ten, shaken but alive, and managed to lift her out and get her into the ambulance with her mother close by.

'My little sister is still under there,' the girl sobbed.

'Get my other girl out, please,' begged her mother.

'We'll do our best,' said Percy. 'You stay with this little one while we get the other girl out.'

The woman did as he said and Percy and his mates continued their work, eventually reaching the other child. But she hadn't been as lucky as her sister and Percy thought his heart would break as he prepared to tell her mother that she hadn't made it. There were times when this job was almost too awful to bear.

★　★　★

The doodlebugs, as the flying bombs came to be known, caused an enormous amount of death and destruction in southern England, but people got on with their lives regardless. The siren sounded so often that people tended to carry on with their daily business.

The post office staff had just shut up shop for half-day closing and were about to leave when there was a terrific crash followed by the sound of breaking glass. Bessie found herself on the floor next to Joyce with something heavy on top of them.

'Are you both all right?' asked Mr Simms, who was lying over them in a protective manner.

'Just about, I think,' said Bessie.

'I'm all in one piece,' said Joyce, clambering up after Mr Simms had moved.

They all got up feeling shaky, and looked around to see broken glass everywhere.

'Thank you, Mr Simms,' said Bessie, realising that had he not pushed them down and shielded them she and Joyce would have taken the full blast of the glass.

'Yes,' added Joyce. 'Thank you.'

'What for?'

'You know what for,' said Bessie, her opinion of him having changed in the last few minutes.

'Well, let's get on,' he said. 'You'll need to be very careful as you go into the staffroom. There is glass everywhere.'

'Oh well,' said Bessie, trying to stay calm as she saw the glassless shop front. 'At least we'll have a nice breeze while we're working.'

Then she went to the lavatory and burst into tears.

★　　★　　★

Although it was her afternoon off and Mr Simms had insisted that she and Joyce went home, Bessie went back to work after she'd had something to eat to see if there was anything she could do to help.

Mr Simms was there and most of the broken glass had been removed. There was a man with him, a stranger to her, but her boss didn't introduce them. She supposed he didn't consider her important enough.

'You've been busy,' she said.

'I've nearly finished,' he said. 'We'll probably have to wait until after the war to get the glass replaced but I've been on to the council and they are coming to put something in temporarily.'

'I'll wait for them if you want to get off,' she offered.

'No, you go home,' he said in a tone not to be argued with. 'I'll stay. I don't think they'll be long.'

Sensing that he really did want her to leave, she said, 'Cheerio then. See you tomorrow.'

As she walked home through the shabby, war-torn streets she was thinking about Mr Simms, for whom she had new respect. Whenever there was a crisis he showed heroic qualities; when the gunman had threatened their lives and today when they could have been cut by flying glass. She wondered who his friend was. Anyone else would have introduced them, but Simms didn't bother with the social graces.

He was of a surly nature and a hard taskmaster as a boss, but when there was an emergency he showed his mettle so he couldn't be all bad. She really would try to be more patient with him in future.

★　　★　　★

Joyce was of the same mind about Mr Simms's good qualities.

'He's a hero when he needs to be,' she said on the way to work the next morning. 'It's a pity he's so flamin' irritating the rest of the time.'

'I promised myself I would be more patient with him after yesterday,' said Bessie.

'It's more a question of him being more patient with us.'

'Yeah, I know, but I am going to try to like him.'

Joyce laughed. 'Good luck with that. I reckon you might last until lunchtime.'

When they arrived at work the windows had been boarded up and Mr Simms was in a foul mood, complaining of a lack of light.

'I don't think I'll even last until breaktime,' said Bessie.

'I'm damned sure you won't,' smiled her colleague.

The customers greeted the patched-up post office with their usual humour.

'Blimey, it's a dark as a ruddy coalmine in here,' said Edna. 'Why don't you put the light on?'

'Because it's a waste of electricity when we can see perfectly well without it,' replied Mr Simms.

'You might be able to, mate,' said the customer. 'But we can't. Anyway, it's so bloomin' dismal.'

Mr Simms gave an irritated sigh, switched the light on and a cheer broke out.

He looked slightly embarrassed then said, 'It's going off again in a minute. We'll have to get used to a dimmer atmosphere.'

'It's your post office so you can do as you please,' said a

woman in the queue. 'But so can we and there are other post offices we can go to.'

'All right, point taken,' he said with an irritated sigh.

Bessie and Joyce exchanged a look.

'I did try,' said Bessie.

Joyce and Stan grew closer and her feelings for him strengthened. They weren't having an affair, as such, but they did enjoy each other's company and shared an occasional kiss. Most evenings he met her from work and walked some of the way home with her, leaving her at a safe distance and carefully avoiding the subject of a future for them together.

Joyce was a very disciplined person but she did struggle to keep her feelings under control as far as Stan was concerned. She wanted to be with him all the time, and knew that he felt the same, but as she was married to someone else there could be no happy ending.

The sensible thing would be to tell him to stay away from her, but she couldn't bring herself to do that because he brought warmth and colour into her life and she couldn't bear to lose those things. All credit to him, he never tried to persuade her to leave Jim, but she knew he wanted more from their relationship. It was only natural that he would.

Obviously it couldn't go on like this forever, but for the moment she was taking it one day at a time and enjoying having him in her life.

As the summer continued so did the doodlebugs. Extra barrage balloons could be seen in the skies but the bombs still roared over, regardless of the added defence. Percy was very busy with his ARP work and out on duty most nights. West Londoners heard that South and East London were the worst hit and Bessie and family sympathised with them. It was bad enough here so they could imagine how awful it must be for them.

'Fancy coming over the park, Bessie?' asked Shirley one Sunday morning when she visited with her daughter, who had now turned one and was sitting in her pushchair. 'Gloria is taking a few steps now so we can get her out and let her show us what she can do.'

'Wouldn't miss it for the world,' said Bessie and they headed off in the sunshine.

'There's going to be some explaining for me to do when the war is over and Joe comes home,' said Shirley as the two women supervised Gloria's walking efforts.

'Yeah. There will be no hiding your daughter who can't possibly be his.'

'Exactly. God knows what his reaction will be,' she said. 'He'll drop me like a hot cake I should think and I won't blame him.'

'I suppose it will depend on how you feel about each other when you meet again after all this time,' Bessie suggested.

'I daren't think about it,' said Shirley. 'Are you going to tell Josh about Ray?'

'Oh yes.'

'Even though Ray is past history.'

'I still have feelings for him though,' she said. 'I have no idea how I'll feel about Josh when I see him again. If I see him. I haven't heard from him for ages, so I don't know if he's alive or dead.'

'I don't hear from Joe much either.'

'How about Bernie? Does the thought of him still send shivers up your spine?'

'God no,' she said. 'The reality of motherhood soon disposed of that romantic dream. But I can't forget what happened because something so wonderful came out of it. Gloria means the world to me. Honestly, Bessie, mother love is overwhelming.'

'I can imagine,' said Bessie. 'I hope to experience it myself one day.'

'Really? You've never said.'

'I thought you'd take it for granted,' she said. 'But at the moment I don't have anyone to make a baby with. Ray gave me my marching orders and so will Josh when I tell him about Ray.'

'Does he have to know?'

'Most definitely,' she replied. 'I really love Ray and that hasn't changed because he dumped me. I don't know how I'll feel about Josh when I see him again, but I know it won't be the same as before. He seems like a pale shadow after Ray.'

'Anyway, we'll have to see what happens when they get back. If they make it.'

'Shirley, what a thing to say.'

'We have to face up to reality,' she said. 'They are both away at war. Every day we hear of people getting the dreaded telegram. It could happen.'

The conversation came to a halt at the sound of the siren followed by the drone of a doodlebug. They looked skyward and then lay on their stomachs on the ground with Gloria beneath them. The robot passed over and they scrambled to their feet.

'What am I doing, Bessie, bringing my child into an open space when there are these awful bombs about?'

'You're taking the bombs in your stride, the same as the rest of us. We are getting on with our lives and not letting Hitler win,' she said as Shirley put Gloria back into her pushchair. 'You weren't to know a bomb would come over.'

'As they're coming over so often it was a fair bet there would be one,' she said. 'Oh Bessie, what sort of a mother am I to put my child at risk?'

'A bomb could have hit the house if you'd stayed in,' Bessie reminded her.

'I should have stayed close to the shelter,' she said.

'You can't do that all the time,' Bessie sensibly pointed out. 'And you go out to the shops with the baby, don't you? And you don't beat yourself up about that.'

'I know you're right but I still feel bad.'

Bessie was reminded again what a mixture her friend was. Ultra-confident in her outward demeanour but desperately vulnerable in reality.

'We are all living under a threat, Shirley,' she said. 'You are doing a really good job as a mum and it's obvious you would give your life for your child, so stop doubting yourself.'

'You really think I'm doing all right?'

'Yes, I do.

'I never used to be so full of self-doubt, did I?'

'No. It's since you became a mum,' said Bessie.

'Oh for those carefree days when all we had to worry about was which film we were going to see at the cinema.'

'Would you really like to go back to those pre-Gloria days though?' Bessie asked lightly.

'Not on your life,' she replied.

'That's what I thought,' said Bessie. 'Come on, let's go home and have a cup of tea.'

'Flamin' doodlebugs,' said Shirley as they broke into a homewards run that made Gloria squeal with delight.

Chapter Ten

The doodlebugs, or V1s, continued through the summer, and many of these lethal machines clattered overhead every day. It was odd to see the robots roaring across the sky at night with flames spurting from their tails, sometimes a few together. But despite the death and destruction these vile bombs caused, and the fact that the siren was in action for most of every day, life and work went on as normal.

The news from abroad was positive and a member of the government came on the wireless to tell the population that 'apart from a few last shots the Battle of London was over'. So, despite constant fear and atrocities still happening, Bessie could sense a feeling of optimism in people, that they were finally coming to the end of this dreadful war.

Then the Germans launched an even more lethal robot bomb known as the V2. These killing machines dropped out of the sky at all hours of the day and night with no warning and a very high casualty rate.

'I was starting to put things aside for my son's welcome home party; the odd tin of fruit and so on,' said Edna in the post office one morning. 'But I'm not so sure now with all these bombs about.'

'I think you still can,' said Bessie. 'I heard on the wireless that this is Hitler's last attempt to beat us.'

'It can't hurt to put a few tins aside anyway,' said Winnie. 'It isn't as though it will go off as it's tinned stuff and the war will end at some point. We all want the celebrations to be special and because of rationing we have to think ahead or there'll be nothing to put on the table at party time.'

'I've started putting things away, too,' said Annie. 'A tin or two of fruit and the odd bottle of laughing water. It's no good leaving it until they're home because there's so little stuff about.'

A girl of about fifteen came to the counter asking for savings stamps. 'I've done really well with my savings,' she said. 'It's the first time I've ever managed to put anything by.'

'Well done,' said Bessie. 'You'll need a new book soon. You're helping your country as well as yourself.'

'Am I?'

'You certainly are,' said Bessie. 'The country needs all the money it can get for the war effort so you are lending them yours and getting interest in return.'

National Savings had been hugely successful during the war. Ordinary people, who didn't go to banks, could buy savings stamps and help themselves while helping their country in its hour of need. Money was one thing that wasn't short among the working classes in wartime because there were plenty of jobs about. Being as she sold savings stamps, Bessie knew how well people were doing. So that was one positive thing in a world full of trouble.

* * *

Daisy invited a boyfriend home for Sunday tea and Tom metamorphosed into a Victorian father.

'So, what do you do for a living, Harold?' he asked the boy, with an air of authority.

'I work in menswear in a department store,' said Harold, who was a thin, pale boy, very neat in appearance and had not a hair out of place. 'Not the same store as Daisy though.'

'That doesn't seem like much of a job for a man.'

'I like it,' said Harold while Daisy turned scarlet and the others looked uncomfortable.

'Will you be going into the services when you're eighteen or are you one of these who gets deferred,' asked Tom as more of a demand than a question.

'I'll be going in, as far as I know.'

'As far as you know? repeated Tom. 'What exactly do you mean by that?'

'Well, you have to pass the medical, don't you,' he said, just about managing to retain his composure throughout this grilling.

'Is there some reason why you wouldn't pass that then?' asked Tom, almost as a demand.

'I'll get some more tea,' said Bessie, picking up the teapot. 'Can you come and give me a hand, please, Tom?'

'I'm talking,' he said.

'Go with your sister, please, Tom,' said Percy angrily.

He tutted but followed Bessie to the kitchen.

'How dare you be so rude to our guest,' said Bessie, having closed the kitchen door. 'I'm thoroughly ashamed of you.'

'What have I done?' he asked innocently.

'You know very well what you have done, cross-questioning the boy like that,' she said. 'You are embarrassing the whole family and what poor Daisy is going through I can't imagine.'

'I'm just making sure he's suitable for her.'

'It isn't your place.'

'Someone has to look out for her.'

'And we all do,' she said. 'You know that perfectly well.'

'Yeah, well maybe she needs a closer eye,' he said. 'We don't want her getting in with the wrong type.'

'I shouldn't think Harold would hurt a fly,' she said. 'So you go back in there and behave decently towards him for the rest of the time that he is here. Make him feel welcome at our table, please.'

'That's pushing it.'

'Just do it,' she said.

'All right,' he said, looking peeved. 'No need to get into such a temper about it.'

'Can you blame me, the way you've behaved this afternoon?' she said. 'I'm ashamed of you. So go back in there and show Harold that you do have some manners.'

'I'm going, I'm going, calm down,' he said and swaggered off into the other room.

'I'm sorry Tom was so rude to your friend earlier,' Bessie said to Daisy later on when Harold had gone home and they were in the bedroom.

'It's not your fault,' said Daisy.

'I know, but Tom is my brother so I feel some sort of responsibility.'

'Honestly, there's no need to apologise,' she said. 'Harold can take it.'

'He seems a nice boy,' said Bessie.

Daisy nodded. 'Yeah, he's a good sort.'

'Have you been friendly with him for long?'

'Quite a while.'

'You haven't mentioned him.'

'Haven't I?' she said. 'I don't know why. Must have slipped my mind for some reason.'

Bessie could sense conspiracy. Daisy wasn't the least bit upset by Tom's behaviour. In fact, she seemed rather pleased about it. So, had Harold been invited to tea to get a reaction from Tom? Yes, it was obvious now. Daisy had been looking rather pleased with herself throughout the whole incident. The sad little girl they had taken in was now a young woman determined to get her man.

'Will you be bringing him home again?' asked Bessie.

'I don't know,' she said.

Bessie doubted it. Daisy had achieved her aim so there was no need to repeat the charade.

In fact, Daisy was absolutely delighted with Tom's reaction. He was as jealous as hell which meant he did have feelings for her. Now she had something to work on.

'Things are changing between Daisy and Tom,' Doris remarked to Percy as they got into bed.

'Yeah, I noticed that,' he responded. 'They are growing up and getting closer. Harold was only invited to get a reaction from Tom.'

'That's what I thought,' she said. 'It worked too.'

'It certainly did,' said Percy. 'But Daisy and Tom are good together so I hope it works out for them.'

'It's early days though.'

'You never know,' he said.

★　★　★

Autumn seemed early this year as the blast from the flying bombs stripped the leaves from the trees. The pungent odour of sap lingered in the air for ages after a bomb had fallen, especially in the parks, as Bessie and Shirley noticed in their local one where they often went with Gloria.

But despite the bombs and destruction there was an air of optimism. People knew that the war was finally coming to an end, but it was a slow process. Half lighting was allowed which meant blackout curtains could be removed, but it seemed a bit of an anti-climax because everyone had been longing for proper lighting and this was only only a partial lifting and was referred to as the dim out.

'It's all a bit of a let-down, isn't it,' said Edna while Bessie was serving her with stamps. 'I thought the war would end in a blaze of glory.'

'It hasn't ended yet,' put in Mr Simms. 'When it does you'll get your blaze of glory.'

'There are still bombs falling,' said Winnie. 'Those V rockets are still coming down.'

'Funny that we're all talking about the end of the war when we are still being bombed.'

'Only rocket bombs, though, not the piloted bomber planes we had in the Blitz,' said Joyce. 'We know Hitler has run out of options.'

'Yeah, that's true.'

'As long as the war is over by Christmas I'll be happy,' said Edna putting her stamps in her bag. 'Our first peacetime Christmas for nearly six years. Won't that be something.'

'Don't hold your breath, love,' said Winnie. 'It might take a bit longer than that.'

'Come on, let's get this queue moving,' urged Mr Simms. 'People have things to do.'

'We certainly have and plenty of 'em,' said Rita, who was an occasional customer and today was wearing a turban with curlers on show at the front. 'But we still like a good old natter in our local post office. Isn't that right, everyone?'

There was a roar of approval.

'You'll never stop the chatter in here, Mr Simms,' said Bessie. 'Not unless you get a police order.'

'Apparently not,' he said. 'And all I want is to run an efficient post office, which isn't much to ask.'

'And you do,' said Bessie. 'But you also run a friendly one.'

There was a shout of agreement from the customers and Mr Simms raised his hands as though in surrender.

Percy Green was in the bus queue on his way home from work. Unusually he wasn't on ARP duty tonight so was looking forward to an evening in the armchair with Doris beside him and any of the kids who were in. His wife and family were his life and he had grown very fond of young Daisy.

It had been a hard few years for everyone with the war dragging on, but they really were coming to the end of it now. The flying bombs Hitler was sending over were his final efforts to try to show that he wasn't defeated, but everyone knew that he was.

When the siren sounded, Percy didn't move. He wasn't prepared to lose his place in the queue because of a damned doodlebug. Most people stayed where they were too until the doodlebug rattled overhead, then everyone darted into shop doorways.

Percy was taking cover in the doorway of a shoe shop when he saw a young woman run across the road, screaming hysterically. His instincts took over and he dashed after her and brought her down to the ground, lying on top of her protectively. The last thing he heard was the engine of the bomb cutting out overhead.

'Dad's late home tonight, Mum,' Bessie remarked when the family sat down to eat without him.

'I hope he's all right,' said Daisy.

'He's probably stopped off for a pint,' said Bessie.

'Yeah, I'm sure that will be it,' said Doris, who always tried not to panic. 'He won't mind us starting without him. I've put his food in the oven.'

'I'll be doing that sort of thing soon,' said Tom. 'Going to the pub and joining the army.'

'Don't mention the last one,' said Doris.

'Why, will you miss me when I go away?'

'Of course we will,' she said. 'At least it will be peacetime when you go in.'

'Will they still call men up after the war?' asked Bessie.

'I should think so,' said Doris.

'Tom a soldier,' said Daisy dreamily. 'I bet he'll look really handsome in his uniform.'

'Blimey, a compliment – from Daisy. What's the world coming to?' he joked.

'Yeah, I forgot myself there for a moment,' she said laughing. 'I'll have to be careful or I might get used to being nice to you.'

'I don't think I could cope with that,' he laughed.

'Honestly, you two,' smiled Doris.

'They like to banter, Mum,' said Bessie. 'Take no notice of them.'

There was a knock at the door.

'I'll go,' said Doris. 'It'll probably be the insurance man, come for his money. You carry on. I won't be a minute.'

They continued eating, but Doris returned very soon with two policemen. She was ashen faced and shaky. 'Your dad has been killed by a flying bomb on his way home from work,' she said and one of the policemen helped her to a chair as her legs gave in.

Of all the bad news Bessie had taken these last few years, her brother Frank's death, her rejection by Ray, this was by far the most devastating. She felt paralysed by it. She could hear the policemen speaking and see her grey-faced mother being helped on to a chair, but Bessie saw it all as though from a distance.

When she saw Tom go to their mother, she snapped out of it and could hear Daisy crying while their mother, who was now deathly white, sat motionless.

'She'll be all right with us now, officers,' Bessie said to the policemen, ushering them towards the front door. 'Thank you for coming to tell us.'

They were all crying and doing their best to comfort Doris, but the youngsters showed a new maturity. Daisy quietly put all the food back in the oven for later and made tea while Bessie and Tom sat with their mother.

'We'll look after you, Mum,' Tom said to Doris. 'Bessie, Daisy and I will take care of everything.'

'That's right, Mum,' added Bessie.

'Thanks, dears,' she said, sobbing. 'It's just that your dad and I have been together so long I don't know what I'll do without him.'

'Aah,' said Tom kindly. 'It will seem impossible to believe now but we'll get through this together. I promise.'

Daisy intervened. 'I know food is the last thing anyone wants, but I think we should all try to eat something a little later on. It's on a low light in the oven.'

'Thank you, Daisy,' said Doris. 'You are all being very grown-up. Percy would be proud.'

And then she started to cry and so did everyone else. Bessie didn't know what they were going to do without Dad. He had always been the backbone of this family. First Frank and now Dad. When would these awful things stop happening?

Because there were so many more funerals in wartime, they were sometimes less well attended, but not so the funeral of Percy Green who had done so much for the war effort with his work for the ARP and had died a hero, having lost his life to save another.

The church was packed and friends and neighbours lined the streets despite the cold and misty weather as the funeral cars went by. Mr Simms closed the post office for a short time as a mark of respect so the staff and regular customers were there to support Bessie.

'All these people,' said Doris to Bessie in the graveyard after the burial. 'I knew that Percy was well liked but I didn't realise the extent of his popularity.'

'He was a quiet hero, Mum,' said Bessie. 'He got on with

his war work for various organisations he supported and didn't say much about it. But people knew.'

'Mm, I suppose they must have because there are so many here today,' she said.

As the crowds began to disperse, a young woman approached Doris.

'Hello, Mrs Green. I am here today because of your husband's bravery,' she told her nervously. 'I am the girl whose life he saved. It should be me in the grave not him. I'm so sorry for your loss. I feel guilty because you are suffering.'

Doris didn't say anything. She just put her arms around the young woman. 'My husband wouldn't want you to feel like that,' she said. 'You are young. He would want you to enjoy your life.'

'I am so sorry for your loss,' said the girl tearfully.

'I know you are,' said Doris. 'But now you must get on with your life and make the most of every minute so that Percy didn't die in vain.'

'I will,' said the girl and quietly went on her way.

It had been very hard for Doris to say those words because her heart was breaking for the loss of her beloved husband. But this young woman wasn't much more than a girl with her life ahead of her and Percy wouldn't want that life to be shadowed by guilt.

'Well done, Mum,' said Bessie, holding her mother's arm as they made their way back to the funeral car. 'That must have been really difficult for you.'

'Everything is difficult without your dad by my side,' she said. 'But we just have to get on with it, don't we?'

'Yes, I suppose we do.'

Daisy and Tom appeared and the four of them headed across

the cemetery together in the mist. Bessie knew that she would never forget this day.

It was the most miserable run-up to Christmas Bessie had ever known. Even apart from the family's personal grief and the lingering sadness of the funeral, there was fog and ice to cope with and the house was bitterly cold as coal was in short supply. People in general had aches and pains in their limbs, and sore throats. It was so cold in the post office with just boards at the windows, Bessie and Joyce kept their coats and scarves on all day.

'Well, the war is supposed to be coming to an end but it's taking its bloomin' time,' said Nellie one bitter morning.

'No chance of a peacetime Christmas now,' added Winnie.

'Never mind,' said Will, an elderly man who came in occasionally. 'We'll have it to look forward to afterwards.'

But no matter how hard Bessie and Joyce tried to stay cheerful, a dismal atmosphere hung over everything as they shivered behind the counter. Then Betty, a regular with a large family who lived across the road, came in with pot of tea.

'I thought this might cheer you up,' she said, smiling. 'My old man managed to get a bit extra so I can spare you a pot.'

Much to her embarrassment Bessie felt tears streaming from her eyes. Things couldn't all be bad when people could still find it in their hearts to be kind, despite their own troubles.

'You're a saint,' said Bessie.

'Far from it, love,' said the woman. 'I just happen to have a husband who is in the know.'

'It's very kind of you,' said Bessie.

'Thank you very much,' added Joyce.

'Yes. Many thanks,' put in Mr Simms and smiled at the customer, a rare event indeed.

'Blimey,' said Joyce in a whisper to Bessie. 'He must have been feeling thirsty.'

Christmas came and still the war continued. Bessie and the family planned to spend the big day quietly. It seemed only right with Percy's death so recent. On Christmas morning Bessie felt extraordinarily depressed and lonely. As well as missing her dad, she still felt sad that it hadn't worked out for her with Ray, who she knew was the love of her life. She loved her family but she felt very much alone today. This was followed by guilt because she knew her mother must be feeling worse. She kept busy helping her mum prepare the dinner and pretending to be jolly because it was Christmas Day, but the awful lonely ache persisted. Then there was a knock at the door.

'Happy Christmas,' said Shirley, giving Bessie a hug. 'From me and Gloria. Give your auntie Bessie a kiss, baby.'

Gloria did her best and Bessie was almost moved to tears.

'Come on in and have a Christmas drink with us, love,' said Doris who, unbeknown to anyone, had hardly been able to get out of bed this morning such was the ache in her heart for Percy. 'Oh, isn't Gloria coming on, what a sweetie.'

They stayed an hour or so during which time the atmosphere lifted, then Shirley said, 'Well, we'd better get back. Mum will be wanting a hand with the dinner.'

Bessie went to the front door with her. 'Thanks for coming. You've cheered us all up.'

'What's up, Bessie, apart from losing your dad, and I know that is bad enough?' asked Shirley.

231

'Nothing,' said Bessie.

'You might be able to kid yourself, but you can't fool me,' she said. 'Is it Ray?'

'Yeah,' she sighed. 'Christmas is such a sentimental time. It's really got to me today what with us losing Dad and all. But it's cheered me up, you and Gloria coming around.'

'That's what friends are for, to offer emotional support.' She grinned and said in a low tone, 'You think you've got problems. What about me?' She looked down at Gloria. 'How am I going to explain her to Joe when he comes home?'

'Maybe you should have written and told him before.'

'No, I didn't think that would be right, what with him being away. Best to tell him to his face.'

'Maybe you're right. You'll have to tell him the truth.'

'I know.'

'How do you feel about Bernie now?'

'As though he was part of a romantic dream,' she said. 'I can't regret what happened because I have Gloria, but I have no feelings for Bernie at all now and I'm deeply ashamed of the affair; letting myself go off the rails like that.'

'One thing is for sure,' began Bessie. 'There is going to be a hell of a lot of heartbreak when the boys come home, as well as joy. We won't be the only women who fell for someone else.'

'True enough,' said Shirley. 'Still, the war isn't over yet and it could still be going on this time next year, the way things are going.'

Bessie laughed. 'Now you really are exaggerating,' she said.

'Well . . . everyone says it's about to finish and still it doesn't,' she said.

'The blackout has been lifted,' Bessie pointed out. 'That's a step in the right direction.'

'Only partly,' she said. 'There are still some restrictions.'

'But they are gradually lifting them.'

'Yeah, I suppose so,' said Shirley, strapping Gloria into the pushchair. 'And when it does end officially we'll all forget our broken hearts and celebrate.'

'Not half,' Bessie agreed.

'Bye for now. Have a nice day. Happy Christmas.'

'Happy Christmas,' returned Bessie and went into the house to help her mother in the kitchen, determined to pull herself together and to stop yearning for something that wasn't to be.

Doris wasn't so immersed in her own grief that she wasn't able to notice what was going on around her, and she perceived a change in Tom since his father's death. He seemed to have matured overnight and was taking his new and self-imposed role as man-of-the-house very seriously. She was proud of him, and all of them, including Daisy. They had been an enormous comfort and made every effort to support her, but no one could heal the void in her life left by Percy. No one ever could. All she could do was endure the pain and emptiness and carry on.

It was evening now and she was glad that this, the first Christmas Day without Percy, was over. Soon she could go to bed and allow herself to wallow in her grief and cry if she needed to. She tried not to in front of the kids because it upset them so much and they were already sad enough. In practical terms, she was lucky in that Percy had taken out insurance soon after they got married so, although she wasn't rich, she was provided for and the kids didn't need to feel they had to help her out.

So, her New Year's resolution was to endure her personal

grief privately and keep going. Make this house a happy place again. It was what Percy would have wanted.

It was a slow process but gradually the signs of forthcoming peace began to appear. As well as the entire abolition of the blackout, certain things became legal again, none of which affected the Green family who had no reason to release a racing pigeon or sound a factory hooter.

'Did you know it is now legal to have a radio on in your car,' said Winnie to Bessie one afternoon in April.

'I don't have a car,' said Bessie.

'Exactly,' said the woman laughing. 'I was reading a list of all the things that are legal again and couldn't see anything that applies to most of us around here.'

'It's good to know that we can do them if we want to and things are gradually getting back normal, though,' said Bessie.

'Hear, hear,' said Maisie and the queue broke into conversation.

'Are you looking forward to the end of the war, Mr Simms?' asked Bessie. 'Will you be celebrating?'

'Of course,' he said.

'Everyone will be out dancing in the streets, I should imagine,' said Edna. 'I know I will.'

'I don't know about that,' said Mr Simms. 'We're quiet sort of people where I live.'

'Oh well, each to their own,' said Winnie. 'We're going to have a right old ding dong in our street.'

'It might be a good idea to put on another concert to welcome the troops home,' suggested Bessie.

There were joyful cries of encouragement and the conversation continued light heartedly. Everyone was happy about the good times ahead, but when two smartly dressed men accompanied by two police officers came into the post office and went over to Mr Simms, a hushed silence fell. The men spoke in low voices, but Bessie could hear enough to know they were about to arrest him. She recognised the words 'in breach of the Official Secrets Act' before the policemen put him in handcuffs and led him away.

'So he's a flaming spy,' said Edna, who was near the counter and had heard everything. 'He's been working for the Germans against us all along, the dirty rotten pig.'

'He hasn't been found guilty yet,' pointed out Bessie, who always tried to be fair.

'He will be though,' said Joyce. 'They wouldn't have arrested him if they weren't sure he was guilty.'

'I suppose you're right,' agreed Bessie.

'There are a lot of spies around, apparently, mingling in with the rest of us,' said a customer. 'That's why there are all those notices about Careless Talk Costs Lives and so on.'

'You don't ever think that you might be working with one, though, do you?' said Bessie.

'You certainly don't,' agreed Joyce. 'I feel shattered by it.'

There was a kind of hush until the current customers left and new ones came in knowing nothing about the drama. A Post Office official came to say he was sending a replacement for Mr Simms tomorrow and would appreciate it if Bessie and Joyce could manage on their own for the rest of the afternoon.

'It will entail cashing up and doing the bank, amongst other things,' said Bessie.

'If you two could manage it today I'll get someone here by tomorrow morning, to fill in until we get someone permanent for the job.'

'We'll take care of it.' Bessie looked at Joyce who was worried because she had family commitments and was not in a position to take on extra responsibility, which might entail staying late. 'I'll look after things. I know what to do. Mr Simms made a point of showing me in case he was ever taken ill or anything.'

'I'd really appreciate it,' said the Post Office official. 'And we'll get a replacement as soon as possible.'

'Well, never a dull moment at Oakdene is there?' said Stan who witnessed the whole thing. This light-hearted comment eased the tension and Bessie and Joyce managed a smile.

Tom was spellbound by the story. 'A spy? Cor! You've been working with a real live spy. How exciting!'

'There's nothing exciting about it, Tom,' said Bessie. 'The man has been working against this country, against us all.'

'I know that and it's terrible,' said Tom. 'But it still has a kind of buzz to it. I mean you don't expect to have a spy working among ordinary people. What was he like?'

'He wasn't easy to get on with, a miserable bugger to be honest. I made excuses for him because I thought he must have problems at home or something. And all the time he was betraying us.'

'Traitor,' said Doris.

'Dead right, Mum.'

'So, you'll be having a new boss,' said Doris.

'Yeah. They'll put someone in from head office temporarily until they've had time to find someone permanent for the job, I should think,' said Bessie.

'Will you apply for it?' asked Tom.

'Don't be silly,' she said. 'Of course not.'

'Why not?' he said. 'You know the job inside out and the bits you don't know they'll teach you.'

'Your brother is right,' added Doris. 'It would probably mean a good pay rise too. You're single and only have yourself to please, so why not?'

Bessie had rarely given such a thing a thought. 'Maybe I'll consider it,' she said. 'I'll talk to Joyce. See what she thinks.'

'Excellent idea,' was Joyce's reaction when Bessie spoke to her about it on the way to work the next morning. 'I was wondering what sort of person our new boss would be. If it's you, it would be marvellous. So long as you don't let the authority go to your head and start throwing your weight about.'

'As if I would.'

'Exactly,' said Joyce. 'So why not give head office a ring and get an application form.'

Bessie had never even considered the idea of a long-term career. She had always thought of a job as something with which to pay her way until she got married. But as that wasn't an option for her now maybe a step up in the workplace might be just what she needed.

'I think I will, Joyce,' she said.

Because of her experience at a post office counter, and a shortage of applicants, Bessie got the job, though she had to adhere to protocol and go through the interviewing process. A replacement for her as a counter clerk came in the form of Ron, an unassuming man in late middle age who was experienced in the job, having worked in several post offices in

London. He was a cousin of Annie's and had heard about the job through her, and he hit it off with his colleagues right away.

'Well, how does it feel to be the boss?' asked Joyce as they walked home together after Bessie's first day in the new job.

'The job in itself isn't much different, except for the cashing up at night and ordering and so on,' said Bessie. 'It's just the new responsibility that is a bit of a worry. I can see why Mr Simms was always having a go at us. If the work isn't done it's all down to the chief clerk. It's the same for me now.'

'Don't say you are going to start cracking the whip.'

'She'd never do that,' said Stan, who was glad to see the back of Mr Simms. He'd been the only drawback in this lovely little post office.

'Of course not. I've no need to,' she said. 'Mr Simms didn't trust us to get on and do the work, but I do. You're good at the job and Ron seems to be on top of things.' She grinned. 'And there's also the fact that you're a good mate and I wouldn't want to fall out with you.'

'Don't worry. I'll soon tell you if you start throwing your weight about.'

'One thing, Joyce, at least all this business with the job has taken my mind off the feverish speculation about the end of the war.'

'It's any time now, apparently,' her friend reminded her. 'So make sure you've got plenty of flags and bunting.'

'Mum has taken care of all that,' she said. 'Exciting, eh?'

'Very,' Joyce agreed.

Chapter Eleven

It was indeed very exciting for them all. Bessie had never experienced anything like VE Day before and knew, somehow, that she never would again. It was a national holiday and everyone was out in the streets imbued with goodwill and keen to share it. Tears of joy spilled from people's eyes; there was singing and dancing and strangers kissed strangers. The thought of no more bombs united everyone.

Bessie and the family joined in the local celebrations by day but in the evening, along with Shirley, who left Gloria at home with her grandmother, joined the ecstatic crowds in the West End. Joyce's husband was celebrating with his drinking pals, so Joyce was also there with Stan. The streets and pubs were packed. Although they had to wait their turn, they managed to get some drinks and they all had a tipple and a toast to their lost loved ones Percy and Frank. Now sixteen, Tom and Daisy were allowed a taste of something stronger than lemonade to celebrate, but they didn't need alcohol to raise their spirits on this wonderful occasion.

The highlight of the evening was Buckingham Palace, which was floodlit and magnificent. The crowds went wild when the

King and Queen and the two princesses came out on the balcony. The people waved and they waved back. Along with other important buildings, Big Ben and the Houses of Parliament were also floodlit. After nearly six years of darkness, this truly was a treat.

They went to a huge bonfire in Hyde Park and walked by the lake in which the coloured lights in the trees were reflected. It was during these wonderful festivities that Bessie realised Tom and Daisy's relationship must now have developed into something more than friends. They were holding hands and kissing when they didn't think anyone was looking. Bessie thought it was rather lovely.

When they got home there were people still celebrating in the street. Bessie and the others went indoors, apart from Shirley, who went home to her daughter. They were all too excited to go to bed so sat around talking.

'Your dad would have loved today,' said Doris. 'A good old knees-up to celebrate the return of peacetime.'

'Yeah,' said Bessie. 'I missed him something awful.'

'I miss him all the time,' said Doris tearfully. 'I suppose I always will.'

'Oh Mum,' said Bessie, giving her a hug but feeling helpless to make her feel better.

'I'll put the kettle on,' said Daisy tactfully, heading for the kitchen while sister and brother comforted their mother.

One evening a few weeks later Daisy and Tom were in the queue for the cinema, hoping to see a Bing Crosby film.

'I'm not sure if we'll get in,' said Daisy, holding Tom's hand. 'There are a lot of people in front of us.'

'I don't mind if we don't make it,' said Tom. 'As long as I'm with you I don't mind what we do.'

'Aah,' she said, lifting her face to kiss him. 'You are so sweet.'

'It's because I love you.'

'I love you too.'

'I'm glad the family know about us,' he said. 'It's nice that it's out in the open.'

'They seem pleased, don't they?'

'Yeah, I suppose they can see that we're right for each other,' he said.

'Ooh, the queue is moving,' she said as people began to shuffle forward. 'We might get in after all.'

'Well, who would have thought we'd be worse off after the war than during it?' said Nelly in the post office one summer day. 'I queued for an hour at the greengrocer's and when I got to the front all they had left was some dried-up swede. My kids can't bear the damned stuff, but what can I give them if there's nothing else?'

'Mine have to put up with whatever's on the table,' said Maisie. 'There's nothing in the shops and the rationing is tighter than ever, so we can only do our best.'

'I suppose it'll take a while for things to get back to normal,' suggested Nelly.

'Let's hope it isn't too long,' remarked Maisie, who had little Joycie with her. 'We had enough hardship during the war.'

'Next please,' said Bessie and greeted her customer with a smile. The atmosphere in the post office had changed completely since Mr Simms left. Bessie hadn't realised quite how tense it had often been until after he'd gone.

They had been told officially that he had been passing information on to the Germans and she and Joyce had been shocked to think that they had never suspected anything, despite his mysterious behaviour at times. But that era was over. Bessie was in charge now and was doing her best to make a good job of it. She had a lot more responsibility as well as a pay rise, but things were going well. Neither Joyce nor Ron needed to be told to do their work; they were both experienced in the job, the latter having worked in a South London post office for many years before applying for this position to be closer to home.

'Yes, I do have a boyfriend away in the army,' she said in reply to a customer's question. 'But I have no idea when he'll be home. None at all. I expect he'll just turn up one day.'

'I'm sure it won't be long,' said the customer kindly.

'I expect you're right,' said Bessie, weighed down with dread at the thought because things had to be said that would hurt.

Shirley had the same thing on her mind the following Sunday when they took Gloria to the park.

'God only knows what's gonna happen when Joe comes home and sees this little one,' she said.

'It will be a shock, that's for sure,' said Bessie. 'You've never hinted at it in a letter have you?'

'Not likely,' she said. 'Something like that could have put him off his soldiering and cost him his life.'

'You do dramatise, Shirley, but I agree that an emotional thing like that shouldn't be said in a letter, especially when they are away at war,' said Bessie. 'Obviously, I'm concerned about him, he is my brother.'

'I know it was terrible, Bessie, my having the affair, and I hate myself for betraying Joe, but how can I regret it when it gave me Gloria?' she asked emotionally.

'You can still regret being unfaithful to Joe.'

'And I do every single day,' she said. 'I beat myself up about it all the time. But I can't go around hanging my head in shame forever. I have a job to do and a child to bring up. It was a wartime thing and you and I aren't the only ones who got carried away.'

'That's true.'

'It isn't only about Joe and me anyway,' she said. 'If he isn't prepared to have Gloria in his life then he can't have me.'

'That is a big ask of any man.'

'I know. But we come as a package now. How can it be otherwise? She's my daughter and I adore her,' she said. 'I know it might sound a bit extreme, but my needs come second to Gloria's now. It's the way it is when you're a mum.'

'Yeah, I suppose that is how it would be.'

'It's a lot to ask of any man, I'm fully aware of that,' said Shirley. 'And I'm not going to force him into anything. I'd fight for my man if it wasn't for my daughter, but it isn't just me any more. He'd have to really want to have her in his life and as she is a complete stranger I don't hold out much hope. She's the most important thing to me now and that will be hard for any man to take. So, I don't hold out much hope for a future with him, Bessie.'

'I think you're right to be cautious,' said Bessie, 'but he might surprise you. You never know.'

She shrugged. 'Anyway, what about you?' she asked. 'Will you tell Josh about Ray?'

'Oh yes,' she replied. 'But my situation seems easy in comparison to yours.'

'It's never easy to break someone's heart.'

'I know because Ray broke mine,' she said. 'He really was the love of my life.'

'So, you are not going to stay with Josh then.'

'I don't see how I can when I'm still in love with Ray,' she said. 'The fact that he doesn't want me doesn't change my feelings for him. But how do we know how we really feel until we see them again?'

'My thoughts exactly,' agreed Shirley. 'I think I still love Joe but I can't be sure until I see him. It's been a very long time and we are different people now.'

'Anyway, it might be months before they arrive home.'

'Exactly,' she agreed. 'We can plan it down to the last detail, but it doesn't mean it will happen that way.'

'Only time will tell,' said Bessie. 'So, shall we go back to mine for a cuppa and let Mum have a cuddle with Gloria?'

'Yeah, let's do that,' she said. 'There's only so much talking and planning you can do when it comes to the emotions. I mean, I might look at Joe and wonder what I ever saw in him and he might feel the same about me.'

'It could happen, I suppose.'

'We've all grown up these past six years.'

'True,' agreed Bessie. 'We'll just have to wait and see what happens and hope it isn't too long.'

They headed back home talking of other things.

Tom gave Bessie and her mother a shock one evening in August when he made an announcement over dinner.

'Daisy and I are getting married,' he said.

Doris smiled, assuming he was joking. 'Oh yeah,' she said.

'And I'm going to tea at Buckingham Palace. Do you have a joke to tell, Bessie?'

'It's no joke, Mum,' he said seriously. 'We really are getting married.'

'Ha ha, you'll be telling me that there's a baby on the way next,' she said.

Four eyes stared at her.

'Oh no, please tell me it isn't true.'

'Sorry, Mum,' he said. 'But we do love each other very much.'

'You're barely out of nappies,' she said, her face and neck suffused with pink blotches.

'That's a bit of an exaggeration, Mum,' said Tom.

She stood up, went over to him and slapped him across the face. 'After all your father and I have taught you about morality. It's a good job your dad isn't here.'

She slammed out of the room and they heard her footsteps on the stairs. Tom got up to go after her but Bessie stopped him.

'I think she needs a bit of time on her own,' she suggested. 'I'll go up in a few minutes.'

'I've never known Mum to be so angry.'

'It's a big thing you've thrown at her.'

'Sorry, Bessie,' said Daisy. 'For upsetting your mum; and you as well I expect.'

'It isn't my place to disapprove,' she said. 'People get into a real state about this sort of thing, especially the older generation. She'll be all right when she's calmed down.' She looked from one to the other, wondering how she could have missed such a dramatic change in their relationship. She'd seen them getting closer and knew they had been going out a lot together recently but she'd never thought they were fully fledged lovers. 'You've kept this very quiet.'

'We've been so wrapped up in each other, we wanted to keep it to ourselves for a while,' said Daisy. 'But I'm sorry we've upset Auntie Doris . . . and you, Bessie.'

'I'm not upset,' said Bessie. 'Just worried for you two because you are so young for such a responsibility. Tom still has to do his military service so will be going away.'

'The wives of the married men who went away to war managed,' Daisy pointed out.

'They were older than you and Tom,' she said.

'Not much.'

'You've got a baby on the way so you'll have to face up to the responsibility.'

'We know that, Bessie,' said Tom. 'And we are. That's why we want to get married.'

'Oh well, if it's what you both want then I wish you the best of luck,' she said.

Daisy flung her arms around her. 'Thank you, Bessie. That means so much to me.'

'And me,' added Tom.

'My little brother, a dad,' said Bessie. 'It doesn't seem five minutes since I was wiping your nose for you.'

'Now you're embarrassing me,' said Tom.

'I do wish we hadn't upset your mum, though,' said Daisy. 'She's been really good to me and I am very fond of her.'

'It was quite a bombshell you dropped on her,' said Bessie. 'She might need some time. Poor Mum. First, she loses Dad. Now this.'

Tom and Daisy had been openly physical in their attitude towards each other, but Bessie had hoped they would have been more careful.

'But this is a joyful thing surely, Bessie,' said Tom. 'A new baby in the family.'

'Yes, of course it is,' she responded. 'But you've put the cart before the horse and Mum has to get used to it.'

Doris was sitting on the edge of the bed, every nerve in her body on edge. If it wasn't one thing it was another, lately. She still hadn't got used to Percy's death and now there was this new situation to deal with on her own. Every problem was enlarged, every situation more difficult without her husband's support.

But what was she doing sitting here crying when there was a young couple downstairs in trouble. Yes, it was of their own making, but it was trouble nonetheless. A baby though, a new life in the family. It might be trouble, but it was wonderful and just what this family needed. So get things sorted, woman, instead of wallowing in self-pity. She stood up, straightened her clothes and headed for the stairs.

'Are you all right, Mum?' asked Tom when she walked into the room.

'After the news you've just given me?' she said. 'No, of course I'm not all right.'

'Sorry,' said Tom.

'I'm sorry too,' added Daisy.

'And so you bloody well should be, both of you,' she said sternly.

They both looked shamefaced.

'But it's happened and we have to get cracking and get things sorted out.'

'I'm not getting rid of it if that's what you mean,' Daisy stated categorically.

'Of course I don't mean that,' said Doris. 'Do you really intend to get married?'

'Definitely,' said Tom. 'I've got some money in my National Savings book. And we'll only have a very small wedding. Just us family and a mate as best man.'

'I think we can do better than that, Tom,' said Doris. 'We can have a few friends and relatives.'

'But we wondered if we could continue to live here until we can get a place of our own,' said Daisy.

'Do you really think I would throw you out on the street?'

'Not really, but Joe will be coming home soon so there'll be quite a crowd of us and Josh will have nowhere to go.'

'There are some bigger families than ours in this street,' she said. 'Next door have six kids and they manage so I'm sure we will too, until you get a place of your own. We'll have to alter the sleeping arrangements around, but that's the least of our problems. The important thing is, we are going to have a new family member. And we will welcome it with open arms.'

'Hear, hear,' said Bessie.

Daisy burst into tears.

'Don't cry,' said Tom, putting a comforting arm around her. 'It's going to be all right.'

'I know,' sobbed Daisy. 'It's this family. You are always so good to me you make me cry.'

'You're going to officially be a part of the family soon and you'll always be very welcome.'

'I'll do my best for you all,' she said tearfully.

Bessie felt emotional because she knew how desperately

Daisy had wanted to be a part of a family, having lost her own. She didn't think she had knowingly connived to get into this one, though, because she obviously adored Tom. They were young to take on the responsibility of marriage and parenthood, but Bessie was confident they could make a success of it and she wished them all the luck in the world.

Because of the short notice and the circumstances, it was a small wedding at the registry office. But friends and relatives were there and the occasion was filled with heart and warm wishes for the happy couple. Daisy looked lovely in a smart red dress with a wide-brimmed cream hat and Tom was proud and handsome in his best suit.

Seeing the couple so full of love for each other, Bessie was overcome with emotion. Looking back, she could see that this occasion had been destined from the moment the couple had met as children. Despite Daisy's hostility to him, there had been strong chemistry between them which had probably been partly to blame for a great deal of their disagreement.

Yes, they were young for the responsibilities that lay ahead but there was a toughness about them. Bessie was confident they would make a go of it.

The reception was at home. Despite the food shortages, Doris managed to put on a tasty spread; just cold meats and mashed potato, but everyone enjoyed it. Bessie made a wedding cake too, despite the shortage of ingredients. There was a real party atmosphere and later the furniture was moved aside for dancing to records on the gramophone.

* * *

Daisy was taking a break from the dancing and sitting down watching. She had thought she could never be happy again in those grim days after she lost her family, but today was the happiest day of her life. Looking back over the years, she could see that there had been a spark between her and Tom from that very first day at the Green house at that most terrible time in her life. She would never have admitted it, even to herself back then, but she had admired him from the moment she had first set eyes on him. They had been children then, of course, but she had always felt drawn to him and had hidden it behind a show of abuse.

Over the years they had fought a great deal. But they had laughed too and there was plenty more laughter to come, as well as commitment and responsibility. He was her soulmate and the love of her life. She looked up to see him watching her from across the room. He smiled and made his way over.

Tom thought he must be the happiest man in London today. He had married the love of his life and things didn't get better than that. He remembered what a little horror Daisy had been for a long time after her arrival, but even then he had felt drawn to her. There had been something strong between them from that very first moment. Now she was his wife and he couldn't be prouder.

'Would you like to dance?' he asked.

'Yes, please,' she said and a cheer went up as the happy couple took to the makeshift dancefloor.

★   ★   ★

'You've worked miracles at such short notice, Mum,' said Bessie in a quiet moment. 'You've given the couple a real day to remember and that isn't easy in these hard times.'

'I've done my best.'

Bessie guessed how much her mother would be missing Dad today as she herself was. 'And all credit to you,' she said, giving her a hug and trying not to cry. 'It really is a lovely event and everyone seems to be enjoying themselves.'

'Thank you, love,' said Doris thickly.

Joyce came over with Stan by her side; both were acquainted with Doris. 'A lovely party, Doris,' said Joyce.

'Cracking,' added Stan.

'Glad you're enjoying it,' said Doris. 'Your husband couldn't make it then, Joyce?'

'No, he had something else to do,' she fibbed. Jim had refused to go with her and tried to stop her from going. He said he couldn't bear weddings and didn't want to socialise with her boring friends and work colleagues. She didn't mind because she knew that Stan had been invited so she would enjoy herself.

'I'm standing in for him,' said Stan.

'Well, have fun.'

'We will,' said Stan and the two of them headed for the dancing.

'What's going on there?' Doris asked Bessie when the couple were out of earshot. 'They seem very pally.'

'Yes, they are friendly but I don't know if anything is actually going on,' relied Bessie. 'I think they are just friends.'

'Seems a bit more than that to me,' said Doris, who was old fashioned about such things. 'She should be with her husband.'

'He didn't want to come, apparently,' said Bessie. 'I think it's a difficult marriage.'

'Oh, that's a shame,' said Doris. 'She's such a nice woman too. She deserves a good man.'

'Yes, she does and I think Stan might just be that man.'

'Oh dear,' said Doris. 'Still, it's none of our business.'

Bessie was saved from further discussion on the subject by Joyce's son, Jack, who had recently been demobbed and came over to ask Doris if she'd like to dance. It was a sweet gesture to make sure the older woman didn't feel left out by the abundance of young people here and Bessie was touched.

'Are you enjoying yourself, Shirley?' asked Doris later on when her daughter's best friend came over for a chat.

'Not half,' replied Shirley. 'It's so good to have a night out. I don't get many of those now that I'm a mum. What a lovely party it is too. You've done wonders.'

'Thank you, dear.'

'I haven't heard from Joe in ages,' said Shirley. 'And I'm guessing that you haven't either because Bessie would have mentioned it.'

'Not a word,' said Doris.

'He should be home sometime soon,' said the younger woman. 'The boys are beginning to appear on the streets again.'

'Yeah, I've noticed a few servicemen around,' said Doris, wondering what was going to happen when her son arrived home and saw little Gloria. 'He'll turn up one day soon.'

Shirley nodded. She was also worried about Joe's reaction to Gloria, but was trying not to dwell on it because there was nothing she could do until the occasion arose. 'Meanwhile we have another concert to prepare for, so that will keep us busy.'

'Yes, Bessie said she was doing another one, a sort of welcome home to the boys. I think it's a really nice idea. They aren't all home yet, but perhaps you can do another one later on for those who'll miss this one.'

'I'm sure we will,' said Shirley. 'But for now, I'm going to enjoy the rest of this lovely party.'

'Yes, go and have fun,' said Doris smiling. She was glad the event was going so well.

Bessie and her friends managed to get the new concert organised for the New Year of 1946. They didn't have the glorious tones of Ray or the thrill of Mr Simms's magic act, and Daisy was feeling too plump to perform, but Stan did an excellent job as compère and they had the regulars. They also managed to find a few new volunteers: a couple of singers and a man who played the trumpet. But the star of the show was Joyce's son, Jack, who did a comedy spot with Stan and together they were hilarious. Jack had such a way of delivering the jokes, the audience was in fits and Bessie thought how nice it was that they had become close friends.

'Well done, son,' said Joyce 'You were a riot. Where did you learn to perform like that?'

'The army. They encourage entertainment to keep the men's morale up. I joined the concert party.'

'You and Stan were brilliant,' said Bessie as they made their way home through the town. 'Absolutely marvellous!'

There was a chorus of agreement.

★   ★   ★

They were all tired when they got home, but still feeling vibrant from the concert. They had just made some cocoa when there was a knock at the door.

'Who's calling at this time of night,' said Doris. 'It's no time to be coming to someone's front door. I hope it isn't trouble.'

Bessie went to answer it and immediately burst into tears of joy. It was her brother Joe. Her mother also gave him an emotional welcome while Tom shook his hand and introduced him to his new wife, who was noticeably pregnant now.

'My little brother a married man,' said Joe. 'Well, well.' He gave Daisy a hug. 'Hello, new sister-in-law.'

'Hello, Joe,' she said, still thrilled to be officially part of this family.

Joe had had something to eat on the journey, but Doris went to the sideboard and took out a bottle of sherry she had been keeping for this occasion.

'Could we keep that for tomorrow, Mum?' asked Joe. 'What I fancy now is a nice cup of tea.'

'Of course, love,' she said and scuttled off to the kitchen, eager to do something for her soldier son.

When the others went to bed, Bessie stayed up chatting to her brother.

'You've not got married while I've been away then, sis?' he asked.

'No. I do have a boyfriend,' she said. 'Daisy's brother, Josh, but we'll have to see what happens when he gets home.'

'You don't sound too sure.'

'He's been away a long time, Joe,' she said. 'None of us knows how we'll feel after so long.'

She was tempted to tell him about Ray, but thought better

of it. She would tell Josh about Ray when the time was right and depending on how she felt about Josh when she saw him again. She didn't want him to hear so much as a whisper from anyone else. The others knew about him, of course, but they had promised not to say anything.

'I hope Shirley hasn't gone off me after so long,' he said.

Bessie's stomach clenched. Shirley has asked her to keep quiet about Gloria, preferring to tell him herself when she saw him.

'The war has changed everyone and everything, but I'm sure all will be fine,' she said.

They talked into the small hours and as it was a Saturday they could lie in in the morning. Bessie was very happy to have her brother back, but not so sure about his romantic happiness with Shirley.

Ray was back from the war, but found it something of an anti-climax. Apart from his family there was no loved one to welcome him, through his own fault, admittedly. His job prospects weren't good either. Following an injury to his foot he was unable to do building work, so with his dreams of setting up his own construction firm shattered, he'd been using his singing to earn a living. He did have quite a bit in army back pay so there was no real urgency, but he wasn't the sort of man to do nothing.

He had never thought of singing as a proper job, despite Bessie's encouragement, but now that he was doing more of it he was beginning to enjoy it as a working tool. It was all very small time: weddings and welcome home parties, twenty-first birthdays and pubs where they provided entertainment, nothing very grand but it was a steady earner. And he had to admit that it was nice to see people enjoying his efforts.

Now that he was back in England he couldn't get Bessie off his mind. When he'd been away in all-male company it had been easier, though he had spent a lot of his time in regret for having given her up. Self-pity wasn't in his nature, but he could be very hard on himself at times.

Still, at least a few of his mates were home from the war so he had someone to have a pint with. He was on his way to the pub now and as he went up to the bar to order his drink, the landlord handed him a slip of paper with a name and telephone number written on it.

'The Guv'nor of the Park Hotel, a mate of mine, is doing an event in their functions room. They've got a three-piece band booked and are looking for a singer. He wondered if you'd be interested.'

'When is it?' asked Ray. 'I'm busy for the next couple of Saturdays.'

'It's well into the future,' he said. 'He just wanted to get you booked up.'

'Oh good. I'll go to the phone box and give him a ring then,' he said eagerly. 'I'll have my pint when I get back.'

'Righto, mate,' said the landlord.

Ray headed for the phone box feeling cheered. The bookings were coming in quite regularly now, and knowing he had work ahead gave him a feeling of security. There were worse ways to earn a living than singing. It still didn't feel like a proper job, but as he was being paid, he supposed it must be.

Singing wasn't really a job for a man like him who liked to feel the aching muscles of a good day's work. But he knew he was blessed to have such a gift and if people were willing to pay him for it he'd do it and see how it went. There were a few people waiting to use the phone box so he joined the queue with a feeling of optimism.

The next day was Sunday and Joe headed off to see Shirley in the morning, feeling simultaneously nervous and excited. It had been a long time. Would they feel the same about each other after all this while?

Shirley's mother answered the door and stared at him blankly before recognition dawned. 'Joe,' she said at last, her voice rising excitedly. 'Welcome home. Come on in, love.' She shouted into the house. 'Shirley, there's someone here to see you.'

Shirley appeared with a little girl trailing behind her.

'Joe!' she said with spontaneous warmth and joy in her voice as she opened her arms to him. 'Welcome home.'

They embraced while Shirley's mother scooped Gloria up and took her away.

Shirley took Joe into the front room, which was only used at Christmas and other special occasions.

'It's a bit chilly in here because we only have a fire going at Christmas, but at least it's private,' Shirley explained. 'Oh Joe, it's so good to see you.'

'Likewise,' he beamed.

Shirley was surprised at how strongly she felt for him after all this time, especially having had an affair with someone else. But she really did love him and wanted them to be together.

'Do you still love me after all this time?' he asked.

'Absolutely,' she said from the heart. 'How about you?'

He took her in his arms. 'You can't possibly know how much I have longed for this moment. To see you and to hold you in my arms.'

'Me too,' she said.

There was a tap on the door and Shirley's mother poked her head around. 'I'm taking Gloria to the park,' she said.

'All right, thanks,' said Shirley.

'Bye, Mummy,' said Gloria.

'Bye, darling,' Shirley replied.

It was absolutely silent in the room as the front door closed.

'It seems things have been happening while I've been away,' said Joe miserably.

'Yes, I'm afraid they have,' said Shirley and prepared herself to tell him all about it.

When Shirley's mother returned from the park with Gloria, Joe was nowhere to be seen.

'How did he take it?' she asked. 'He didn't even stay for a cup of tea.'

'No. He has a lot to think about so needs to be on his own.'

'Yes, of course,' she said, glancing towards Gloria.

'He was shocked, naturally,' Shirley said.

'Bound to be,' she said. 'Such a nice boy, too.'

'Yes, he is,' she agreed sadly. 'He really is.

When Joe got home from Shirley's he asked Bessie to go for a walk with him.

'Why didn't you tell me she had a kid, Bessie?' he asked as they headed for the river.

'I didn't think it was my place.'

'It was such a shock,' he said. 'It was all going so well then this little kid calls her mummy.'

'Yeah. She's a lovely little thing, isn't she?'

'Not to me she isn't,' he said. 'To me she is the proof of my girlfriend's unfaithfulness.'

'You were away for a very long time, Joe, and Shirley is young and only human.'

'So, what happened to faithfulness?' he said. 'Has that been eradicated by the war?'

'Of course not, but we've all been living under extra-ordinary circumstances,' she said. 'It was just a fling, probably brought about by the fact that she was missing you. He was a real chancer. Full of charm and not an ounce of decency in him. Disappeared when she got pregnant. Left her to face it on her own and didn't leave an address. She had a hard time for a while.'

'I'm sorry, of course, but it doesn't make it any easier for me,' he said. 'I feel absolutely betrayed.'

'Do you still love her?'

'Of course,' he said. 'If I didn't it wouldn't bother me.'

'Are you going to end things with her then?'

'That's what I should do.'

'And lose a precious thing because of something brought about because Shirley was lonely and missing you.'

'It's like a physical pain, Bessie.'

'I know, Joe.'

'Anyway, how can I bring up another man's child?' he said. 'It would be a constant reminder.'

'I suppose it would,' she said as they walked beside the river, grey and muddy on this cold afternoon, a pale sun reflected in its moving tidal waters, busy with traffic, barges carrying coal, boats loaded with tea and other provisions.

'I really don't know what to do, Bessie,' he said, sounding anguished. 'I want to be with Shirley, but I'm full of resentment so the relationship wouldn't work.'

'Let me tell you something, Joe,' she said. 'I fell in love with someone else while my boyfriend was away. But unlike Shirley I am still in love with him, even though he doesn't want me. So, I have to tell Josh when he comes home that I can't be with him any more. I can't pretend, Joe.'

'Oh, Bessie, that will be hard for him,' he said.

'I feel awful about it, but I can't stay with him just because I don't have the courage to tell him,' she said. 'We're not engaged or anything.'

'Was there an understanding though?'

'Not as such, but we were serious about each other,' she said. 'I feel terrible but it's happened and I shall have to tell him. Sometimes we are just not in control of our emotions. At least Shirley loves and wants you.'

'Mm, I know,' he said. 'I want to accept it and be with her. But this thing is there all the time, nagging away.'

'Shirley really wasn't in love with this other man, you know,' she said. 'She was missing you and he really did know how to turn on the charm. She was dazzled by him, I think.'

'Good looking, I suppose.'

'It was more his self-confidence that was so attractive to her, I think,' she said. 'I mean, I thought he was conceited and overbearing, but Shirley was taken in by it all for a while. She wouldn't have given him a second glance if you had been around.'

'Maybe I should try to see it from her point of view, but

at the moment I am hurting too much,' he said. 'A child, though, Bessie. You must be able to see how hard that is to take. A constant reminder. I don't know if I'm strong enough for that.'

'You might surprise yourself, you never know,' she said. 'But it has to be your decision.'

'Of course. I still love her and want to be with her, but I don't know if I have it in me to bring up another man's child.'

'It's a huge commitment and I can imagine how difficult it must be to make the decision,' she said. 'Only you can know if you are prepared to take it on.'

'I know,' he sighed as they headed towards Hammersmith Bridge, its gaudy grandeur brightening up the grey landscape on this cold and gloomy day.

Later that day, as dusk began to fall, Joe was striding through the streets of Hammersmith on his way to the pub, hoping that some liquid refreshment might make him feel better. What a disappointment his homecoming had been! After all the years of looking forward to a future with Shirley she had betrayed him and broken his heart.

The state of London had come as a shock too. It was shabby and bomb damaged. Like a different place. The people must have been though hell during the air raids too. Seeing the destruction had made him realise. He slowed his steps, lapsing into thought. What was he doing wallowing in self-pity when he had been through a war and survived when plenty hadn't? He'd lost mates at the front and he knew many lives had been wiped out at home, including his beloved father's. So what if

Shirley had been unfaithful? Surely they were strong enough to put that behind them and look to the future. The child was a challenge, but he was sure he'd soon get the hang of fatherhood with Shirley by his side. He hurried on his way, almost breaking into a run in his eagerness to get where he needed to be.

Shirley opened the door. 'Joe,' she said in surprise. 'I didn't expect to see you.'

'Marry me,' he burst out.

'But I thought . . .'

'I love you,' he said. 'Nothing else matters.'

'What about Gloria?'

'I'll do my best to be a good dad, I promise,' he said. 'Please say you'll be my wife.'

'Of course I will,' she said, melting into his arms.

'Isn't it lovely to see our boys back on the streets,' said Edna while Bessie dealt with a registered parcel for her, securing the knots with hot sealing wax. It was almost closing time and Edna had been told that her parcel wouldn't go off until the next day.

'Yes, it really is,' agreed Bessie.

'Is your young man back yet?' asked Edna.

'No, not yet, but my brother is.'

'Oh lovely,' she enthused. 'I bet your mum is pleased.'

'I'll say,' said Bessie. 'She's spoiling him something awful.'

'I'm sure he deserves it,' said Edna. 'They all do after all they've been through to serve their country.'

'Indeed,' said Bessie. 'I think we're all giving him special treatment at the moment.' She put the parcel on a pile behind her ready for the postman to collect the next day and took the customer's money.

'Ta ta, dear,' said Edna when the transaction was complete. 'I hope your boyfriend gets home soon.'

'Me too,' said Bessie. 'Thank you for your wishes. Ta ta for now.'

Joyce gave Bessie a nudge. 'It might be sooner than you think,' she said. 'Isn't that him waiting outside?'

Chapter Twelve

Such was Bessie's anxiety, her hands were shaking as she served her last customer of the day.

'I'll do the cashing up,' Joyce offered. 'You get off and see your fella. Ron will help me close up, won't you, Ron?'

'Course I will,' said their colleague, who was a very friendly and obliging man.

'Thanks, both,' she said and as she went into the staff-room to get her coat she took a few deep breaths to try to calm herself before heading out of the shop, hoping that by some miracle she would fall in love with Josh again when she saw him.

She didn't. There was a deep affection for him, but it wasn't the sort of love she'd had for him when they were last together. She went through all the motions. She returned his kiss the best way she could manage and said how pleased she was to see him, which was true. Then as they set off for home he said, 'So, what's his name?'

'What do you mean?'

'You've either met someone else or absence hasn't made the heart grow fonder.'

'There isn't anyone, Josh,' she said.

'So what's wrong then?'

'Nothing.' How could she break his heart when he was just back from all sorts of hell?

'Please don't insult my intelligence, Bessie,' he said. 'I knew the moment I set eyes on you that things had changed.'

'Well . . . there was someone, briefly,' she admitted at last. 'It didn't work out but he was special.'

'You wanted to be with him?'

'At the time, yes.'

'And now?'

'I've accepted that it isn't to be.'

'So, you thought you'd have me as second best.'

'No, absolutely not,' she said. 'I didn't want to tell you in a letter, so I was going to tell you as soon as the time was right. Obviously I wouldn't throw something like that at you as soon as I clapped eyes on you after all this time.'

'Good job I'm an observant sort of a bloke then, isn't it?'

'I'm so sorry, Josh,' she said with deep sincerity. 'I'd give a lot to turn the clock back, but it isn't possible. If it's any consolation, the man doesn't return my feelings.'

'Do you really think I can take pleasure in knowing that?'

'I thought it might help.'

'It doesn't. If anything, it makes it worse.'

'I'd give anything to change things back to how they were,' she said. 'But you've been away too long.'

'If your feelings had been sincere it wouldn't have mattered if I'd been away ten years.'

'In fairy tales, maybe,' she said. 'In real life, it isn't always that simple. We're all only human.'

He shrugged. 'I'll move in with a mate until I can find somewhere else to live,' he said.

'Oh Josh, there's no need for that,' she said. 'Don't make me feel even worse by moving out.'

'Do you really think I can live in the same house as you, under the circumstances?'

'I suppose not,' she agreed, riddled with guilt. 'But accommodation is really scarce in London at the moment.'

'I'll be all right at my mate's place,' he assured her. 'His mum will probably be glad of the extra rent. They have a box room that will do for me.'

Bessie felt terrible. What an awful homecoming! To lose his girlfriend and his home in one fell swoop. But she knew it would be awkward for everyone if he stayed at the Greens'. Daisy would be furious with her on his behalf, though she was so wrapped up in Tom and her pregnancy, maybe she wouldn't be quite so protective of Josh.

'Don't worry about it, Bessie,' he said in a warmer tone and to her amazement she suspected he might be relieved. 'I'm not really sure how I feel either, if I'm honest, so it's probably for the best.'

'Why didn't you say so instead of letting me go through all that?' she asked.

'I didn't get a chance to think about my feelings because it all happened so fast. When you're away at the war, all you live for is coming home, the happy ending. Truth be told I don't really believe in happy endings any more. I have a lot of readjustment to do so I'll probably be better on my own for a while. I need to work out what to do with the rest of my life.'

'How do you mean?'

'There are other places in England besides London,' he said. 'Maybe I might want to explore a little.'

'But you've only just got back.'

He shrugged. 'Perhaps the war has made me realise that the world doesn't begin and end with Big Ben,' he said. 'It might be nice to see some other places as a civilian. Daisy is settled with Tom so she'll be all right, bless her. I thought she would burst with happiness when she saw me, but she isn't reliant on me any more.'

'Maybe not, but she still adores you,' she said.

'And I her so I'll always keep in close touch wherever I am. But I have no plans as such, I'll just enjoy being back for a while.'

'I hope you and I can still be friends,' she said.

'I'm sure we can work something out,' he said. 'We'll still be in each other's lives because of Daisy and we'll never be enemies. But bosom pals? I really don't know. Let's see how it goes, shall we?'

'Of course.'

'So why don't you bring me up to date with what else has been happening while I've been away,' he said. 'I know the main event about Tom and Daisy getting married and expecting a baby.'

'I'm not sure where to start, but I'll give it a try,' she said. 'There is plenty of news after all this time. My friend Shirley and my brother Joe are getting married soon.'

'Sounds good,' he said.

'Yeah, that's all anyone is talking about in our house at the moment,' she said. 'Shirley's parents aren't short of cash so it'll be quite a big do. White wedding with all the trimmings and reception at a posh hotel afterwards.'

'I suppose you'll be bridesmaid,' he said.

'Yeah, and Shirley's daughter, little Gloria, is their flower girl.'

'I need to know more about this daughter of hers,' he said. 'Like who is the daddy?'

'That's a story for another time,' she said as they reached the house.

'I'll look forward to hearing about it,' he said.

As they went into the house Bessie was thoughtful. She'd hated having to hurt him, but sensed it had only been a surface wound. He was full of ideas for the future and marrying and settling down didn't seem to have been a top priority.

Bessie was still on Ray's mind and he was longing to see her. He had even toyed with the idea of going into the post office for some stamps to that end, but thought better of it because he was ashamed of the way he had behaved. If he'd not been so stupid as to give her up when they had been together, she might be his wife by now. She certainly wouldn't want to get together with him as he was now with a smashed-up foot, so it would be best to stay away for her sake.

Still, at least he was kept busy with singing engagements so he was able to pay his way and keep his self-respect. He enjoyed it, too, now that he had managed to convince himself that it was proper employment and that maybe he could carry a tune. All right, so he didn't work normal hours or have aching muscles at the end of the day as proof that he'd done a good day's work, but he did have the satisfaction of knowing that he pleased people and got paid for the privilege.

So, all in all, life wasn't bad. It was all a matter of acceptance. He'd managed to take things in his stride when he got wounded, so why couldn't he accept the fact that there was no future for him with Bessie? Love, mate, that was the problem, he told himself. Hope springs eternal when you're in that condition.

Shirley was in the Saturday shopping crowds in Hammersmith's King Street with her daughter.

'When can we go to the café for a bun, Mummy?' asked Gloria.

'Not just yet,' said Shirley. 'We have to get you some new shoes first.'

'Can I have pretty shoes with bows on like the girl in my story book?' she asked.

Most unlikely, thought Shirley, in these days of shortages and utility goods. 'We might not be able to find any today because we are looking for everyday shoes,' she said. 'But you'll have pretty shoes for the wedding if I can possibly manage it.'

They went into a shoe shop and sat down waiting to be served. It was busy in there and a family was dominating events. They were three exuberant boys and their parents. The boys were full of high spirits and laughing and joshing with each other; they were very noisy and seemed to fill the shop.

'Calm down and be quiet,' said the woman.

'It's him, Mum,' said one boy pointing at another: all the boys looked very alike.

'No, it's not,' said the other, pushing his brother. 'Why do I always get the blame?'

'Because it's usually your fault,' said the man.

'Aw, come on, Dad,' said the boy. 'That isn't fair.'

'They are all as bad as each other, darling,' said the woman.

'Well, we are not going to put up with them showing us

up when we're out,' said the man sternly. 'So sit down all three of you and wait quietly until we are served.'

'But, Dad,' began one.

'Enough,' said the man raising his hand in a halt gesture.

All the boys sat in silence. Shirley was thinking how good looking they all were when their father sat down next to them, right opposite her. When he looked ahead of him she saw that it was Bernie. Instinctively she smiled. He looked blank, showing no sign of recognition, but a hint of threat, warning her to keep quiet. He didn't want to know. She got up and left the shop holding her daughter's hand and heading for Lyons.

'Where are we going now? asked Gloria.

'To the café.'

'Goodee,' she said.

A bun and a glass of milk in Lyons teashop was a real treat for Gloria in these hard times, when everything was in short supply. The days of plenty after the war that everyone had looked forward to hadn't arrived. Instead they had been plunged into even tighter rationing and shortages of absolutely everything.

But the state of the nation was the last thing on Shirley's mind as she queued to get served. She was still reeling from the blow of being snubbed by Bernie. He didn't know that his daughter had been right there in front of him. He wouldn't have cared if he had. He was a married man with three children and judging by the ages of his sons he had been when he'd been having a passionate affair with her.

Any lingering romantic notions she might have occasionally harboured about him were now eradicated completely. He was a happily married man and she had just been his 'bit on the side'. It wasn't a pleasant conclusion and it hurt, but it was also closure for her. She could now marry the love of her life with no hint of hankerings for the past.

She was counting her blessings as she and her daughter got served and went to find a table. She would put all her energy into making Joe and Gloria happy. Her daughter would never know her half-brothers, but she had adoring grandparents and family friends who loved her. Shirley was hoping too that Gloria would have some siblings before too long. She and Joe wanted to have kids.

'Where are we going next, Mummy?' asked Gloria as she finished her refreshments.

'To get your shoes.'

'Back to that shop?'

'No, we'll go to one of the others,' she said, not wanting to take a chance on seeing Bernie and his family again. Once was more than enough and he had to be put firmly into the past.

There was great excitement in the Green household when Daisy gave birth to a son. They were calling him Frank after Tom's brother they had lost to the war, but he was going to be known as Frankie.

'Yippee, I won't have to wear maternity clothes to the wedding,' said Daisy, nursing her new baby. 'Thanks, Frankie, for not keeping me waiting.'

Bessie was so pleased for the young couple. Everything had seemed so bleak for Daisy when she had first come into their lives, but the family was richer for having her and now she had started a family of her own, which was also a new branch of the Green family. Tom's military service was delayed because of his apprenticeship so he would be around to give Daisy his support in these early days of motherhood.

Much to her shame, Bessie felt a stab of envy. Everyone seemed settled. Tom and Daisy had started a new chapter in their lives and Shirley was about to get married, while Bessie didn't even have a boyfriend. Oh well, she thought, people had worse things to cope with. The sight of so many men who had been wounded in the war was proof of that.

The sun shone for the wedding of Shirley and Joe. Bessie was bridesmaid and Gloria a flower girl, both in pale-blue taffeta, while the bride was radiant in white alongside Joe smart in civvies. Bessie felt emotional and an awful feeling of loneliness persisted.

Shirley's parents had really pushed the boat out for their only child and as well as a grand wedding reception in a hotel had also organised an evening do with a band and dancing. Helped by a few glasses of something with a bit of a kick, Bessie began to enjoy herself and had no shortage of dancing partners.

It was only when they introduced the singer that she was thrown into confusion. 'Now, ladies and gentlemen, please give a warm welcome to our singer for the evening, Mr Ray Brownlow.'

And there he was, dressed in dinner jacket, white shirt and bow tie, as handsome as ever but walking with a limp. Bessie knew instantly that she was still in love with him.

★　★　★

Everyone was enjoying his performance as he gave a marvellous rendition of 'That Old Black Magic', his rich deep tones filling the hall as people danced, his talent and charisma reaching every corner of the hall.

Deeply affected by this unexpected sighting of him, Bessie decided to take action. She'd stood back waiting for things to happen for too long. He might be married or spoken for and if he really didn't want her, she would accept it, but she wasn't going to give up without a fight. He had ended things between them because he was afraid of commitment, but as he had reappeared in her life she was going to do everything she could to get him back. This time she wasn't going to give up without a fight. But even as the thoughts came, he finished his song and left the stage, heading in her direction.

Joyce and Stan were sitting down near the dancefloor enjoying a glass of wine together, she in a smart blue dress, he in his best suit.

'Thank goodness for a sit down,' she said lightly. 'I'm worn out after all that dancing.'

'I don't believe you,' said Stan lightly. 'You've got more energy than the entire postal service.'

She laughed. 'Now you really are exaggerating,' she said.

'Well maybe a little, but you are very lively.'

'For a woman of forty-seven, you mean.'

'No. I wasn't even thinking about your age,' he said. 'Just your energy.' He paused. 'You are two years younger than me but I won't hold it against you.'

They were both smiling, happy to be together. They had

become very close. The intimacy in her marriage hadn't existed for years. She cooked and cleaned for Jim and that was about all, but still she couldn't bring herself to leave him, even though Jack was grown up so no longer an obstacle.

'Jack seems to be enjoying himself,' mentioned Stan, looking across the room. 'He's getting on well with that pretty girl over there.'

She smiled. 'Yeah, he does seem to be,' she agreed.

'He'll be the next one to get married,' said Stan.

'Yes, he probably will,' she said thoughtfully.

Doris was dancing with an uncle of Shirley's, a pleasant man of about her own age.

'Are you enjoying yourself?' he asked.

'I'm doing my best, but I don't find enjoyment easy these days.'

'Yes, I heard that you lost your husband.'

'Mm.'

'It's a bugger isn't it,' he said. 'My wife died a couple of years ago, so I know what it feels like.'

'Was it the bombing?'

'No. Pneumonia.'

'I'm sorry.'

'Thank you.' He looked at her with kindness in his eyes. 'It does get easier with time, you know.'

'I'm not sure I want it to,' she said. 'I'd feel guilty if I was enjoying myself.'

'I've been through the same thing, but I can now laugh without feeling bad about it.'

'Oh, it does come back then?'

'It has for me and I'm sure it will for you eventually. I am enjoying this wedding party; a year ago I would have wanted to leave as soon as I got here.'

'That's how I feel now.'

'Kindred spirits, then.'

'I suppose so.'

'Since we are both here we might as well enjoy ourselves.'

'We can try anyway.'

'The singer is good, isn't he?' he said.

'Very good,' she agreed. 'He was a boyfriend of my daughter's at one time.'

'Looks as though they're about to get together again,' he said as the dance ended.

Doris looked towards the stage to see Bessie and Ray engrossed in conversation. 'I do hope so,' she said to her new companion. 'Those two were meant for each other.'

'Bessie,' he said, his face wreathed in smiles.

'Hello, Ray.'

'I'm surprised you can bear to speak to me after the way I treated you,' he said.

'I don't hold grudges,' she said. 'Anyway, you were free to do as you pleased.'

'I've never stopped regretting it.'

She shrugged. 'I was hurt and I got over it. It's in the past and I don't want to go back there again. I certainly don't want to spoil the wedding party with bad feeling.'

'Of course not. But honestly, Bessie, I don't know what I was thinking,' he said. 'Giving you up was the worst decision of my life and I've regretted it ever since.'

'Why didn't you get in touch to say you had made a mistake if you felt that strongly about it?'

'I got wounded in the foot and it affected my confidence,' he explained. 'I accepted that I would never be able to be a builder and I wasn't sure if I could provide for a wife from what I can make as a singer.'

'You seem to be doing all right.'

'Yes, I am, but I don't know about the long-term prospects.'

'Neither do any of us.'

'Can we go outside?' he asked. 'It's too noisy in here. I'm not onstage again for a while.'

They went through the swing doors into a lobby and sat down on a sofa. 'So what happened to your foot?'

'A bullet,' he replied. 'I lost some toes.'

'I'm sorry.'

'Don't be. It's nothing compared to what some of the blokes came home with, those that made it back.'

'The terrible cost of war, eh?'

'Exactly.'

'Did you know that this was Shirley's wedding and that I would be here?' she asked.

'No. It was just a job as far as I was concerned,' he told her. 'The bandleader gave me the time and place. It was his booking; he's paying me. I didn't know any details except the address. I was thrilled when I spotted you.'

'You don't deserve to hear this and part of me wishes I'd never seen you again, but I am very pleased to see you.'

'You can't hate me any more than I hate myself.'

'I don't really go in much for hate,' she said. 'It's too draining. It was pain I felt.'

'Oh Bessie,' he said with feeling. 'Please give me a chance to make it up to you.'

'What's the point when you don't want commitment?' she asked.

'I do, with you,' he said. 'Seeing you again was meant to be. I'd already realised what a fool I'd been to let you go and fate brought us together. I . . . I want to marry you, Bessie.'

'Oh Ray, please don't do this to me,' she said. 'I can't go through all that again when you decide you don't want to settle down. Marriage isn't for you; you told me.'

'I was wrong and you won't ever have to go through that again,' he said emotionally. 'I promise.'

'How can you be sure?'

'Because I realise that I was being selfish and immature,' he said. 'I know it's a bit late in the day, but I have finally grown up.'

Nature took its course and she was in his arms.

'Don't think this means we're back together,' she said, drawing back.

'Marry me, Bessie, please,' he said.

'I'll think about,' she said.

A year later they were at another wedding and this time he wasn't the singer and Bessie wasn't the bridesmaid. She had needed time to be sure that Ray was ready to settle down and was now confident that he was. They had had a wonderful year of engagement, during which they had loved and laughed, had fun and looked forward to this wonderful day.

All their family and friends were there, her colleagues

from the post office, everyone wishing them well. Most of the regulars had turned up at the church with good wishes. Bessie looked up at Ray and smiled. Being in love with him hadn't always made for an easy life, but she was so happy to be married to him and proud to be his wife.

Gloria made a gorgeous bridesmaid in pink, and even little Frankie, dressed in a pageboy outfit, had managed a few unsteady steps down the aisle holding his mother's hand, with his daddy Joe hovering protectively. Family and friends together and united in their love and best wishes for the happy couple.

It wasn't easy to look good in these hard times of shortages and rationing, but this wedding party managed it. There were big hats and ribbons and guests in their best clothes. Centre stage was the bride in a long white dress, her radiant smile captured by the photographer. It was the happiest day of her life.

A BRIGHTER DAY TOMORROW

Pam Evans

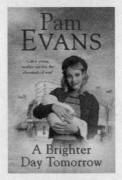

Despite air raids and rationing in wartime London, sisters Liz and Dora Beck find time for fun and laughter at the local ice-rink. Then a handsome American serviceman catches their attention, and so begins heartache between the sisters. Dora is increasingly jealous of her sister's blossoming romance with Victor. But when Victor is killed in a bomb attack, Liz makes a shocking discovery that upsets her whole family.

Forced out of her home, Liz finds support where she least expects it. And, with almost nothing left to lose, she hopes for a brighter day tomorrow . . .

www.pamevansbooks.com
www.headline.co.uk

HEADLINE

DANCE YOUR TROUBLES AWAY

Pam Evans

It is three years since the Second World War claimed the life of Polly's beloved husband George and not a day goes by without her wishing he was still alive. Polly is grateful that her mother is on-hand to look after her daughter Emmie while she works day and night to make ends meet. She can't help worrying about the future but at the Cherry Ballroom, where she works for her aunt Marian, Polly is able to forget her fears.

Then one night a handsome Canadian airman asks her to dance and in James's arms her troubles slip away. But the war cannot last for ever and James must return home, leaving Polly to face the future alone. That is until she is reunited with someone she never thought she'd see again . . .

www.pamevansbooks.com
www.headline.co.uk

HEADLINE

WHEN THE LIGHTS GO DOWN

Pam Evans

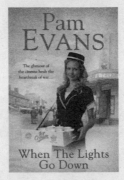

It is 1938 and the threat of war looms on the streets of London. But, when the lights go down in the cinema aisles, usherette Daisy Blake is transported to a world of glamour and romance.

Among the staff there is much merriment and Daisy soon falls in love with the handsome organist, Al Dawson. Then war is declared and, just after Al leaves for the frontline, Daisy discovers she's pregnant. Her mother is distraught; she doesn't think Al is right for her daughter and when Daisy's letters to him go unanswered, her mother encourages her to marry John, the cinema's projectionist, to spare her further heartache.

As the blitz rages over London and disaster strikes, Daisy's morale is boosted by her work and her young son, Sam, brings her comfort and joy in the troubled times ahead . . .

www.pamevansbooks.com
www.headline.co.uk

HEADLINE